C000133219

Praise for Dana Marie Bell

"*Bear Necessities* was a fun and sexy story with entertaining characters. I really like your voice and am looking forward to reading more from you."
—Dear Author

"The characters are fun, imaginative, snarky and could easily pass for someone you might know—minus the fur."
—Romance Junkies Reviews on *Cynful*

"What I love about the Halle Shifters series are the smexy heroes with the strong heroines."
—*USA TODAY* Happily Ever After Blog on *Bear Naked*

"Dana Marie Bell has a way of drawing you into her books; you immediately love the characters because they talk to each other the way you would speak to your friends and family."
—Long and Short Reviews on *Bear Naked*

"This book had me laughing non-stop."
—Book Junkiez on *Figure of Speech*

Look for these titles by Dana Marie Bell

Now Available:

Halle Pumas
The Wallflower
Sweet Dreams
Cat of a Different Color
Steel Beauty
Only In My Dreams

Halle Shifters
Bear Necessities
Cynful
Bear Naked
Figure of Speech
Indirect Lines

The Gray Court
Dare to Believe
Noble Blood
Artistic Vision
The Hob

Siren's Song
Never More

Heart's Desire
Shadow of the Wolf
Hecate's Own
The Wizard King
Warlock Unbound

Poconos Pack
Finding Forgiveness
Mr. Red Riding Hoode

True Destiny
Very Much Alive
Eye of the Beholder
Howl for Me
Morgan's Fate
Not Broken

Indirect Lines

Dana Marie Bell

SAMHAIN®
PUBLISHING

Samhain Publishing, Ltd.
11821 Mason Montgomery Road, 4B
Cincinnati, OH 45249
www.samhainpublishing.com

Indirect Lines
Copyright © 2015 by Dana Marie Bell
Print ISBN: 978-1-61923-394-2
Digital ISBN: 978-1-61923-364-5

Editing by Tera Cuskaden
Cover by Kanaxa

This book is a work of fiction. The names, characters, places, and incidents are products of the writer's imagination or have been used fictitiously and are not to be construed as real. Any resemblance to persons, living or dead, actual events, locale or organizations is entirely coincidental.

All Rights Are Reserved. No part of this book may be used or reproduced in any manner whatsoever without written permission, except in the case of brief quotations embodied in critical articles and reviews.

First Samhain Publishing, Ltd. electronic publication: December 2015
First Samhain Publishing, Ltd. print publication: March 2016

Dedication

To Mom, who consoled me when my eleven-year-old told me he *might* have a girlfriend. When questioned, he admitted right now they're friends, but they might be more in the future.

Help. Me. I'm not ready yet.

To Dad, who would probably pat my eleven-year-old son on the back with a "That's my boy!" At least I know he'd horrify the boy with stories of dating Nana back in the day.

To my sixteen-year-old who told me ain't nobody got time for dat. He'd rather concentrate on school, thank you very much. Yes, son. Thank you. Thank you so much.

And to Dusty, who listens to my psychotic ramblings about boys and girls and "he's too YOUNG, damn it!" with a patient ear and a 3 Musketeers bar. The man knows me well.

Chapter One

"You have *got* to be kidding me." The spate of Spanish that followed sounded anything but cheery. Heather stopped sketching the tattoo she was working on to find Cynthia Reyes, her boss, stomping around the tattoo shop, her steel-toed boots making squeaking noises on the newly cleaned floors. Her multicolored hair in was disarray and her lips clamped tight in frustration. The vision brought a smile to Heather's face.

Of course, Cyn was always stomping around, but it was the hair, that carefully colored and pampered hair all standing on end, that made Heather grin. Something was up with the owner of Cynful Tattoos, and Heather wanted to know exactly what that was. Heather got off the chaise she'd been lounging on. "What's wrong?"

"The ink company sent me the wrong fucking order." Cyn glared at the box on the glass display case. "Now I have to pull some green out of my ass, and since I don't shit grass, I'm wondering where the fuck I'll get it."

"No problemo. I can mix some up." Heather walked into the back room, looking for the colors she'd need. She'd been studying art since middle school. Whatever color Cyn wanted, Heather could whip up with ease. "What shade do you need?"

"See? This is why I hired you, to do the dirty work." Cyn cracked her knuckles. "But I do seem to have an excess of Ass-Slapped Red."

Heather giggled. "I don't think I'll ever get over the names of some of the inks." Heather was still thinking of tattoo ink like paint, with simple names like burnt orange or sunset red. She still had a lot to learn.

"Not all companies name their inks like that, but I love how the colors stay true longer. That's why I use them." Cyn followed her into the back as Heather gathered what she needed to mix the inks.

She pulled down some mixing cups and grabbed the colors Cyn pointed out. "Isn't there another shop across town?" She glanced at the shelf containing the needles. "We're running low on round shader needles. You were going to put that in this week's order, but maybe we can trade?"

Cyn shot her a sharp look. "Not exactly what I was thinking, but..." She rubbed her chin, then nodded sharply. "I'll give them a call. What could it hurt?" Cyn headed for the counter and the phone. "Good thinking, kiddo." Cyn winked and grinned at her, obviously pleased.

Heather tried not to blush. With her bright red hair and pale complexion, any color in her cheeks wound up taking over her whole face. She looked like a ripe tomato when she blushed. "Thanks, Cyn." It meant a lot to her that the woman who'd taken Heather under her wing was happy with her.

Heather settled back and concentrated on mixing the color Cyn wanted. Cyn's muffled voice came to her through the curtain as she called the other tattoo shop in town. Odds were good he'd have the needles, and hopefully he'd take the ink in exchange.

She'd just finished mixing the inks when the doorbell jingled. Heather left the tattooing area, eager to see Cyn's customer. She was expecting a regular, someone whose tattoo was in progress since Cyn was so intent on getting the correct green.

Who she got instead was Tabby Bunsun, her cousin Alex's mate, with a baby carrier in one hand and a diaper bag in the other. Tabby entered with wild eyes and the sharp, staccato sound of dropped keys on hardwood floor. "Help!"

Heather, laughing, rushed to help the new mother. Cyn was still on the phone, rolling her eyes at Tabby even as she spoke to the owner of the other shop. Heather grabbed the keys and took Tabby's diaper bag. "What's up?"

"Me." Tabby gently placed baby Wren's car seat on the floor before collapsing into one of the two turquoise chairs decorating the shop. "All night, every night." Her head fell back. Her lime green hair was longer than it had been since before she'd had the baby. Tabby's neat bob wasn't quite as neat and the roots were dark brown. "And every time I complain to Alex about the baby needing to be fed every two hours, he starts humming 'Hungry Like the Wolf'. Bastard."

That sounded just like Alex. "You need to get him to take better care of you. Want me to call Aunt Barbara? She'll straighten his ass out."

Tabby shook her head. "Nah, we've got this. It's just, I didn't realize how hard this would be, you know?" Tabby's Georgia drawl was slurred with exhaustion.

Heather crouched to get a better look at her new cousin. The baby was sleeping, her little bow lips pursed and sucking, her tiny fists on top of her jade green blanket. A wee knit cap kept her dark curly hair under wraps. "She's so beautiful."

Tabby's lips curved in a sweet smile. "She is." Tabby lifted her head as Cyn hung up the phone. "Trouble?"

"I have a client coming in and a wrong ink order, so yeah." Cyn walked from behind the counter and nudged Heather out of the way, taking her place before the baby carrier. "Hello, *mija*." Cyn touched the baby's brow with one finger. "Look at you."

"She's getting so big," Heather added. She glanced at Tabby with a smile. "By the way, everyone's been asking about you." It had been a month since Tabby gave birth, and everyone missed her around the tattoo parlor.

"Tell them I'll be back in two weeks." Tabby glanced down at the baby. "She'll be with me when I'm here."

"Don't worry, we'll all take care of her." Cyn touched the baby's arm again. "Right, *mija*? Aunty Cyn will show you all you need to know about life."

"Lord help me," Tabby muttered, wincing when the baby started to squirm.

Cyn scoffed as she picked the baby up out of the carrier. "Gimme the bottle. I'll feed the squirt while you rest."

"Thank you thank you thank you." Tabby dug into the bag and dragged out a baby bottle, handing it and a white cloth to Cyn.

Heather eyed the two as Cyn began feeding the baby, wondering what a child of hers and Barney's would look like. *Probably like a blond John Wayne, including tiny little cowboy boots.* "What about your client?"

"She can wait." Cyn nudged Tabby with her foot. "I think she needs a nap more."

Ah, that explained why Cyn was so upset about the ink. Tattooing a friend was a lot more nerve racking than doing a client. "Did the guy have the needles?"

"Yeah, he's willing to do the exchange thing for us. Think you can run over and pick up the box?"

"Not a problem." Heather went and got her purse and the red ink. "Anything else while I'm out?"

Cyn didn't even look up from the baby. "Grab some lunch, sweetie. We've got a light schedule today, so just make sure you're back by three. You have a client then."

"Thanks, boss." Heather waved bye as she ran out the door. First stop, the tattoo parlor.

It didn't take her long to reach the place, and less time to drop off the red and pick up the needles. She didn't bother to chit-chat with the owner, a large, leather-wearing bald guy by the name of Gus who was sweet as pie despite his scary looks. Gus was talking with a customer and didn't have time to chat. "Thanks again for the needles, Gus."

Gus shot her a warm smile. "No problem, kiddo. You tell Cyn if she needs anything else just to give me a call, okay?"

Gus's place wasn't nearly as nice as Cyn's, and his tattoos were far more traditional than the work the girls did. No 3-D tattoos or artsy ink adorned his customers, and Heather thought that was just fine. Art was art, after all, and always in the eye of the beholder. Some of his stuff was just as awesome as the stuff Cyn and Tabby did, just different from what Heather wanted to do. "I'll do that. See you around, Gus."

"If you ever get tired of working for Cyn, you come see me, okay?"

She smiled and waved. She'd never leave Cynful. "Thanks, Gus. You take care."

"You too. See ya." Gus was back to his customer, talking about the tribal tattoo the man wanted on his bicep.

Her errand done, Heather decided the best thing to do was what Cyn had said. Lunch sounded wonderful, and she had a new book on her e-reader she'd been dying to get to. She'd have to set a timer and make sure she didn't get too caught up in the tale or she'd miss out on helping Cyn with Tabby's tattoo.

It wasn't where she'd seen herself when she'd been sixteen and plotting her life. She'd planned on becoming an artist, perhaps working with paint, but she'd never managed to settle on what exactly she was trying to do. Watercolor was pretty, but got boring after a while. Oils and acrylics took time and patience, something she had, but for some reason it didn't satisfy her.

Then she'd met Cyn, Tabby and Glory and been invited into their world of ink and skin and marvelous body art. While her family had been skeptical, especially her cousin Eric, Heather knew she was where she belonged. Her parents wanted her to go to college either for art or to learn the landscaping business and become a landscaping architect like Alex.

Working with flowers was the last thing Heather wanted to do. Unless they were made of ink.

She was so busy thinking she missed the curb. Down she went, scraping her knee and her hand. The box of needles rolled to the middle of the street and almost got run over.

Heather pulled herself to her feet, limping after the box. She hissed as she picked it up. Geez. She was going to get one hell of a ribbing when she got back and told them she'd tripped on air.

As she passed one of the stores she stopped to stare at her reflection in the window. Tilting her head at the image she made, she grimaced. Long red hair, messy from the summer breeze, blew past her pale face. Nondescript green eyes stared back. Her skin was so white it practically glowed, showing off her freckles. Her cut-off jean shorts and white tank top were nothing special, the

Doc Martens on her feet worn and comfortable. Thanks to her tumble, she now had brand-new scuff marks on the toes.

No wonder Barney doesn't want me. I look like any other campus kid running around Halle. I'm a complete mess. All I need is a backpack and the look would be perfect.

Halle was a college town, but it was also home to the Halle Puma Pride, led by the Cannons, Max and Emma. Because of that, the college was deemed a safe place to send shifter children for further education. It allowed shifters to leave their home territories and enter colleges that not only had the major they wanted to study but where their parents knew they'd be safe.

It hadn't been so safe for her cousin Chloe, but Heather tried not to look back on the time Chloe was in the hospital, fighting for her life. She tried to focus on the fact that her cousin was alive and well, and back in school. Even better, Chloe had her mate, Jim Woods, cheering her all the way.

I wonder if Barney would cheer for me.

She squared her shoulders and glared at her reflection. Grunting in disgust, she moved on. She wasn't going to change, not for her parents, and not for Barney. Nope. If anything about her changed it would be because she wanted it to.

Of course, there were a few things she'd like to change. Like her mated status. Watching her cousins getting all cozy with Glory and Tabby was driving her crazy. Meanwhile her mate kept her at a distance, refusing to acknowledge the pull at all unless it suited him. Hell, he'd ordered her to have nothing to do with some weird chick and her brother who were currently guarding Chloe and Jim. Why, she had no idea, but the fact that Barney had done so gave her hope. It was slim, barely breathing and crawling on all fours, but it was there.

"Heather?"

She froze as a deep baritone washed over her, making her shudder in want. "Barney." She turned to find him just behind her, his image towering over hers in the plate glass window.

He was the epitome of everything she'd been terrified of before she'd met him. Tall, blond, with shoulders as wide as a Mack truck, she should have been running for her life.

Instead, she wanted to climb him like a tree and plant a damn flag on his head that declared him hers.

"What are you doing?" He studied her with an amused smile. He always looked at her like she was something amusing. She had yet to see him looking at her with desire.

"Getting something for Cyn. You?"

His brows rose. "Nothing. Just out for a stroll." He gestured toward the box. "Want me to carry that for you?"

"Pfft. It weighs maybe two pounds. I think I got it, Barney."

He patted her on the head. "Of course you do. Hobbits are stronger than they seem." He bowed and waved, his T-shirt stretching over his shoulders. "After you."

"Oh no," she replied. "Age before beauty."

His brows rose, but he took the lead with a small laugh. "Do I need to tuck you under my arm?"

"Only if you want your ass bit," she muttered, falling into place beside him with a wince. Damn, her knee hurt.

"Not in this lifetime." He took a few larger steps, effectively putting her behind him. "Keep up, shorty. I'm on a timer here."

"Really? I thought you were just out for a stroll." She quickened her pace, taking two steps to his one to remain at his side. She clenched her hand, hissing when pain shot up her arm.

"You're hurt." Barney stopped and pulled her under the awning of one of the local businesses. He tugged her fingers open and glared at the bleeding scrape on her palm.

"I tripped crossing the street." She showed him her scraped knee as the pain in her palm eased.

He hissed in sympathy. "That looks nasty." He knelt in front of her, brushing his hand gently over her knee. To anyone else, it would look like he was brushing something off, but for her the soothing heat of his power washed over her, taking the pain away.

He'd healed her, using his Bear's power to do so. As far as she knew, Barney never healed *anyone*. As he stood, he took her hand again, checking her palm once more.

She smiled at him, needing him to know that it meant something that he'd done for her what he'd done for no one else. "Thank you."

Their gazes locked together, her hand still in his. The world around them went silent and still. His thumb caressed the skin of her palm, making her shiver with a desire so sudden she almost dropped to her knees. Only his hold on her kept her on her feet.

Barney slowly let go of her hand, bringing the world crashing down around her senses once more. "You're welcome."

Without another word he took the box and carried it to the front door of Cynful. He handed it over, nodded once, and was off to whatever it was Hunters did when they weren't in their home territories.

Heather shook her head and carried the box into the shop. "I'm back…"

Chapter Two

"Get off my couch, cat."

The only answer Barney got was a yawn. A yawn with huge teeth involved. A striped tail swished lazily as the big white head settled on the arm of Barney's leather sofa.

"Don't you scent mark my shit, you asshole." He threw his pencil at the big pain in his behind. "Get the hell out, Artemis."

The Tiger grunted and stretched. Barney could hear the distinct sound of leather popping before the cat landed on the floor.

Barney wanted to inspect his couch for damage, but the Tiger was there, getting changed. While nudity among shifters wasn't uncommon, it was still considered polite to give someone a little privacy when their bits and pieces were dangling out. "Why did you come here?"

"Apollonia kicked me out." Artemis moved with all the slow, graceful movements cats were known for as he dressed. Barney wanted to tell him to hurry the hell up. "She thinks I damaged her car. Again."

"Did you?" Not that it mattered much to Barney, but if the two Tigers had a real fight he'd be the one trying to get them to knock it the fuck off.

"Maybe." Artemis pouted. "She called me a pain in the ass."

Barney kept his lips clamped. Artemis *was* a pain, and lazy, and one of the deadliest shifters Barney had ever met.

Still, if Artemis had ripped Barney's couch, he'd have a brand new Tiger-striped rug.

"Are you done yet?" He had shit to do that didn't involve babysitting Artemis Smith.

Another grunt and a yawn. A plain T-shirt went over Artemis's head, his words muffled by the cloth as he replied, "Yup." His head popped out. "I'll be out of your hair in a minute."

For one of the Tiger twins, a minute wasn't what it was for most other people. It was like they moved on Island time, getting there when they got there, not bothered in the least if they were early or late. Mostly late. "Get your fuzzy ass gone. I have work to do, you know."

"Yeah, yeah. You've been grumbling all afternoon." The Tiger shot him a wounded look. "Didn't you know I was trying to sleep?"

Barney wanted to throw the table at him. "Two becomes one, one becomes three. Bear knows the way, but Fox holds the key."

Artemis blinked lazily. "Huh?"

"That's what I'm working on." Barney shook his head. No way was he explaining himself to Artemis. The Tiger could just suck up his curiosity like the cat he was and choke on it. Artemis's sole job was to protect Chloe Williams and nothing more.

Artemis stared at him blandly. "Want some help?"

"No." He'd rather eat fire ants. Live ones. Hold the honey.

"You sure?" The Tiger tilted his head, his dark hair falling across his forehead. One strand of white showed.

Barney scowled. That strand of white meant that the Tiger had been using his powers, and for a Tiger, that meant fighting. Biggest of the shifters, Tigers had the ability to take on a half-man, half-Tiger form, making them the most formidable fighters in the shifter world. "What have you been up to?"

Artemis shrugged. "A little of this, a little of that. A little trip down to a certain tattoo parlor to check on a cute little redhead." Artemis licked his lips, and Barney wanted to deck him. "She's delicious."

Holding his rage by a thread, Barney pointed toward the door. "Out."

"But—"

"Now!" The roar echoed off the walls of his tiny apartment. Damn it, the neighbors would probably complain again.

"Your funeral." Artemis strolled to the door, pulling it open. "Just remember, Fox holds the key." The door shut behind him with a soft click.

Barney ran for the door, pulling it open, ready to demand that the Tiger come back. But somehow, some way, that lazy ass Tiger was gone, a bare hint of his scent left in the wind. "I hate that fucker." Barney slammed his door shut.

Barney stared at around the tiny, one-bedroom apartment he'd gotten when he'd come to Halle to investigate Chloe Williams on the Leo's orders. This thing with the white shifters was becoming bigger than he'd thought possible. There was Senate involvement, mercenaries, a riddle and attacks on innocent people. Chloe Williams had nearly died, Julian's mate had been attacked, and Hunters were popping into the area faster than Wawa's with gas stations.

Normally Hunters worried themselves over rogue shifters, those who either couldn't or wouldn't abide by the laws laid down by the Senate for the protection of all shifter kind. But if the Senate was clandestinely hunting white shifters, people who'd done nothing wrong, something had changed dramatically. As annoying as Artemis was, he hadn't done anything to set Barney's Hunter instincts tingling. If anything, his Bear was actually amused by the lazy S.O.B. Chloe had been a simple college student. And Julian was a Kermode, one of the rarest of the Bears, so his presence in Halle was something of an anomaly. He was the only one of his kind to leave his home territory since…

Ever. Barney didn't think they ever left British Columbia. Yet this all started when Julian appeared, searching for something he couldn't name and saving Chloe's life.

Hell. The only way Barney would be able to solve the case was by solving the cryptic riddle told to Julian DuCharme and Chloe Williams by Fox and Bear. It had haunted Barney day and night, and the more he learned the farther away the answer seemed to be. He wished he could speak to the spirits the way they did, but that privilege was granted to only a few, and they were all white.

He sat back at the table and stared at the message the spirits had sent.

Two becomes one. Well. That one, and the second line, *One becomes three,* confused the hell out of him. The list of things that could go from two to one were staggering, but he was slowly narrowing it down. But then to have it go from one to three? It made no sense whatsoever, no matter how he twisted it around in his head.

His Hunter senses weren't just tingling, they were singing the goddamn "Imperial March". That symphony was all for the Senate, who'd sent him here to investigate, and, if necessary, bring in Chloe Williams, the white Fox. But the Leo had given him completely different orders, and it was those he intended to follow.

The Senate was a loose conglomerate of all of the shifter species. Its main purpose was to see to it that humans did not learn of the existence of shifters, with the only exception being human mates. Over the years the Senate had also instituted certain laws that all shifters abided by, one of them being the sanctioning of new Packs and Prides. Every six years the different races would elect one of their own to a seat on the Senate.

The shifter Senate also ran a legal corporation, the Wildlife Conservation Federation. It was a charitable organization that was mostly concerned with the conservation of endangered species, funding those places that gave sanctuary to them. It was the shifters' way of thanking the animals for giving their human half not only the ability to shift, but a lifetime companion. The foundation only accepted donations from shifters, so they didn't fall under public scrutiny. As far as Barney knew, they didn't even have a website.

And it was all headed by the Leo, a white Lion born of the Lowe family. It had been that way for centuries, and no one had expected that to change anytime soon.

So what did the riddle have to do with all of this? It was burned into Barney's brain, driving him insane. The connections between Chloe, Julian and the Leo were thin at best. Add in Artemis, the white Tiger, and none of it came together in a neat, tidy package.

The only part that made any sense was *Bear knows the way but Fox holds the key.* If that didn't scream the Bunsuns, Williamses and Allens, he didn't know what did. That family was chock-full of Foxes and Bears. But according to Chloe, she wasn't the Fox spoken of in the rhyme. And the Bear wasn't Julian DuCharme. So who were they? And were they the two becomes one? And was the key something physical, or metaphorical?

Worst of all, he and some of his compatriots had uncovered evidence that half-breed children, like the daughter of Tabby the Wolf and Alex the Bear, were being targeted and killed before their first shift. But he didn't know who was targeting them or why, or if it even had anything to do with the riddle or the white shifters.

The worst thing he could think of was that those in the Senate organizing the attacks here in Halle and elsewhere had already figured this riddle out. If they were using it to make sure that whatever it was the spirits wanted never came to pass…

That couldn't be good.

The thought that the riddle had nothing to do with the white shifters had crossed his mind, but it was quickly dismissed. Too many factors pointed right toward them. There was no way they weren't involved somehow in whatever was going on.

Thank God Heather isn't one of them.

Barney sighed and rubbed his eyes. Well. That made ten whole minutes without thinking about Heather Allen. It might be a new personal best. He'd been avoiding her all week, and his Bear was giving him fits about it.

The thought that Heather, rather than Chloe, could have been the white Fox, could have almost died, drove him insane. He had nightmares where Heather was beaten, half-dead, kidnapped or worse. The thought that he might have lost her before he even knew she existed was too much to bear. Alex had told him all about the attack on Heather when she'd been ten years old, how some adult male Bears had tried to force his tiny cousin to shift when she wasn't physically ready. It had puzzled him for some time, and still did. They'd ripped her clothes, taunted and teased her, terrified her to the point where she probably still had nightmares.

But they hadn't done the unthinkable. Either Alex got there fast enough to stop that horror, or they'd never intended to rape her to begin with. Sometimes he wondered if those men hadn't attacked her because she was a mixed-blood Fox and might be a white shifter. He still hadn't figured out why mixed-blooded shifters would sometimes turn up white, but he had the feeling that someday he'd find the answer to that riddle as well.

Thank God Heather *wasn't* the white Fox. The life of a Hunter was dangerous enough. If he'd been mated to a white shifter, things would have become far more deadly than anything he'd ever dealt with before. He would have given up everything to ensure her safety, even his own sanity.

This was why Barney had always felt that Hunters shouldn't mate. His focus wasn't split, it was twisted around the object of his mating instincts. Everything in his life seemed to lead right back to Heather, and it was driving him insane. He wasn't certain anymore if he could trust his own hunches where this case was concerned, but calling in another Hunter to protect Heather was out of the question. Only Barney was capable of taking care of her the way she needed.

Pushing her away had worked in the beginning, but it was becoming more and more impossible to drive her out of his life. One look into her big green eyes and his world came alive in ways he'd never experienced before. One smile and he was ready to hand her anything she desired. One sad little sigh and he wanted to eviscerate anyone who'd made her cry—past, present or future. He had to figure out a way to bring her into his life but keep her safe at the same time.

Maybe bubble wrap would work. But then he'd have the urge to pop all the bubbles, and that couldn't end well.

The desire to head to the tattoo parlor to check up on her was so strong he was at the front door before he even realized he'd moved. His hand was on the knob, his Bear growling with anticipation. He needed to see her and make certain she was safe. It didn't matter that Ryan was there, another Hunter, protecting the Cynful girls. No one had the right to watch over Heather but Barney.

Barney forced his hand off the doorknob, successfully pissing his Bear off. Now wasn't the time to be thinking about mates and whether or not they were as bendy as they looked. Nope. He wasn't going to think about putting her pert little ass over the arm of the sofa. He wasn't going to imagine all that bright red hair spread out beneath her as he fucked her into oblivion.

Nope.

Wasn't gonna.

So why was he standing on the front porch?

"Fuck my life." Barney dug out his keys and locked his apartment door. Fine. He'd drive by Cynful Tattoos, but he wasn't going to get out of the car. He was going to head over to the diner and have lunch, then come back and work on the riddle some more. He wouldn't mate Heather until he was certain he could protect her from not only rogue shifters but the Senate itself.

He considered himself a reasonable Bear, but when it came to his mate all bets were off. He'd yank the balls off anyone who so much as touched a hair on Heather's head.

It didn't take long for Barney to make it to Cynful Tattoos. His apartment was only a few blocks away, but he didn't want to be seen strolling by Cynful without having anything new to tell the girls. What was he going to say, that he'd gotten a headache from trying to figure shit out?

Barney closed his eyes and shivered as the sweetest sound in the world drifted to his ears. Heather was laughing, the sound bright, young and full of an innocence he'd kill to protect. His mate should be sheltered from all the dark things that lurked in the shadows. It was his right as her mate to keep them at bay.

If that innocence was shattered, he didn't know what he would do.

Heather glanced out the window, almost as if she sensed his presence. Before he could find out if that was true or not he put the car in gear and headed for Frank's diner. It was almost time for Cynful to close for the night anyway. Ryan would take care of getting Heather home, so Barney didn't have to worry about her. Maybe grabbing a bite to eat would help clear the cobwebs from his mind.

Nothing much could make them worse.

Chapter Three

Heather shook her head. She could have sworn she saw Barney's car out there, but that couldn't be. Could it? Or was she finally getting to the point where she saw him everywhere?

If Glory had sprouted a Barney head Heather was checking herself into Chez Crazy as soon as possible. But if that *had* been Barney out there, why hadn't he come in? "I just don't get it. Why is Barney avoiding me?" It had gotten worse since she fell and scraped her palm. He'd avoided her for a week now, and it was starting to make her itch.

"Because he's a chicken-shit coward?" Glory Walsh blinked, her baby blue eyes filled with mischief. Her powder blue curls were up in a ponytail today with loose strands flying around her face. Her multicolored gauze skirt was matched with a plain tank top and a chain belt.

Heather wasn't fooled by the fairy-like appearance of her co-worker. Glory Walsh was one tough female. She'd been through hell and back, and anyone who thought her prey would quickly find out just how predatory she could be.

"A lot of men are yellow-bellied when it comes to 'the one'," Cyn added. She was behind the front counter, scowling at something Heather couldn't see.

Heather pretended to put a phone up to her ear. "Hello, Kettle, this is Pot. I'm calling to tell you that you're just as black as me."

Both women glared at her before continuing on with their tasks.

Heather wasn't about to let it go. She started with Glory, since she was closest. "I'm just saying, Ryan should have athlete's foot, he chased you so hard."

"I have issues, okay?" Glory stuck her tongue out, but Heather knew she'd struck out at a sore point by the look on Glory's face. Glory had abandonment issues and sometimes had panic attacks so severe she passed out.

"You know what I mean." She hugged Glory to show she meant no harm. "And I understand why you ran, but you still did. It's the not knowing why Barney's running that's killing me."

Glory hugged her back. "It's okay, baby girl. You know Mama Glory loves you to pieces."

Heather did. The women of Cynful were awesome that way. "What do you think I should do?"

"Jump his ass." Cyn grinned at them. "Bite him until he's humping your leg."

Heather giggled as a mental image of a tiny Barney clinging to her leg and going to town filled her mind's eye. He looked so cute as a *chibi* she might have to draw him that way.

"What she said." Glory let Heather go and got back to her inventory. "We're closed up for the night. If you want, I can finish this."

"But—"

Cyn pointed toward the front door. "Go. Get food, go home, count Bears and go to sleep. Everything will look better in the morning, I promise."

Before Heather could say anything else her cousin Ryan came out from behind the employees-only curtain. "You almost done, SG?"

Ryan always worked in the shop when Glory was scheduled for the day. He'd bring his laptop and do the accounts for Bunsun Exteriors while making sure Glory knew he was there for her. Since he'd begun doing that, a lot of her anxiety had dissipated. And if, for some reason, he couldn't be there for his mate he made sure that one of the other men was.

Glory smiled sweetly at her mate. "Almost. I'm finishing up inventory, then we can head out."

"Great, because I'm starving." Ryan glanced at Heather. "You need someone to walk you home?"

It was both touching and aggravating, how protective her cousins were of her. "I'll be okay. I'm going to head to Frank's for a burger, then head home."

Ryan scowled. "You want to wait for us? Glory and I could go with you."

Heather waved him off and grabbed her purse. "Nah, I'm fine. You worry about Glory, I'll take care of me."

Ryan didn't look happy, but he backed off. "Okay, but if you need anything you have my number."

"Thanks." Heather gave Ryan a peck on the cheek. "I promise I'll call you if I'm uncomfortable walking home." Ryan was a brand new Hunter in training, which took his natural urge to protect to the extreme sometimes. "Don't forget the family dinner this weekend, by the way. Mom's looking forward to having us all there."

Glory looked like a deer in the headlights for a moment before smiling weakly. "Ryan? Why didn't I know about that?"

Cyn chuckled behind her hand. "Busted."

Heather made a run for it as Ryan began to stammer out excuses. Glory was still getting used to having a large family around her, and finding out there was going to be a family gathering always made her uncomfortable. "Bye!"

Through the window she could still see Cyn chuckling, but Glory and Ryan had disappeared.

"What's going on in there?"

Heather jumped, almost shrieking in fear.

"Easy, there." Julian DuCharme, the handsome Bear who'd won Cyn's heart, gently took Heather's chin in his hand. "Are you all right?"

Yikes. Another overprotective Bear, but this one had superpowers. He was Kermode, a Spirit Bear, one of a rare breed who consorted with the spirit world on a regular basis. His healing skills were amazing, but they came at a terrible price. They'd almost killed him more than once.

"I'm fine, Super Bear." Heather patted his cheek. Really, the guy was too nice for his own good. "Cyn's just finishing up, I think."

His gaze immediately went back to the window, a wicked grin on his face. "So I see. Time to go get my lady." He glanced back at Heather. "Where are you headed?"

She bit back the urge to roll her eyes. "Frank's."

"Ah." He looked up and down the street, then shrugged. "Be careful on the way home, all right? If anything happens to you the entire clan will be on my furry ass."

She laughed. He was the one who'd first termed their family a clan, but it fit. "I will. Oh, family gathering Sunday."

"Your Aunt Laura already ordered my attendance." He chuckled. "Cyn and I will see you then." He strode over to the front door of Cynful and waved, catching Cyn's attention. "Later, Heather."

"Bye." She smiled as she heard Cyn greet her mate. Maybe she should just bite Barney and get it over with. Once bitten, he'd have no choice but to finish the mating. The heat generated by the bite would ensure it.

But…

Damn it.

Taking away his free will wasn't something she wanted to do. He had to need her as desperately as she needed him. He got on her last nerve, argued with her, refused to explain things and was a general pain in her ass. He was bossy to the extreme, cautious, arrogant, gorgeous and everything she never thought she'd want in a mate.

Just thinking about him made her want to hit something. Preferably Barney's stubborn head.

Walking to the diner took longer than she'd thought. She'd been so busy grumbling about Barney that she'd slowed down, but the smell of those delicious burgers sped her up once more. Her stomach grumbled as she opened the door.

Another scent hit her then like a freight train. Barney was in here somewhere.

She started moving around the diner, looking for him. The moment she spotted him she slid into the booth with him. "Hey."

He looked up from the menu and winced. "What?"

Heather smiled despite the sting of his dismissive tone. "The bacon cheddar barbecue burger is my favorite."

Barney shrugged and looked back at the menu. "Good for you." She couldn't see his face, but his fingers clenched around the edges of the menu, turning his knuckles white. Maybe this was as hard on him as it was on her.

They sat in silence until a waitress appeared to take their order. When she left, Heather tried once again to talk to her mate now that he couldn't hide behind the menu any longer. "How's the investigation going?"

"Peachy." He sat back in his seat and crossed his arms. His gaze was stony, encouraging her to drop it.

He stared at her with such indifference her heart started to pound in fear. "Barney. Please? Give me something, anything."

For a moment his expression softened. His hands clenched, but then he put the on the table. His expression hardened again. "It can't happen. Not yet."

Not yet? What the hell did that mean? "I just—" She was interrupted as the waitress brought them their sodas. "Thank you."

Barney grunted and opened up his straw, surprising her when he thrust it into her drink. "You look tired." His tone was far less brusque. If anything, there was a hint of concern that made her heart race with hope.

"Long day at the shop, but I love it. There's something new to see every day." She loved what she was doing, so the long hours were worth it to her. "We had this one client come in who wanted a lobster tattooed on his ass. Full color, 3-D and everything."

Barney choked on his drink. "A what?"

She shrugged. "Don't ask me, but there was some kind of story behind it. Sometimes they tell us, sometimes they don't. This guy just lay there and let Cyn and I work on him."

Barney growled. "You touched his ass?"

She held up her hands. "They were covered in plastic gloves."

He huffed and sat back. "I still don't like it."

She raised her brows. "Until you bite me, you don't get a say."

His blue eyes turned brown. "The fuck I don't."

The deep, rumbling tone made her shiver. "It's my job, just like Hunting is yours."

Barney stared at her, still looking aggravated.

"Cyn let me be the one to draw the lobster and the client almost cried over it."

His smile was tight. "I still don't like it."

"Would it help if I told you he farted?"

"Nope." His expression lightened. "Maybe."

"Cyn made me shave his butt."

Barney's lips twitched.

"He had a pimple on one side that—"

He held up his hand, laughing. "Okay, that's enough." He shook his head. "TMI, baby."

She shivered happily despite his grimace. "For a while there I thought you didn't want us to be mates."

He sighed. "That's not it at all. There's more going on right now than this thing between you and me. I have to focus on my duties first, and if I'm mated my attention will be split. Can you understand that?"

"Nope." She leaned toward him. "Both Gabriel Anderson and Ryan have mates, and they're both Hunters. Neither of them would think twice about doing their jobs."

"But part of their attention will always be on their mates, wondering if they're safe." He put his finger over her lips when she tried to protest. "I'm not saying never, Heather. I'm saying later. Once I know no one is going to go after you for what I'm investigating. There are people who will kill you just for having the last name Barnwell. Others will discover you exist and…" He shuddered. "I can't let anything happen to you. If we're not mated—"

"They won't smell me on you?"

He nodded soberly.

Shit. She hated that his reasoning made sense. "Damn it."

"It's the best way to keep your little Hobbit ass safe."

Hobbit. That was his nickname for her. It sucked that she only came up to his armpit, but he could have come up with something cuter to call her than Frodo Baggins.

Still, she always got goosebumps when he called her that. It was *his* name for her, and she was becoming pretty fond of it. Not that she would ever tell him that.

"And if the Senate is after your family, then I *have* to keep them *all* safe, and not just because you're cute. If they know I'm mated into the family, they could take not only you but any of them as hostages, and I'd do almost anything to get them back."

Goddamn motherfucking shit humpers. How in hell was she supposed to argue with that? "This sucks rocks."

"It does." He put his hand over hers, twining their fingers together. "But not forever."

She bit her lip, conflicted by his reasoning and her own desires. The mate dreams were driving her crazy, but she couldn't find any words to use to argue with him. "Damn it."

"I can't push you away anymore." He winced. "I can't see that pain in your eyes. Not again."

"You should have told me all of this before, jackass." But she caressed his hand, hoping to take out some of the sting of her words. "I'm not stupid, you know. I can understand 'Danger, Will Robinson! Danger!'"

That earned her a laugh. It might have been the flailing robot arm that did it. He was still holding her other arm hostage. "You're cute. Like a Pomeranian, only louder."

That did it. She glared at him. "One year."

"Hmm?" He blinked, looking confused.

"That's my time limit." The burgers were placed in front of them, forcing their hands apart, but Heather's focus was all on Barney. She shook her finger at him. "If you haven't claimed me by then, I'll track you down and give you a bite to remember." She picked up her burger and held it out. "Deal?"

He smiled as he clinked burgers with her, like the bun-wrapped meat was the finest crystal champagne flute. "Deal. I figure my Bear won't hold out longer than that anyway."

She blushed brightly. If his Bear was getting as pushy as her Fox, she might just be mated well before the deadline.

With a contentment she hadn't felt in quite some time, she bit into her burger, happy just to be in her mate's company.

Chapter Four

Barney was packing his overnight bag, but his mind was stuck on the conversation he'd had with Heather the day before. She'd actually understood why he needed to wait, acceded to his wishes and given him a time limit he could live with.

He was still reeling with surprise. He'd thought she was going to fight harder to mate him after seeing what Chloe and Jim, her cousin's mate, had gone through. Chloe had waited four years for Jim to claim her, suffering through the mating dreams while struggling with a traumatic brain injury that left her with a serious speech impediment. And while part of him was pleased Heather had understood his need to wait, another part of him, the Bear part, had wanted to yank her over that table and mark her right over her barbecue bacon burger.

Barney zipped his overnight bag shut. Thinking about Heather wasn't going to get him any closer to a solution. For that to happen, he had to head to Sedona, Arizona, the current seat of the shifter Senate and home of the Leo, Sebastian Lowe. Sedona was a perfect city for the Senate to make their home, with plenty of open spaces, parks and enough tourism that people visiting from other states wasn't anything remarkable. Barney showing up with two idiots in tow shouldn't be noticed by anyone other than a Senate employee.

If questioned, he planned on explaining that he was there for the Leo's business and nothing else. It was the truth, so even a Coyote wouldn't question him, since Coyotes could smell lies like Barney could cheese fries.

The knock on the door came just in time. He picked up his bag and headed for the door, opening it to see the mercenaries who'd been sent to take out Chloe

Williams. Instead, they'd wound up bonding with her, becoming her strongest allies. They were just as dedicated to finding out why they'd been sent to bring her in as Barney was.

"Hey, y'all ready to head out?" Casey Lee, his blond hair tousled, his pose relaxed, was a Fox. Upon discovering Chloe's existence and scenting "family" on her, he'd sworn to do his best to protect her. Barney still didn't understand what that was all about, and all Casey Lee would say was that his momma would kick his ass if he did anything to harm Chloe.

Barney let it go. When a Southern man said his momma would kick his ass, he meant it. Casey Lee was no more a threat to Chloe than a ladybug was.

His partner, Derrick Hines, was a tank on legs, with thick biceps, wide shoulders and dark hair and eyes. His body language screamed predator, the Wolf easily the more threatening of the two. He'd decided to follow his partner's lead where Chloe was concerned, making Chloe's safety a priority. As scary as the man was, it was Casey Lee Barney was going to keep an eye on. The Fox was swift and silent, and since Foxes could hide their scent they often went unnoticed, making them deadly assassins.

Barney handed Derrick his suitcase. "Let's go."

"Did you let Darien know you're coming?" Derrick slid into the driver's seat of a quad-cab truck.

"Do I look stupid?" Barney took his seat in the back, allowing Casey Lee to ride shotgun. "I want to see his honest reaction."

"If anyone catches wind of this they'll let your cousin know for sure we're in town." Casey Lee rolled down his window and stuck his head out. "Man, it's a nice day."

Barney's cousin, the Bear Senator, was Darien Shields's boss. The orders that sent Casey Lee and Derrick to Halle, Pennsylvania, were supposedly from him, but Darien had told them that no such orders came through Carl's office. Yet the orders bore Darien's signature. It was just another part of the mystery that was driving him crazy. "Don't worry about Carl. I'll deal with him. Worry about Darien."

"Has Francois found any hint of Vaughn Clark?" Derrick's voice matched his looks. Deep and kind of grumbly, the man probably made kittens piss in fear when he spoke.

"Not yet, and that worries me." Francois was another Hunter who'd been sent after Chloe and was now working with them. They'd forced him to acknowledge that the unique Hunter ability to detect rogues wasn't activating around either Chloe or her mate, Jim Woods, making the Hunter's orders suspect. He'd agreed to help them figure out what the fuck was going on, and had taken on the task of hunting down the Hunter liaison to the Senate. The Cheetah hadn't found any sign of the missing man. Barney was beginning think Vaughn was dead. "We'll need to inform the other Hunters soon."

"They must know he's missing by now." Casey Lee pulled his head back in as Derrick began to speed down the road out of town. "Y'all are Hunters, after all."

Barney shook his head. "I'm not Miss Cleo. I can detect rogues, but not whether or not Vaughn is dead or hiding in Cleveland."

Casey Lee turned in his seat. He stared at Barney with a dumbfounded look on his face. "Why Cleveland?"

Barney rolled his eyes. "Turn back around, dumbass."

Casey Lee did, still muttering. "I'd hide in Reno. Or Vegas."

"I'd hide in New York," Derrick added, turning onto the highway.

"You gonna go to Coney Island and join the circus sideshow?" Barney hid his smile. "You can bill yourself as 'The Man Without a Brain'."

"Nah." Derrick tilted his head. "The burlesque show, on the other hand…"

Casey Lee laughed. "No way I want to see your hairy ass in a bikini, jiggling all over the place."

"You should be so lucky." Derrick pushed at Casey Lee's arm when the other man started gagging. "Seriously, though. If Vaughn had to hide he'd go somewhere where he wouldn't be noticed. Somewhere with either a shit-ton of shifters or none at all."

"Vaughn's also a Hunter. He'd know how to hide." Barney rubbed his chin. "I'll pass that along to Francois. The feelers he's put out haven't returned anything he can sink his teeth into."

They rode in silence after that. Barney texted Francois, who texted him back with *Heading to NYC now*. Francois would probably check in with the New York Coyote Pack. Their Alpha, Nathan Consiglione, was a friend of the Poconos Pack Alpha, Richard Lowell. No doubt he'd give Francois the assistance he needed to find Vaughn.

"How's Heather doing?"

Barney grimaced at Derrick's question. "She's fine."

"She sure is," Casey Lee drawled. "I wonder if all the women in that family are just as fine as your mate?"

Barney shrugged. "Dunno. Haven't looked."

That was a blatant lie, but the only women he knew were Chloe, Heather and the assorted aunts. Heather shared her bright red hair with her father, Raymond, and her Aunt Laura—Raymond's sister and Chloe's mother. But she got her petite frame and bright blue eyes from her mother, Stacey. Barney knew her older brother and sister, Keith and Tiffany, were still out west, working on moving the offices of Bunsun Exteriors to Halle from Oregon. He had no doubt they'd arrive in nanoseconds if they thought Heather was in any danger. The clan just seemed to work like that. "She has an older sister, but I've never seen her."

"Almost there." Derrick pulled off the highway, following the signs for the Departure section of Philadelphia International Airport. "Do you have anyone watching Heather? Chloe's covered by Apollonia and Artemis, but Heather could be used against them."

"I know. Ryan and Alex Bunsun are going to keep an eye on her."

Casey Lee frowned. "Not real acquainted with Mr. Bunsun."

Barney's grin was evil. "Alexander 'Bunny' Bunsun might seem like a teddy bear, but the man beat the shit out of seven men who harassed Heather when she was ten. Crippled one of them, in fact. Trust me when I tell you Heather's safe with him."

Casey Lee whistled low. "Dayum."

"Why would seven men go after a ten-year-old?" Derrick was scowling as he parked the truck in the short-term lot.

Just remembering what he'd learned had him clawing at the seat in anger. "They tried to force her to shift."

"At *ten?*" Casey Lee's face twisted into a disgusted grimace. "That's sick."

Barney nodded, barely holding back his own growl. "When I found out about it, I tried to get Alex to tell me the names of the men. He wouldn't. He said they were on the other side of the country and weren't a threat to her anymore."

"Do you agree?" Derrick pulled his overnight case out and handed it to Casey Lee before grabbing Barney's.

"No." Anyone who tried to use shifting to force a child into puberty wasn't simply playing around. They were after something else. But unless Barney saw them for himself, there was no way to know if they were rogues or were telling the truth. "Without more information there's nothing I can do." Barney grabbed his bag. "Let's focus on the Senate and what they're up to."

"For now," Derrick grumbled.

Casey Lee nodded in agreement.

Shit. Barney was beginning to like these guys. "You read the info I gave you on Darien Shields?"

Casey Lee responded first. "Male Black Bear, twenty-nine years old, five foot ten and weighs a hundred and seventy-five pounds. Lives alone in Sedona, Arizona. Owns one cat and two goldfish."

Barney blinked. "That's a bit more than I told you."

Casey Lee merely smiled. "I know."

Barney shook his head and followed the two mercs into the airport. Working with them was going to be interesting. Casey Lee had access to information not even Barney could get ahold of easily. "Remember, when we get there, I do all the talking."

"Got it. You're the official honcho, the man with access, yadda yadda." Derrick pulled onto I-76 heading east. "What's the plan other than interrogating Shields?"

"Wing it. I have no idea yet what we're walking into, but if it comes down to it you two are now working for me. Anyone gives you grief you send them my way."

"I like that." Casey Lee leaned back, crossing his arms behind his head. "I stick my ass out, you cover it."

The visual had Barney smacking Casey Lee on the back of his very hard head. "Damn, your skull is made of concrete."

"That's what his mama always says." Derrick grinned at his partner.

"Speaking of which…" Casey Lee lowered his arms. "You okay leaving Heather behind?"

"Nope, but it has to be done. She understands, thank God." She would be a good mate eventually. She'd never once backed down or showed fear of his size, something that made him surprisingly proud of her. Anyone else giving him that kind of sass would have been on the wrong end of his claws, but his itty bitty mate just made him laugh.

Maybe it was the itty bitty part. Who did she think she was she kidding? She couldn't beat up the Pomeranian he'd compared her to, let alone a full-grown Grizzly shifter. But she still stood up to him, her little shoulders thrown back like she was daring him to start something.

Derrick sniffed, his lip curling in disgust. "Can you stop thinking about your mate?"

Casey Lee rolled the window down. "Some days I hate being a shifter."

Barney snarled. "Dickheads." It was considered somewhat rude to mention another shifter's arousal, but he doubted that mattered to these two.

"Please don't mention dicks right now." Casey Lee stuck his nose out the window and breathed deep. "Ah, Philadelphia funk at its finest. Still better than what's in the car right now."

"Wait until you find your mates." Barney smiled, making sure his fangs showed. "I'm going to torture you two."

"Aw, we love you too, brother." Casey Lee winked and turned back toward the open window.

"Can you close that?" Derrick winced and put one hand over his right ear. "I feel like one half of my head is a drum and your open window is the drumstick."

Casey Lee rolled the window up, grumbling about dick smell the entire time.

"Fuck off." Barney closed his eyes and prayed they hit the airport before he killed the Fox in the front seat.

Chapter Five

The ringing of the front door startled Heather. She'd been so engrossed in her book she hadn't realized how much time had passed.

"Heather, get the door for me!" her mother yelled from the kitchen, where she'd disappeared to with Heather's father some time ago.

"Okay, got it." She put her book down and padded barefoot to the front door. She grinned as she swung it wide open. "Bunny!"

"Heather!"

She laughed as he mimicked her. "What's up, cuz?" She let the big, burly Grizzly in, delighted to see him. It had taken her some time to get over her fear of him, but now she was glad every time she saw him. He'd protected her when no one else could, and she was grateful for that.

"Um." Bunny scratched his bald head. "Yeah. See, Barney left for Arizona about an hour ago. He wanted me to let you know so you didn't worry about him when he didn't stalk you for a few days."

"He did *what*?" Heather tapped her foot and glared at Bunny. She ignored the whole stalking thing. After all, keeping an eye on your mate made sense to her, especially because her Hunter hadn't claimed her yet. "What the fuck?"

"Now hold on." Bunny held up his hands like she was holding a gun on him instead of a glare. "You know he needs to investigate the Senate, right?"

She blew out a frustrated breath. "Yes, but I didn't think he'd go so quickly." She was being childish and she knew it, but the thought that her mate was out there, possibly in trouble, was giving her hives. Big strong Hunter or not, he was *hers*. He should have been the one to tell her he was going, not Bunny. Wasn't that what mates did for one another? And hadn't he acknowledged that she was his mate?

Bunny patted her on the head. "It's okay, Heather. He probably didn't want you to worry any more than you already are. And he's not going to be gone long, you know?"

"Pfft. I call bullshit. He didn't want me to yell at him." She pulled out her cell phone and dialed Barney's number. "Give me a sec, I have a message to leave someone."

To her surprise, he answered. "Hello, sweetheart."

"Why didn't you—" *Sweetheart?*

He laughed, the sound low and wicked. "Why didn't I what?"

Grr. He was *not* going to distract her from her righteous wrath. "You didn't tell me you were going away."

"Nope. I'm a strong, independent Bear, and I don't need no woman to—"

"Oh fuck yes you do," she snarled back. Being cute wasn't going to get him out of trouble. Besides, she could hear two other yahoos laughing in the background. She just bet he'd brought Casey Lee and Derrick with him.

"You just want me barefoot and pregnant all the time." He sniffled. "You don't understand the struggles I face."

"Asshole." She wished she could see his face. "How difficult is it to dial a phone?"

"With my big fingers? Do you have any idea how often I've accidentally called 1-800-SEX-MEUP?"

"Oh, I bet it was an accident." Heather was seriously considering some sort of child safety lock for his phone. They made that kind of thing, didn't they?

"Hey, the plane is going through a—" he made a bizarre buzzing noise, "—and I think the signal is—" that buzzing noise again before he hung up on her.

"Grr." She put her phone back in her pocket. "You weren't even on a plane yet, dickhead." She glared at Bunny again just for good measure.

He put his hands up in the air. "I didn't do it."

She wanted to snarl some more, but he wasn't the one who deserved it.

"Fine. But I reserve the right to kick his shins when he gets back."

"He'll love that." Bunny hugged her cautiously, as if afraid she'd break if he used even a fraction of his strength.

He was always careful with her. It still hurt to know she was the reason that Alex had become so passive that he'd earned the nickname Bunny, but she'd truly been terrified by his rage when he'd defended her from her attackers. That was eight years ago, though, so maybe she could get him to understand that she wasn't afraid of him anymore. The more she was around him, the more comfortable she became. He wasn't some angry avenging angel, he was just a man who'd tried to protect her the best way he knew how. "I'm not made of glass. You can hug me tighter. Maybe I'd feel it then."

He chuckled and let her go. "I'll try to remember that." He winked at her. "And I've got an even better surprise for you."

"Oh? What is it? Are we kicking puppies next?"

"Not quite." He rubbed his hands together gleefully. "You ready?"

"Sure." She crossed her arms and stared at him. Whatever it was, he seemed mighty pleased about it.

Heather was startled when he walked right back to the front door and opened it up. "Come on in!"

In walked—

"Holy crap!" Heather raced toward her brother and sister, squealing in delight. "When did you guys get here?"

Keith picked her up and twirled her around. He was the spitting image of their mother, dark haired and blue-eyed, with a swagger that was all his own. "Hey, squirt, how's it going?"

Tiffany hugged Heather hard once Keith let her go. She kept her dark hair short, and her blue-green eyes were a perfect blend of both their parents. "Just now. Alex picked us up at the airport."

Bunny was grinning so wide Heather was surprised his head didn't split in half. "It was hard keeping it a secret from you. I thought for sure Tabby was going to blab."

Tiffany held her at arm's length and looked her up and down. "Damn, girl, you look good."

Keith tapped her on top of her head. "And what's this about tattoos? Aren't you too young for that?"

Heather rolled her eyes and pulled away from her siblings. "I'm a big girl now, Keith. I've even gotten my own tattoo." She turned around to show off her two-tailed kitsune tattoo. It was one of two that she had, but this one signified her new life, one where she wasn't afraid of large men like her mate. The little red fox had sprouted wings and was ready to fly. Her fox was high up on her right shoulder. She hoped someday to put her mate on her left.

The other one, the one she couldn't show them without taking off her shirt, was a beautifully detailed Victorian birdcage, and inside that cage was a blue and green bird, its head bowed and its eyes closed. Outside the birdcage was a palette of bright colors, a paint brush and an easel with a halfway-finished portrait of the bird and cage, but the bird in the painting was lively and happy, unlike the one in the cage. It filled the space between her shoulder blades and continued halfway down her back. It had been immensely painful, as the needles kept striking her spine, and utterly worth it.

It represented her family's desire to see her go to school for bookkeeping, when all she wanted to do was be an artist. Until she'd met Cyn, she'd never have had the courage to stand up to her parents and demand that she be allowed to apprentice at the tattoo shop, but when she explained it was a way to make a living at something she loved, they'd bowed to her persuasions. It helped when the Cynful girls agreed to watch over her while she was there, making it a family business Heather was entering. Without the connection of mates, marking the Cynful women family, they might never have agreed. "I'm even working there as an apprentice tattoo artist."

Keith scowled. "What happened to bookkeeping?"

Heather gagged. "Ugh. No thank you. Numbers make my eyes bleed."

Tiffany popped Keith in the back of the head as they followed Bunny into the dining room of the house they'd rented. "She never wanted to do that. She's always wanted to be an artist."

Heather nodded. "Cyn told me to try for art school, but honestly, I like what I'm doing now. And the shop is amaze-balls!" She bounced toward a seat, knowing her parents would probably bring in drinks and snacks for Tiffany and Keith. "You'll like Cyn, Glory and Tabby. They're awesome. And family. And, like, the best thing to ever happen to me, other than Barney."

Keith sat across from her while Tiffany sat next to her. It was clear where the interrogation was going to come from. "I'm not sure about Cyn, but Glory and Tabby are family."

Mom entered the room with a huge pitcher of iced tea and a stack of glasses. "So is Julian. I told you about this, remember?"

Behind her, their father had a platter of sandwiches. "He saved Chloe's life and almost lost his own. He's bound to her and is her mentor, and your Aunt Laura adopted him into the clan. So that makes Cyn and Julian family."

Keith shrugged. "I still need to meet him."

"That's fine, but you'll treat him with the respect he deserves or you'll hear it from me." Mom put the pitcher down and began passing out glasses.

"I'm more interested in finding out more about this mate of yours." Tiffany leaned her chin on her hand, her green eyes wide with curiosity. "I hear he's a Hunter?"

Heather nodded proudly. "Yup. He's working on Chloe's case right now. In Arizona. Damn it."

Keith laughed. "He hasn't marked you yet."

"Nope. He wants to wait until he decides I'm safe." Part of her still wanted to tell him to shove that idea where the sun didn't shine, but she'd chosen the compromise instead of the argument. "I gave him one year."

"Good for you." Tiffany patted her back. "You shouldn't have to go through what Chloe did."

"Speaking of Chloe, how is she doing?" Keith smiled in thanks as their mother handed him a sandwich. "I heard she's as good as she's going to get speech-wise, but how are things between her and her mate?"

"Good. Better than good, actually. He's just as protective of her as anyone could wish for. In fact, he's encouraging her to finish her degree and become a vet technician." Their father sat down at the table with a handful of napkins and passed them around. "Dig in, guys. You've had a long flight, you have to be hungry."

"That's all I wanted to know. I figured if he needed his ass kicked Ryan would take care of it." Keith bit into his sandwich and gave his mother a thumb's up. "'S good."

"Thank you, and please swallow before you speak again." Mom shook her head and turned to Tiffany. "Anyway, Jim's really come around. We have high hopes for Barney as well."

"Barney?" Tiffany blinked, then huffed out a laugh. "You're mating someone named Barney?"

Keith's expression went blank as he stared at Tiffany. "I love you…"

Tiffany put her hands to her chest. "You love me…"

"I will beat you both senseless if you keep going." Dad reached out and swatted at both of them.

"It's just a nickname." Heather balled up her napkin and threw it at Keith. "His name is James Barnwell."

"So he calls himself Barney." Mom pointed to the floor, where the napkin had landed. "Pick that up please."

Keith didn't argue. He picked up the napkin and tossed it back at Heather. "So why not call him Jim?"

Heather started to laugh. "Well, there's Chloe's mate Jim—"

"And Jamie Howard, who's going to mate Glory's sister," her mother added.

"Too many people in this family are named James." Dad handed Keith another sandwich. "If he wants to call himself Pluto I'm not going to argue."

Mom tilted her head. "Or Mercury. That's a cute name." Mom turned to Heather. "Isn't that the name of one of those sailor girls Bunny likes?"

Bunny nodded. "But I like Sailor Moon better. Tabby looks killer dressed as her."

Heather nearly choked on her sandwich. "I can't see Barney in a sailor scout uniform, Mom."

"Please, just not Uranus." Keith held up his hand. "I really don't want a brother-in-law named after a gassy giant."

"He is pretty big," Heather muttered.

"Just…" Dad groaned. "Call the man Barney, please?" He turned to Mom. "Now I'm going to picture him in a powder-blue sailor dress every time I see him. Thanks for that."

Mom patted him on the hand. "You're welcome, dear."

Heather grinned at Keith and Tiffany. "Aren't you glad to be home?"

They rolled their eyes, but Heather could tell both of them were pleased to be back with the family once more. Now if Barney could solve the mystery surrounding them all, things would be damn near perfect.

"Is the Oregon office closed down?" Bunny, who'd helped run the business with his father, was sort of Tiff and Keith's boss.

"Everything's taken care of. There's a skeleton crew dealing with a few minor details, but otherwise it's done. Bunsun Exteriors is officially an East Coast operation." Keith held up his glass. "More tea, please?"

"Good." Bunny finished off his sandwich in two bites, then stood. "I need to get back to Tabby. Thanks for the sandwich, Aunt Stacey."

"You're welcome, Alex." She tilted her head, smiling when Bunny kissed her cheek. "Tell your mate I said hello and to bring Wren over whenever she wants."

Bunny beamed. "She is a cute little bit, isn't she?"

Stacey patted his side. "Looks just like her grandmother."

Bunny left, no doubt heading home to coo at his daughter and his wife.

"So." Keith put his hands on the table and folded them together. It was never a good sign when he did that. "Tell me about Barney."

Heather nodded. That was fair. Besides, she'd been waiting for the big-brother interrogation since she'd found out she had a mate. "You've probably heard from everyone else what they think of him, but I'll give my side. He's tall, broad, strong as hell and just as stubborn. He's a Grizzly shifter, like Bunny, but he's got a wicked sense of humor and can move silently when he wants. He's a Hunter, and he trained Gabriel Anderson, the sheriff here, and is also training Ryan."

Keith waved at her for her to continue.

She blew out a breath as she leaned back and thought of her mate. "He's nothing like I imagined my mate would be."

"So he's not Prince Charming rolled up with Ken?"

Tiffany giggled at Keith's description. "Oh, I could totally see that."

"No wonder Barbie goes to G.I. Joe for some lovin'." Heather was about to lose it herself. "Ken's totally bending over for his Prince."

"That's sick." Keith wrinkled his nose.

"I think it's hot." Tiffany chuckled. "Blond, buff Ken, bent over the sofa, his ass up in the air, just begging for it."

"And the Prince, all nice, making sure Ken is properly stretched out." Heather tilted her head and tapped her chin. "I bet he buys the best lube for his butt-buddy."

"Ladies." Her father's voice overrode the sounds of Keith banging his head on the table. "That's enough. No one gets to break Keith's brain but me."

"Ahem." Their mother cleared her throat.

"And your mother," their father amended.

"I hate you all," Keith groaned.

It was so good to have her family back.

Chapter Six

Every time Barney came to the Senate building, he was surprised at how normal looking it was. The headquarters of the Wildlife Conservation Federation were a well-guarded secret. Only those on official Senate business were allowed in or out of the gated compound, but Hunters were the exception to the rule. It was assumed a Hunter was always on Senate business, given access to most of the buildings and offices. Only one building was off limits to the Hunters, as secret Senate business was held there.

It was the one building Barney most wanted to check out. The Senate archives were located there, and who knew what else. But wanting and doing were two separate things. Planning a break-in to the most guarded building in the shifter world was going to take time. For now, he'd focus on the original plan and head straight to the offices of his cousin, Carl Barnwell.

Casey Lee opened the door to the offices, holding it for Barney and Derrick. "Thanks," Barney muttered. He glanced around, noting the lobby was quiet. Even the receptionist was missing. "Huh."

"Did we come on a holiday?" Derrick's voice was quiet, with an edge to it that had Barney's hackles rising.

"Not that I'm aware of." Barney's sense of smell wasn't as good as a Wolf's. "Smell anything out of the ordinary?"

Derrick lifted his head as Casey Lee began walking the perimeter of the room. "Nope. Not a thing."

"Hmm." Casey Lee picked up a flyer off of the receptionist's desk. "Maybe we came at lunch time."

Barney glanced at it. It was for a popular local eatery, close enough to the Senate compound to make it a great spot for lunches and dinners. He relaxed slightly. Nothing was setting off his Hunter instincts. "Perhaps."

It was unusual for him to be so on edge when coming here, but Barney had a lot more at stake than he normally did. If they could find out who'd really sent the order to take out Chloe and Jim, then maybe he could follow the trail to which Senators were involved and which weren't. "Let's get to Carl's office."

"Maybe we can take a look around there too, if he's out to lunch."

Casey Lee's idea was sound. Barney nodded his approval.

Here and there they found occupied offices, but everyone seemed to be relaxing or working quietly. No wonder the place felt dead, everyone was either out or taking an open-eye siesta. Once in a while someone would wave a greeting. Trying to keep nonchalant, they'd wave back but continue on their way to Carl Barnwell's office.

No one tried to stop them. No one had reason to. If Barney was there, then Casey Lee and Derrick must be working for him. Either that or they were used to seeing the mercenaries around the offices. Barney would have to ask them when he had the chance. It hadn't occurred to him that they would be well-known figures in the Senate building.

Carl's office was one of the occupied ones. Darien Shields, Carl's secretary, sat at his desk facing the door and guarding the doorway to Carl's interior office. He glanced up when they entered, a smile on his face until he saw Derrick and Casey Lee at Barney's back. His expression became wary as he stood. "Can I help you, Mr. Barnwell?"

Barney smiled, hoping to put the secretary at ease. "It's okay, Darien. We just have some questions for you."

Darien sat back down, but his expression remained the same. "What do you need?"

"Take a look at this." Barney pulled the letter out of his jacket pocket and handed it to Darien. It was the one that had sent Casey Lee and Derrick to Halle to apprehend, dead or alive, one Chloe Williams. It bore the seal of the Senate and was signed by the Bear Senator, Carl Bunsun.

"Yes, I've seen this before. You sent me a photo to verify that it was my signature." Darien frowned. "But now that I've got the real document, I can tell you that it's got the official seal on it."

Barney's brows rose. "Can you fake that?"

Darien shook his head. "Let me…" He rummaged in his desk drawer and pulled out a magnifying glass. "See here?" He held the magnifying glass over the image of the seal. "There's a faint glitter to the ink, right?"

"Right." It was there, a faint hint of silver.

"We put silver in the ink, sort of a nod to the old days when people thought it took silver to kill us. You could easily duplicate the stamp itself, but the pad of ink is only made by Senate workers who ship them directly to the Senator's offices."

"Is there any chance a shipment could have been deflected?" Barney handed the magnifying glass to Casey Lee, who took his turn looking at the silver flecks.

"Anything is possible." Darien pushed his glasses up his nose. "We wouldn't hear about it, though. That's a different department."

"Who's in charge of ink distribution, then?" Derrick also looked at the silver flecks over his partner's shoulder. "Once it arrives here, who hands it out?"

"Oh, that would be—"

"James Barnwell, as I live and breathe."

Barney winced, then stood and faced the doorway. "Ian Holmes." The last person Barney wanted to see today. Ian Holmes was the Lion Senator. Ian was one of the Senators who believed Hunters should be restricted to their territories and work solo, while Barney was of the opinion they needed to train and fight together to stop rogues. It was tradition versus progress, and while Barney could understand some of Ian's arguments, he'd be damned if he'd see the Hunters he trained die from a simple lack of communication. "I'd say it's a pleasure, but we both know otherwise."

The Lion Senator didn't bat an eyelash. "Come to see Carl? I'm afraid you just missed him. He's out to lunch with Kris Jennings."

"Kris Jennings? The Ocelot Senator?" Kristen Jennings was a four-foot-eleven ball of fire, and Carl was secretly terrified of her. "I see."

"If you have no further business here, I suggest you return to Montana." Ian tilted his head and frowned, looking confused. "Speaking of which, why haven't you been guarding your territory, Hunter?"

It was all Barney could do not to swear. "Carl has me working on something." The lie rolled easily off his tongue. "I'm a Bear as well as a Hunter, after all." Hopefully Carl would back him up when he returned, or there would be hell to pay. Lying to a Senator and supposedly ignoring his duties could land Barney's ass in shifter jail. Hunters rarely did well there, as most of the rogues they'd captured were incarcerated in the same facility. Accidents had been known to happen on more than one occasion. It was a fate Barney had no desire to pursue. And claiming to be working under the Leo's direction, even if it was the truth, wasn't an option. Sebastian Lowe had instructed Barney to be as discreet as possible, and he was going to follow that order to the best of his ability. There was no way Barney wanted to face Kincade Lowe, Sebastian's cousin and chief bodyguard. Barney had seen Kincade fight, and he was terrifying in his single-minded lethality.

"Indeed, Senator Holmes." Darien placed himself between Barney and the Senator, the slimmer man's back stiff as he confronted Ian. "I was instructed to greet Hunter Barnwell and provide him whatever he wished until Carl returned."

Ian looked less than pleased, but nodded reluctantly. "I see. Very well then, Hunter. Just remember what I said. You're in charge of Montana and training new Hunters. Don't let Carl keep you from your duties for too much longer. Understood?"

"Understood." Barney smiled blandly. It was his intention to be permanently relocated to Halle come hell or high water. He'd retire if he had to. It was unheard of for a Hunter his age to quit, but he couldn't imagine taking Heather away from her family and friends. He'd have to be the one to make the sacrifice.

After he solved the riddle, of course.

Hell, perhaps he'd persuade the Leo to allow him to train Hunters in Halle. There were enough of them there to give recruits plenty of experience working with other Hunters. He could probably get Julian DuCharme to assist as well. Having access to one of the rarer species of shifter, like a Spirit Bear, would be of immense value to future Hunters.

Ian Holmes nodded once to Barney, eyed Derrick and Casey Lee sharply, and left without another word. Barney turned to Darien and held out his hand. "Thanks, man. I appreciate that."

"You're welcome." Darien scowled at the door. "The Lion Senator has been a thorn in my paw for months now."

"Oh?" Casey Lee sauntered over to Darien's desk and leaned casually against the edge. "Do tell."

Darien shook his head. "I wish I could, but this is Senate business. I'm afraid it has nothing to do with you."

"Or me?" Barney folded his arms across his chest.

"I'm afraid not." Darien settled back behind his desk. "Carl should return shortly."

"About the letter, Darien." Derrick took the opposite corner from Casey Lee, but unlike his partner he stood straight, his arms loose at his sides. "Did you type it?"

Darien shook his head. "No. I told you before, I had nothing to do with this letter."

"Yet you agreed it's your signature." Casey Lee picked up a pen and twirled it between his fingers. "So how'd that happen?"

Darien sighed. "You're not going to intimidate me into an answer I don't have." He pointed to a stack of papers on his desk. "These are all of the documents I need to sign this afternoon. Carl's stack is larger than mine. Carl decided we should sign documents on Thursdays so that orders arrive for Hunters and Senate workers on Mondays."

"So this could have been put into the stack for your signature?" Barney stared at the pile of about twenty documents. "When does Carl stamp them?"

"Carl stamps them all in one go, then I stuff the envelopes and send them out." Darien rubbed his eyes. "Since you contacted us, we've been making sure every letter we sign and stamp was actually written by us."

"So you think Barney's right, that someone slipped this into the pile?" Casey Lee was scowling at the pile of papers. "It's still on official Senate letterhead."

"Which anyone in this building has access to, from the secretaries to the janitors, not just the Senators."

Barney turned with a relieved smile at the sound of Carl's voice in the doorway. "Carl, buddy." He held out his hand.

Carl grasped it firmly, pulling Barney in for a guy clench. "Cousin. Good to see you." He patted Barney's shoulder hard enough to move Barney back a step. "Darien answering all of your questions?"

Barney nodded. "We also got a visit from Ian."

Carl grimaced. "Pain in my ass Lion. What did he want this time?"

"For me to go back to Montana." Barney crossed his arms over his chest. "How much of a pain has he been?"

"Enough so that I'm thinking of complaining to the Leo." Carl gestured for them to enter his office. "So. You've spoken to Darien, and you know some of the precautions we've put in place. You can't open an official investigation into this without alerting the whole Senate. How are you planning on handling it?"

Barney grinned. "My way."

Carl sighed. "Damn it. That's what I thought." He shook his head. "I'll do what I can on my end, but the brunt of it will be on you, I'm afraid."

"We're helping." Derrick shook Carl's hand. "Nice to see you again, sir."

"You too, Derrick." Carl held out his hand for Casey Lee. "How're things with you?"

Casey Lee took it, shaking Carl's hand firmly. "Fine, sir. My momma says hi."

Carl grinned. "Tell her to send me some of that homemade bread of hers, will you? I've been dreaming about it for months."

"Will do, sir."

Carl eyed the two mercenaries. "I need to get you access to the grounds in case Barney has to leave, but it will take time to make up a reason for your presence."

Casey Lee and Derrick exchanged a glance. It was Casey Lee who spoke first. "We're mercenaries and bodyguards. Say you've got a need for us, but you don't want to go into details until the situation has been resolved. Make it personal, rather than Senate related. That should do for now."

"If we need more details than that we can manufacture something," Derrick added.

Barney shrugged. "It's not a bad idea. It's been done before, and will grant them access to the Senate buildings you work in."

Casey Lee nodded. "And it will allow us to move around inside your office as well, see if anyone is using you."

Carl glanced at Darien, who grimaced. "Agreed, but I want Darien under protection as well."

Barney's eyebrows shot up. "You think he might be a target?"

"I'm not sure, but I'm not taking any chances."

Carl's worried expression had Barney's hackles rising. "You think *you're* in danger?"

The nod he received was emphatic. "Most definitely."

"Casey Lee—"

Before he could finish, the mercs were already in place, Casey Lee with Carl and Derrick with Darien. "Don't worry, big guy. We've got this."

"You take care of your end, we'll take care of ours." Derrick crossed his arms over his chest.

"Then I'll start trying to figure out how our guy got hold of the ink pad." Barney gave his cousin a guy hug. "I'll be around."

"Me too," said Carl, chuckling.

Chapter Seven

"Just one more store. Please?" Chloe batted her lashes at Apollonia, giving the best puppy-dog eyes Heather had seen in quite some time. This was the first time in weeks Chloe had been available for a little shopping spree and Heather was enjoying the hell out of it. Just watching Chloe smile was worth listening to Jim's lecture on keeping Chloe safe. Even Apollonia, the female Tiger assigned to protect Chloe, was ready to strangle him by the time he was done.

Apollonia groaned. "Can't you people shop on Amazon? Hello! Free shipping, and you can shop braless."

"Pfft." Heather grabbed hold of Apollonia's arm. "We might have to revoke your girl card."

"I spent an hour and a half in Sephora. Isn't that enough for you two?" Apollonia rubbed her cheek. "I might never get the blush stain off."

"Oh hush. You look gorgeous." Chloe rubbed her hands together as they headed straight for the accessories aisle.

"Can't Jimmy-boy take you shopping?" Apollonia fingered a silky navy blue scarf.

Chloe shuddered. "His idea of shopping is 'Ugh. Me find T-shirt. Me buy T-shirt. Now hunt steak.'"

"My kinda guy." Apollonia winked at Chloe, who bared her teeth at the huge Tigress.

"My guy." Chloe sniffed. "Don't make me go shoe shopping."

"Christ, anything but that," Apollonia groaned. "I could see shopping for video games. Oh! We could hit Hot Topic! They have this awesome *Doctor Who* tank top I'm dying to pick up."

"That does sound awesome," Heather muttered.

"Next blip, I promise." Chloe held up the ugliest floral cargo backpack Heather had ever seen. "What do you think?"

"I think you should bury it and put it out of its misery." Apollonia grabbed a different backpack, this one in a simple black and white check. "Here. This one's on sale. And it doesn't make my eyes bleed fuchsia."

"Don't you think it's too plain?" Chloe held up the two backpacks. "What do you think, Heather?"

Heather pointed at the checked bag. "Honestly, Chloe. That other one is colored just so people won't steal it."

"Feh." Chloe put the ugly backpack down and was off again, this time squee'ing over a messenger bag covered in comic book heroes.

"She seems happy." Apollonia was making sure to stay within five steps of Chloe at all times, even when it meant crowding Heather out of the way. Since she was assigned to guard Chloe, Heather couldn't complain.

"Yeah. It's good to see her smiling and happy. She wasn't for the longest time." Waiting for her mate had made Chloe dismally unhappy, but with Jim by her side she was back to her sunshiny self.

Heather began trying on different hats. She picked up a black trilby and put it on, turning this way and that. "What do you think?"

"I think she's addicted to purses." Apollonia shook her head at Chloe.

Chloe squealed over a teal purse. "I glove this one!"

"It's adorable." Heather pointed to her head, or rather the hat perched on top of it. "What do you think of this one?" She posed with it on, making cutesy faces until Chloe was tugging the hat off her head.

"Silly. Looks good." Chloe clutched the purse, her expression bittersweet as she fingered Heather's hair. "I kiss my hair."

Heather took the hat back and grabbed Chloe's arm. "You're silly. Your hair might be a lot shorter than it used to be, but with the edgy bangs and the cute way Cyn shaped it, you look like a red-headed Anne Hathaway."

"Your hair is awesome, and don't let anyone tell you otherwise. I'll eat them for you if you like." Apollonia yawned, delicate little fangs making an appearance. "Speaking of food, when are we heading to lunch? I'm starving."

Heather ignored her, choosing instead to focus on Chloe. "Let's get you a hat too."

Chloe glanced toward the display. "They have one like yours but in purple?"

"You'd look great in blue." Apollonia dropped a navy blue newsboy cap with a cream band on Chloe's head. "Yup. Perfect."

Heather had to admit it. Apollonia was right. The hat did look good, highlighting Chloe's cheekbones and the fall of her bangs. "Nice pick, Polly."

Apollonia scowled. "I told you not to call me that."

"I don't understand why not." Heather headed for the registers. "Apollonia is way too long."

Chloe nodded. "And we can't call you Appy. You're not an iPad."

"Loni could work." Heather handed her purchases to the woman at the register. "Sounds sexy as hell."

Apollonia examined her nails. Like a lot of the feline shifters, she could produce claws at will. While they were in public she kept them hidden, but the gesture spoke more than words could. "Punting you into the parking lot could work too."

"I like Apollonia. It twerks." Chloe grimaced. "You know what I mean."

Heather bit her lip to keep from laughing. Chloe's aphasia was nothing to laugh about, but sometimes the wrong words she spoke were absolutely priceless. She could just picture Apollonia shaking her booty in the clothing store.

"I do. Don't worry about it." Apollonia followed them to the registers, keeping watch over them while they bickered amiably about who had the better purse.

It was a good day. No, a fantastic one. Chloe smiling, laughing, acting like nothing had ever happened to her made this the best day Heather had spent in the longest time.

They made their purchases and headed into the parking lot. They were going to Noah's for lunch, something Heather had been looking forward to all day. This lunch was on Apollonia, who'd decided she was tired of Frank's and wanted a change. They'd offered to go to one of the other places, like Heather's favorite taco place or Chloe's sushi place, but Apollonia had refused. She'd decided Chloe needed a treat, so she was going to get one.

Heather wasn't going to complain. Noah's was one of the best restaurants in town, a popular date spot for those who could afford it. As an apprentice tattoo artist, Heather only ate there when someone else took her, usually her parents. Having Apollonia treat them was just the icing on the cake.

"Thanks for taking us to Noah's." Heather tucked her bag in the trunk of Apollonia's car alongside Chloe's. She hadn't been able to afford much, but she'd enjoyed the day nonetheless. "I can't wait."

Apollonia smiled. "See? Don't listen to anything Barney says. I'm really a good person."

Heather's brows rose. "As good as homemade gnocchi?"

Apollonia wrinkled her nose. "Nah. No one's *that* good."

Just as Heather started to laugh Chloe screamed. Heather whipped around to find a strange man standing there, his arm around Chloe's throat and a gun pointed at Heather and Apollonia. He began to slowly back away from them, Chloe helpless in his hold. "I just want the white Fox. You two stay still and nothing bad will happen."

"You know I can't let you take her." Apollonia's claws were out. She took a stance that looked remarkably like something from a martial arts fight. "She's my responsibility."

"You want the reward?" The man tilted his head and eyed Apollonia appreciatively. "I guess we could split it."

"I don't think so." Apollonia's eyes had turned greenish gold. "It's just not my style to share."

The man backed up, still holding Chloe. Chloe was pale, her eyes wide in terror. "Tiger, huh? Haven't seen one of you in a while."

"You know us cats, we like to be fashionably late." Apollonia began to circle toward the man. "Heather, get in the car, please."

Heather stood there, shaking like a leaf. One wrong move and Chloe was gone. "I..."

"Go." One of Apollonia's clawed hands pointed toward the car. "Now, Heather. I don't need you getting hurt too."

Heather's eyes went wide. Too? So Apollonia was expecting that someone would bleed before this was over.

God. No. No no no. Not again.

The man waved his gun toward her, making her cry out. "You heard the nice Tiger lady, kid. Get in the car and let me walk away."

That must have been what Chloe was waiting for. He screeched as Chloe bit down on his arm, her fangs digging deep into his flesh. He shook her off, lifting the gun and shooting her as she ran toward Heather.

Heather screamed, her Fox demanding she find a place to hide, to stay safe. It was the same thing that happened when those men had cornered her when she was a child. Her Fox, desperate to protect her, had tried to force her to hide, but she'd been surrounded by huge men and too young to shift. She couldn't get away, couldn't find a safe place, not even in her own head. She was terrified, desperate to keep her soul intact as the adults tried to force her Fox out. If that happened, if she was forced into premature puberty...

What they wanted to do to her once she'd changed hadn't sunk in until she was older. Instead, she'd been terrified by visions of her cousin Alex decimating her attackers, leaving her with years of nightmares. But the real horror had been in the men he'd beaten nearly to death. She could see them now, all of them, bigger than life and laughing as they tore at her clothes, taunted her Fox to come out and defend her. She'd cried out, screamed in terror, but nothing had stopped them. She'd been trapped, unable to defend herself.

The gun went off again, waking her from her nightmare.

She opened her eyes and looked around, horrified at what she saw. Chloe was on the ground, Apollonia was fighting with the gunman, and Heather was still standing there doing nothing. She had to do something, to help in any way she could.

She ran forward and began tugging on Chloe, trying to get her cousin to the cover of the car. Chloe helped, but she was bleeding from her shoulder, her arm hanging uselessly at her side. Heather helped Chloe up, shoving her into the car as the sound of fighting continued behind her. She didn't dare stop to look. She had to get Chloe out of there. Apollonia could handle one man, but Heather and Chloe weren't Hunters like Apollonia. Their best bet for survival was to take away what the man was fighting for: Chloe.

She scrambled into the driver's seat, her limbs barely obeying her commands. Her hands were shaking so hard she couldn't close the door. She'd get Chloe to the hospital, or better yet, to Julian. Julian could heal Chloe, no problem. Julian could handle anything. He'd saved Chloe once before.

"Ja ja ja ja ja." Chloe's hand slammed into the back of the passenger seat.

"Jim?" Heather slid behind the wheel, fumbling to see if Apollonia had left the keys in it.

Chloe nodded furiously, tears in her eyes, either of frustration or pain. Or both.

Heather was near tears herself. "I need to get you to Julian first, but we can call Jim on the way." Damn it, where the fuck were the *keys*?

Another shot rang out. Chloe screamed just as white-hot agony ripped through Heather's arm. She shrieked at the pain, clutching her arm and sliding sideways, praying the gunman didn't fire off another shot.

A Tiger's roar was all she heard before the sound of flesh hitting flesh sounded once more. Heather closed her eyes and prayed that Apollonia would get them out of this. Without the car keys, Chloe and Heather were totally boned. Everything was going dark, the world around her tilting sickeningly as she tried to stay conscious.

She lost track of time or consciousness, she wasn't sure which, but Apollonia was gently shaking her. "Kid, I need you to sit up, okay?"

"Uh-huh." Heather lifted herself up with Apollonia's help. Her arm was throbbing fiercely and was coated in blood. "Chloe?"

Apollonia helped her into the passenger seat, but even with the help Heather's vision kept going in and out of the dark. "Out cold in the back." Apollonia slid into the driver's seat, ignoring the blood Heather had left behind. "He got away."

Heather sighed wearily. "Shit."

"Yeah. Got distracted by the sirens and the hot sheriff. Someone in the mall or the parking lot saw what was happening and called the cops." She shook her head. "Stupid amateur. This was the last place he should have tried his shit."

Hot sheriff? "You mean Gabe Anderson?"

Apollonia grinned. "Is that his name?"

Heather groaned as the car jerked into gear. She tried to distract herself with thoughts of Gabe. "His mate's name is Sarah."

"Shit." Apollonia's grin disappeared. "I swear, all the cute ones are taken."

Heather's vision began to darken once again. Her heartbeat was heavy sounding, her pulse running a mile a minute. She began to shiver, cold creeping over her like fog.

"Wait." A familiar figure, one white streak in his hair, came to the window. Julian was there, his dark eyes glancing over both Chloe and Heather. "She's losing a lot of blood."

Apollonia snarled. "I'm getting her to the hospital if you'll move."

"Hi, Julian. We're gonna be on YouTube." Heather chuckled. Her teeth were chattering, her limbs beginning to shake with the cold.

"I can't fix that, but I can do something about the cold."

She didn't know how or when he'd gotten in the car with them, but they were already moving and Julian was doing something that felt really painful. "Owie."

"Just a little bit more, okay?"

"Hurts." Hell, his healing hurt just as bad as the gunshot.

"Can't heal it all. Too many witnesses," he muttered. She opened her eyes (when did she close them?) to see him talking to Apollonia.

"Agreed. Just make sure she lives, okay?"

"She will. I'm going to check Chloe now. Heather was worse off, but she'll make it to the hospital now."

Heather didn't hear the rest. It was all just murmurs and lost words as she sank into the cold darkness once more.

Chapter Eight

Barney was scared shitless. While he was in Arizona meeting with Carl, his mate had been shot, gone into shock and had to have surgery to repair the damage. Now he was back in Halle and ready to pound someone's head in. His Bear was in a rage, ready to tear apart anyone who got between him and Heather.

Fuck this shit. Fuck it to hell and back again. Heather was his to protect, and no one would lay a paw or claw on her again. He'd been an idiot to leave her behind without proper protection. He should have had Apollonia assigned to Chloe and Artemis watching Heather. But no, he'd foolishly believed Heather was safe so long as he didn't mark her as his.

That was about to fucking change. Heather would be his before he headed back to Sedona.

The overriding need to be near her and confirm that she was safe had driven him to the airport, leaving Casey Lee and Derrick to continue the investigation in Arizona. They would get back to him at some point, but for now his place was here. They were more than capable of working with Carl while Barney dealt with the threat to Heather and Chloe. It was the only option open to him. Leaving Heather alone and hurt?

Not gonna happen. He didn't care how many of her clan surrounded her. She'd been hurt while with a Hunter and the white Fox. If they couldn't keep her safe…

Grr. His Bear was riding him hard, eager to find the one who'd made Heather suffer. If he had the fucker's scent, he'd be out there right now, making sure he'd never hurt anyone else ever again. Ripping the guy's head off was his number two priority, number one being Heather.

He strode through the hospital doors like death himself rode on his coattails, ready to send the Smith twins through a wall. They were the ones who had been tasked with guarding Chloe, and they'd failed him miserably. He was going to skin them both for making Heather bleed, and then he'd kill them for almost losing the white Fox.

Barney tried to smile at the receptionist, but it was damn near impossible. From her reaction, a terrified lurch, he'd failed miserably. "Heather Allen?"

"One of the gunshot victims?" She blinked. "Um, are you a relative?"

"Fiancé." His voice was beginning to turn, to pick up the rumble of his Bear. That wasn't good. He understood now what Ryan Williams had gone through when Glory Walsh had been shot. No wonder Ryan had gone on the hunt for her attacker. Barney's Bear was ready to do the same thing. Considering he had far more experience than Ryan, he had no doubt he'd be covered in the blood of his enemy in no time.

The tapping of keys forced him to focus once more on the receptionist. "Room 311."

"Thanks." Past the receptionist, take a left, and he was at the elevator. He'd spent more time in this hospital than he cared to remember, but never before had he been this pissed off.

He strode through the open elevator doors and punched the number three, scowling so fiercely that an elderly woman actually backed away from the doors. "I'll take the next one."

He felt bad for, like, two seconds before the memory of Gabe's voice floated through his mind. *"Heather's been shot."*

Heather's been shot. Those three little words had sent him scrambling so fast even Carl had been stunned. They were going to echo in his mind until he saw for himself that Heather was whole, that she'd suffered no lasting damage from her brush with death.

Getting off the elevator was no better. He stomped toward Room 311, his gaze stuck on two people who seemed to be guarding the door. One of them was going to decorate the floor of his apartment. "Apollonia!"

"Shit," he heard her mutter. She straightened up. "I tried, boss."

"Not hard enough." He grabbed her by the throat and lifted her off her feet. His claws were extended, his fangs dipping over his bottom lip. "She nearly died."

Odd. Apollonia wasn't fighting him at all. If anything, her head lowered, almost like a subordinate shifter to an Alpha.

"Put. Her. Down."

Barney shivered as a deep voice rolled over him, forcing him to put Apollonia back on her feet. He'd heard that voice before, been forced to obey it as he was being forced now. His Bear refused to fight that voice.

Julian DuCharme was here and wasn't going to allow him to kill Apollonia. Damn it.

"Now step away."

Barney was driven to obey. He did as told, putting a little more than an arm's length of distance between himself and the Tiger shifter.

"Look at me. Focus on me."

His feet shuffled him around without any input from him. Terrified, he stared into the silver eyes of the only Kermode Bear in Halle, Pennsylvania.

"Good." Julian's hair was pure white, his silver gaze demanding. "Now calm down. Heather's surgery went very well, and she's awake and waiting for you."

He felt his Bear calm at the command of the Spirit Bear. "I fuckin' hate you."

Julian patted him on the cheek. "I know, dude. Now go in there and kiss Heather's boo-boos." Julian winked, his silver eyes turning their normal brownish-black. "But don't bite her yet. She did lose a lot of blood."

At that, Barney's Bear tried to rise once more, ready to strangle Apollonia.

"She did the best she could," Julian said softly. "Look at her. She's beating herself up enough for both of you."

Barney took the time to really look at Apollonia. Her shoulders were slumped, her usual carefree smile gone. In its place was a weak frown. Her skin was bruised and cut, and there was a powder burn on her right hand. "Who did this?"

She shrugged. "Dunno. Bounty hunter, I think. He offered to share half the reward with me."

"What reward?" There was a fucking *reward* now? Jim Woods was going to go ballistic when he found out. Barney wasn't sure if he should tell him or not.

"Again, I don't know." She pushed off the wall and glared at him, her shoulders finally square, anger overriding the earlier despondency. "He got away from me when we heard the sirens. I couldn't let any humans catch us fighting."

"Since there was no way for her to know it was Gabriel who would show up on the call, I think she did the right thing. She stayed with Heather and Chloe, making sure no one else got to them except Gabe and I." Julian got in-between them, as if afraid Barney would start fighting Apollonia again. "He'll show his face again."

"Or another one will." Barney shook his head and stared at Heather's door. "This just keeps getting better and better, doesn't it?"

Julian sighed. "Tell me about it. Canada is nice this time of year, you know?"

"Thinking of going back?" Since the Kermode Bears lived out on some island in British Columbia, going back there was always an option for Julian since he wasn't officially a citizen of the U.S. Carl was working on that, but even with the backing of the Senate these things took time.

"Nope." Julian's smile was wistful. "Cyn would hate it."

And that was all the Bear had to say. His mate would hate it, so Julian would stick around this crazy-ass town until hell froze over, because Cyn would never leave her friends. "Gotcha."

Barney was afraid he was going to share Julian's fate. He'd stay here for as long as Heather wished, no matter what the Senate said. She would need her family while he was out Hunting, and he wouldn't take that away from her, or the friends she'd found at Cynful Tattoos.

He opened the door and stepped inside. "Heather?"

She turned, smiling as she saw him. She looked so pale against the white sheets that his Bear rose once again. He could practically count the freckles on her face from across the room. The urge to heal had never been so strong.

The relief on her face when she saw him staggered him. Her sweet, welcoming smile nearly floored him. "Barney."

He smiled and entered the room. "Didn't I tell you to keep your little Hobbit ass safe?"

"A girl's gotta shop when a girl's gotta shop." She shot him a weak, yet cheeky grin. "Besides, Apollonia offered to pay for lunch. Couldn't pass that up, could I?"

He shook his head, reluctantly amused by her. The fact that she was smiling at him was the only thing that kept him from ripping the damn room apart. "What happened?"

"Someone nearly got Chloe. Came up from behind and grabbed her around the throat. He pointed a gun at us and told us he'd let us go if we let him take her." Heather shuddered, wincing a bit. It must have tugged on her IV. "I...froze."

"Froze?" He took hold of her hand, gently caressing her fingers. They were so small, so delicate. His own thick fingers were almost sacrilegious against hers. Heather's hands were the hands of an artist, made to create, not destroy. His had shed more blood than he ever wanted to admit to her.

"Yeah." She plucked at the blanket with her free hand, refusing to look at him. "I just...stopped. I couldn't move. It was like being ten all over again. I even saw those men, the ones who attacked me back then." She shuddered so hard she nearly shook loose of his hold. "I couldn't help Chloe or Apollonia."

"Look at me, Heather." He tilted her chin up, forcing her to lift her head. "Everyone, and I mean *everyone*, has a moment like that."

"Sure they do." She rolled her eyes at him. "Bet you haven't."

Between that cute little pout and the way she said it, he was once again reminded of exactly how young his mate really was. He sighed, feeling like an ogre. "I have. First time I faced off against a Tiger rogue."

"Yeah?" Heather glanced at him through her lashes.

"Yup." He sat on the edge of the bed. "When that fucker shifted into his other form, I damn near shit a horse."

"A horse?"

Man, that soft little giggle was going to be the death of him. "It was way too big to be a kitten. And considering how hard my ass was kicked, I'm pretty sure hooves were involved."

"I bet that made it difficult to fight." Her gaze had gone distant. He just bet she was picturing a horse-shaped turd in his jeans.

"Smelly too."

She played with his fingers. "I managed to get Chloe in the car, though. Tried to find the keys, but Apollonia must have still had them on her." She grimaced. "I wasn't thinking clearly, or I would have just ducked down, locked the doors and called 911."

"You trusted Apollonia to protect you." Something Barney would have to thank the Tiger for, damn it. He still wanted to be pissed at her, but she wasn't the one he needed to fight. He had to discover who'd put a bounty on Chloe's head, after he was certain his little Hobbit was safe and sound.

"I did. Or if not me then at least Chloe." She stared into his eyes, her own pained. "I was shot while looking for the keys so I could get Chloe to the hospital." She shook. "I haven't been that afraid since I was ten."

The scent of her fear filled the room. His Bear reared, ready to eviscerate the threat.

"Shh." Dainty hands curled around his arms. "Please, Barney. For me?"

He blinked, his Bear backing down immediately. "I will keep you safe."

She smiled and snuggled against him despite wires and medical tape. "I know."

And that was all she wrote for James "Barney" Barnwell. He couldn't remember the last time someone had leaned so trustingly against him. When was the last time someone had been genuinely glad to see him? His parents, who'd died three years ago? No one was ever happy to see him. He was their pain in the ass trainer, the one they called only when they were in trouble. He wasn't invited to family barbecues, he was asked to join Hunts gone bad.

Barney stroked her hair, listened to her content little sigh, and fell down a hole he'd never intended to even see in his lifetime.

Damn it. It was bad enough he had a mate, but to fall in love with her? That sucked big hairy donkey balls. "I'll be here every day, so don't go dancing without me."

"Can you?" She tilted her head back, the dark circles under her eyes more prominent now that she was so close. "I mean, you have to work."

"Nothing can keep me away from you." He kissed her, careful to keep it soft and sweet. She was hurting, and he wasn't going to add to her pain. "Now. How about a rousing game of Tic-Tac-Toe?"

She shook her head, her smile weary. "I think I might sleep some more." She lay back down with a tiny yawn.

This wasn't how he'd envisioned seeing her hair spread out beneath her for the first time, but he wasn't going to complain. She was alive, and that was all that mattered. "Sleep. I'll be here when you wake."

Her bloodshot eyes closed on a sigh, but one of those small hands of hers had a grip on his arm stronger than steel. She might as well have wrapped it around his heart, because from now on it beat only for her.

Chapter Nine

Heather flipped channels on the hospital TV, bored out of her mind. She'd been in the hospital for two days now, and each successive day made her want out in the worst way. But until the doctor cleared her, no one would let her leave. Even Julian was coming down on the side of the doctors, refusing to take her home no matter how much she begged. Cyn wouldn't allow him to come to the hospital more than necessary. Once they'd made sure that neither Chloe's nor Heather's lives were in danger he'd waited around long enough to deal with Barney's Bear before heading for home and some rest.

She understood, since she had family who were Bears. For a normal Bear, being in a hospital made them…itchy. They wanted to help, to heal, even though they could only heal minor wounds. But for Julian, that itch was unbearable. If left on his own he'd go from room to room, draining himself to death taking care of the sick. He'd almost killed himself more than once healing those he cared for. Cyn was the only one who could stop him, and she did, demanding he save his powers for those truly in need.

But it didn't make Heather's situation any better. The wound ached and itched at the same time, and her boredom was about to reach new heights. Her parents, aunts and uncles visited all the time, but they worried over her until she was ready to pull her hair out in frustration. Keith and Tiffany were bearable but didn't stay long enough to counteract their parents. Those visits were usually accompanied by some minor healing from her Bear relatives, but it would still take time for her to be fully functional again.

To make things worse, the shot was to her dominant side, so she couldn't even draw. The desire to put pencil to paper was a worse itch than her wound.

"Knock knock."

She breathed a sigh of relief. "Barney." Finally, someone who wasn't going to fuss over her and make her feel worse. She grinned, eager to see what her mate had in store for her today. The day before he'd brought Yahtzee and played with her until visiting hours were over, chatting casually with her family as they came in and out of her room. When he was there, they barely fussed at all.

If she could, she'd strap him to the bed and never let him out until they released her.

He held up a deck of cards and a wooden board. "Think you can play Cribbage?"

She frowned, intrigued. "What's that?"

"It's easy, but it takes some strategy to win. Interested?"

She shrugged, wincing a bit at the pull in her stitches. "Sure, why not?"

"Good." He pulled the hospital table over her lap, then sat down on the bed, facing her. He opened the cards first, shuffling them. "I deal out six cards. You choose two to take out of your hand, and I choose two. This forms the crib, and gives the dealer extra points."

"Well that's not fair." She pouted up at him and wiggled the fingers of her right hand. "I'm not sure I can deal." She was in a sling to keep her shoulder still.

"I'll shuffle and deal for you." He dealt out six cards. "This is called a Cribbage board." He placed four pegs into the board, two silver, two gold. The pegs were placed one behind the other. "You're gold."

"Okay." She didn't care what color she was. She could be chartreuse if he got rid of her boredom.

"So, here's how you play…"

Heather frowned in concentration as he explained the rules. It was all about counting and points and moving the pegs around a wooden board, with extra points awarded for different things like a run of numbers or making fifteen. "You'll correct me if I make a mistake?"

He shrugged. "The first couple of rounds, sure." He shuffled the cards quickly and efficiently. "After that, you're on your own."

She eyed him for a moment as he started doling out cards. "You play this a lot, don't you?"

He nodded. "Sometimes the job is to babysit someone, like when I trained Gabriel. It helps to have different games you like to play that can be done with two players. And this one I really enjoy, so I talk everyone I can into playing it."

She smiled, pleased that he wanted to share one of his favorite pastimes with her. "Then let's play. I want to learn how to kick your butt."

He chuckled. "You can try, newbie."

They played quietly for a while, Barney correcting her as she learned the game. Heather was enjoying herself more than she wanted to admit, groaning when the cards didn't go her way and laughing like a lunatic when they did. Barney watched her with open affection, touching her hand or stroking her hair and making her blush. By the time they'd finished the first game, she could picture doing this with him on quiet nights, sipping wine and just enjoying each other.

"What has you smiling like that?" Barney's tone was soft as he reset the pegs.

She shrugged, unwilling to share her vision of a happy life with him. "Nothing."

"Mm-hm." He shuffled the cards, dealing them out deftly. Barney was turning out to be remarkably gentle despite his size and growly exterior.

But that didn't mean he wasn't without his own worries, and it was her job as his mate to try and ease them. "How's the investigation going? Have Derrick and Casey Lee gotten back to you?"

He grimaced. "Yeah, but they're having a hard time getting anything out of anyone. Since they aren't Hunters, they don't have instant access to people the way I do, so they have to do things differently. Add in the fact that they can't tell anyone *why* they're questioning them, and it gets awkward fast."

"What do you mean they're doing things their way?" Heather had barely met the mercs, and what she'd seen made her uneasy. Chloe trusted them, but

Heather wasn't so sure. Casey Lee was funny, but Derrick? He looked like he ate babies for breakfast and drank kitten smoothies just because.

"They're probably doing things I'd rather not know about. I prefer to do things the legal way, or at least legal by shifter standards." He sighed, putting his cards on the table. "I feel like I'm running around in circles, and all the answers are somewhere in a square or an octagon."

She bit her lip, uncertain what to do for him. He looked so frustrated she wanted to help in the worst way. "Is there anything I can do?"

His gaze bored into her. "Just talking to you helps." He made a disgruntled face, glancing away from her. "That sounds so fucking lame."

She patted his hand. "I liked it. Very suave."

He chuckled and turned back to her. "I try." But the humor didn't last long. "I keep thinking that if I can figure this all out then everything will be fine, but I know that's wrong."

She squeezed his hand, hoping to convey her feelings, confused though they were. "Gabe and Alex both told me this thing with the white shifters has been going on for longer than any of us thought. This goes deeper than just Chloe or Julian."

He stared at her intently. "Tell me what you're thinking."

She blinked, startled. "Me?"

Barney nodded. "What's going on in that little Hobbit brain of yours?"

"I keep telling you I'm not *that* short. And I swear my toes aren't hairy." She made sure the blanket covered her feet, just in case he decided to check. There might be a *little* fuzz on her big toes, but he didn't need to know that.

He smiled, but didn't comment.

"You sure you want to know what I think?"

He nodded firmly. "Give it to me."

She took a deep breath. "Why are they going after white shifters? And why children of mixed parentage? What's the connection between them? They're killing kids, Barney. There has to be a connection there somewhere."

"You think there's something linking white shifters and mixed blood?"

Heather shrugged. "You have a better idea?"

"It's something to look into." Barney freed his hand and scratched his chin. "It's definitely something I can have Derrick and Casey Lee look into. I've had the same thought, but I didn't want to focus all my attention in that direction in case I was wrong."

She could understand that. It made sense not to get hooked, only to find out the trail you'd been following led to a dead end. "Birth and death records should be easy to access."

"If there's a greater instance of white shifters among those of mixed parentage it would explain why they're going after those kids."

She held up her hand. "There's one problem, though. Chloe's of mixed blood, but the Kermode are not."

Barney held up his finger as if making a point. "But not all Kermode have Kermode children. They bite their mates, and if they're human the spirits determine what kind of shifter their mate becomes. They might not even become a Bear."

"Really?" She'd never heard of such a thing. As far as she knew, if you bit a human, they became the same kind of shifter as you. A Fox created a Fox, a Bear created a Bear. "Does that mean that Chloe could bite someone and have them become, say, an Ocelot?"

"I have no fucking clue."

"Then maybe we should find one."

He gently tapped her forehead. "What's this 'we' shit? Your Hobbit ass is sitting right here and recovering, end of subject."

"I can still use my brains, big guy. Trust me, the last thing I want to do is face another gun." She shuddered, remembering last night's nightmare. She'd been frozen, staring at the barrel of a gun that seemed the size of her head. There'd been no one there to save her, to keep her from—

Heather gasped as Barney pushed aside the hospital table and grabbed hold of her. He hugged her tight, his chin resting on top of her head. "Nightmares again?"

She nodded, unwilling to speak.

He grunted. "Would it help if I told you how brave you were?"

"Nope." She snuggled in, sniffing at his shirt. His scent soothed her, driving back the memory of the nightmare. "Just…hold me for a sec."

His grip tightened. "Can do, sweetheart."

Barney sat with her, silent and still, the only sound his heartbeat and the hum of the machines she was hooked up to. The quiet, patient care he was showing her touched her far more deeply than any growl or snarl of protection could ever hope to. This contentment was something she'd thought she wouldn't have with him.

She'd been wrong, and she couldn't be happier about it.

"What are you smiling about?"

The smile she hadn't even known she had widened. "It's a secret."

He grumbled a bit, but even that was somehow adorable. And that, too, was a secret she'd never tell him.

"I have to wonder, was the attack on you when you were a child meant to kill you?"

"What do you mean?" She didn't understand what he was saying, but a shiver worked its way down her spine.

"When you were attacked and Alex saved you. Is it possible you were targeted because you're mixed blood?" Barney's arms tightened around her, making it difficult to breathe.

"That's…scary." She pushed against him and he eased his hold. "That's super scary."

"Yeah." He rested his chin on her head and began rocking her. It wasn't clear to her if he was comforting her, or himself. "Adrian has set guards on your door. Chloe's too."

"I saw." The Pumas had waved to her, both of them ensuring her that they were volunteers. One even mentioned having protected the Poconos Pack Luna when she'd been severely injured saving Adrian Giordano's mate, Sheri, from being run down. "So Max knows what's going on."

"And if Max knows, then the Little General knows too. Don't be surprised if you get a visit from her."

She laughed at Barney's description of the female Alpha of the Puma Pride. Emma Cannon was known for her bossiness, but she had a heart of gold. "I'm looking forward to it."

"Lord help us all," Barney muttered into her hair.

Chapter Ten

Barney pulled into the hospital parking lot, wondering if today they'd finally let Heather go. Heather had been due to be released from the hospital the day before, but because she'd run a fever in the night they'd decided to keep her for at least a day or two longer. An infection wasn't something to fuck around with, but at least she was in the right place to deal with it.

While he understood their concerns, Barney just wanted his mate out of the hospital. He was sick of the smell of the place. It lingered on his skin, in his hair, and nothing he did seemed to get rid of it. And it had to be worse for Heather. As a Fox, her nose was more sensitive than his. The antiseptic smell must be stinging her sinuses like crazy.

Once she was cleared to leave the hospital, Barney could get back on the trail of the Senator or Senators who'd hired the fucker to harm his mate. Oh, Barney would *love* to get his paws on the man who'd shot her, he really would. He'd shove the man's head up his ass the hard way. Backward. But the gunman was only a footnote in a bigger problem. To catch the *real* person who'd hurt his mate, he needed to find the one who'd put the bounty out on Chloe. He was certain he'd find that person somewhere in the Senate.

He parked in the first clear spot he could find, eager to get inside and see his mate. Visiting hours were just beginning, and he had plans to spend the whole day with her. The boredom was tough on her, leaving her with only her own thoughts and fears for company. Her parents tried to soothe her, but for some reason it didn't seem to be working. She was tense and pale until Barney walked through her door. Only then did she seem to relax. Was it because he was her mate, or because he was a Hunter?

"Yo."

Barney froze, one leg out of the car, the engine still ticking. "What do you want?"

Lounging against the car next to him was Artemis. The white Tiger was staring at the sky. "How is she?"

Barney got out of the car and closed the door. He gripped the keys tightly, wondering what the hell Artemis was up to. "She spiked a fever, so they're keeping her for another day or two."

Artemis nodded once. "Apollonia's still there, watching them both."

Barney knew that. The female Hunter had been there every day, unmoving, refusing to sleep unless either Gabe, Barney or Ryan was there to take over for her. She didn't care if there were Puma guards on the doors, she trusted no one but another Hunter. Not even Artemis could get her to move. She was taking Chloe and Heather's injuries far more seriously than Barney would have given her credit for.

Artemis was watching him, his expression inscrutable. "Fox holds the key, you know."

"You said that before, but what does it mean?" Barney held still and tried to rein in his temper. Maybe if he stayed calm he'd actually get something out of the flighty Tiger.

Artemis yawned lazily. "I can't tell you much more than that."

Barney gritted his teeth. Man, Artemis annoyed him. "Why not?"

Artemis returned his gaze to the sky. "It breaks the rules."

"What fucking rules?" Barney could feel his anger rising.

"Rules older than you or I. Older even than the shifters." Artemis turned his gaze to Barney once more, but this time they were pure silver. "Even if I knew more, I couldn't say it without hurting the very outcome we're all wishing for."

Barney was even more confused than he'd been before, but the anger had left him. Artemis was speaking on behalf of Tiger now, and apparently there were rules involved he knew nothing about. "I have no clue what you're talking about."

"Sometimes neither do I, and I'm okay with that." Artemis smiled, the silver fading from his eyes. "Maybe you should follow your instincts. What are they telling you?"

Barney wanted to strangle Artemis. So much for remaining calm. "I guess I should go talk to some Foxes."

"Guess so." Artemis stood, his hands shoved in the pockets of his jeans. "See ya."

Artemis sauntered off across the parking lot, going God knew where. Artemis seemed to have two speeds: off and *holy-fuck-a-Tiger's-gonna-eat-me!* And he switched back and forth with the same ease as flipping a light switch.

Barney stared at the hospital doors and cursed. He climbed back in his car and pulled out this cell phone, dialing Heather's hospital room. As soon as she picked up, he spoke. "It's me. I'm going to be late today."

"Hunter business?"

Her tone was solemn, making him feel even more guilty. "Yeah. Artemis dropped by and reminded me that Fox holds the key. It's the second time he's done that."

"Oh. And since he's the white Tiger—"

Barney nodded, even though he knew she couldn't see him. "I figure I should listen to him."

"Are you going to speak to Chloe?"

"Man, I love a smart girl."

Heather choked.

"You okay?" He pulled out of the parking lot and headed toward the animal clinic Chloe worked at.

"Fine," she gasped. "Never mind me. I'm good. Just tried to breathe water, that's all."

"I hate to tell you this, but you're not a fish, sweetheart."

"Asshole," she grumbled, coughing again.

"Uh-huh." Barney pulled out onto the street and started driving toward the animal clinic Dr. Woods ran. He was pretty sure Chloe would be there with her mate. Jim hadn't taken the news that there was a bounty on his mate's head very well and was keeping her close at all times. Something Barney planned on doing with his own mate.

"You do what you have to do and I'll see you later, all right?"

"Definitely." He turned down the street the clinic was on. "I'll bring you lunch. Is there anything you want?"

"Not pudding." She gagged. "I swear, if I eat any more pudding I'm gonna hurl."

"Burger, fries and a nice, thick shake sound good?" He laughed when she whimpered. "I'll see you soon, baby."

"Bye, Barney." The call disconnected, and Barney was left feeling the same. He wanted to be in that hospital room, playing games and talking softly with his mate. She was going to worry a hole in her hospital blanket. He'd seen the pulled threads, the way her fingers tightened on the fabric until she was certain it was him coming to her side. Leaving her, even in the hands of family, just wasn't sitting right with him.

But like he'd often told Gabe and Ryan, he was a Hunter first, a mate second. He had a job to do, and he'd do it no matter how badly he wanted to be with Heather. Besides, by finding the bad guys he'd be doing his job toward his mate as well, protecting her from whoever had set this whole chain in motion. He had to trust in her Puma guards and Apollonia. She was as safe as anyone could make her.

He pulled up outside the animal clinic, smiling when he saw Chloe and Jim sitting on a bench outside. Their heads were together, Chloe's red hair vibrant against Jim's more muted blond. Chloe was smiling at something Jim was saying, looking none the worse for having been shot. She'd been released the day before. Both of them looked his way as he got out of his car, the lunch they'd been eating forgotten in a moment of worry.

Barney had no intention of making them uneasy. He did his best to look unconcerned, hoping they'd pick up on the fact that nothing was wrong. "Hey, guys. You have a moment?"

Jim straightened. A brand new Wolf shifter without a Pack, he should have been setting off alarm bells in Barney's mind. Instead, the Wolf seemed to be one of the rare ones who didn't need a Pack to be whole. Instead, his life simply went on. Max had declared him Pride, but how much impact that had on Jim Barney didn't know. "What's wrong?"

Guess that didn't work. Considering how often Chloe had been hurt, Barney couldn't blame the Wolf for his caution. "Absolutely nothing." Barney crouched in front of them. There wasn't room on the bench for all three of them, and he'd rather be able to see Chloe's face.

"Hey, Barney." She scratched her hand. She'd also been shot in the shoulder and her arm was in a sling, but unlike Heather she wasn't looking at a possible infection. "How's my cousin?"

"Hungry. I'm bringing her lunch when I'm done here."

Chloe sagged in relief. "That's good. If she's hungry she must be feeling sweater." Chloe bit her lip. "So why are you here?"

"Fox holds the key." Barney grunted. "Artemis keeps coming to me and saying that, but—"

Chloe held up her good hand. "I'm not the Fox you're looking for. Fox himself told bee that. And Julian isn't the Bear."

"I know, but I was hoping you could point me in the right direction." Barney ran his fingers through his hair. "It's one of your relatives. It has to be. There aren't any other Foxes around here. You and Heather know them best, but with her still in the hospital I didn't want to bother her with this."

"What about the Fox Senator?" Jim glanced between Chloe and Barney, watching their reactions. "Could he have something to do with it?"

"*She*, and I have no idea." Chloe stared at the ground, frowning in concentration. "Nicole Reed hasn't exactly come by for tea and crumpets."

"Has she contacted you at all?" That surprised him. A white Fox capable of speaking with the spirits should have been someone the Fox Senator would be highly interested in.

Unless, of course, she thought Chloe's abilities to be nothing more than the delusions of a woman with a traumatic brain injury.

"Nope. And I'm kind of scared to contact her myself." Chloe took hold of Jim's hand. "I don't know what would happen to me if I did, considering it's the Senate that's after me."

Jim scowled. "Then we're definitely not contacting her, or any other Senator. Not until we know for certain it's safe to do so."

"Carl knows about you, but I'm not sure who else does." Barney filled them in on what he'd learned from Darien before having to leave the Senate buildings. "I left Casey Lee and Derrick to continue the investigation. They're posing as Carl and Darien's bodyguards."

"Speaking of bodyguards…" Jim and Chloe exchanged a worried glance. Jim spoke, his tone concerned. "Apollonia is watching Heather day and night. I don't think she's sleeping at all."

"Even Hunters sleep. She's probably cat-napping here and there when I'm with Heather." But even so, that meant that she was severely sleep deprived. "I'll ask Gabe or Max to assign a Puma to watching her."

"Heather, or Apollonia?" Chloe smiled mischievously.

"Apollonia, of course." There should be someone in Halle other than him who could bully the Hunter into resting. "If necessary I'll sic Emma on her."

Jim laughed. "That would teach her not to mess with you."

Chloe put her hand on Barney's arm. The scarred fingers of her hand tightened briefly. "Fox holds the key."

Startled, Barney took his eyes off of Chloe's hand and stared at her face. The Fox's eyes were silver, her pupils dilated. "Chloe?"

Jim must have heard something in Barney's voice, because he was suddenly fully focused on his mate. "What's happening?"

"I don't know." Barney patted Chloe's hand. "Chloe?"

"Fox holds the key." She blinked, her eyes turning their normal, pretty green. "I don't know why it's so important that you know that, but Fox was pretty insistent that I tell you."

"Okay." Barney didn't pretend to understand the relationship between the white shifters and the spirits, but he accepted it for what it was. "Anything else he wants me to know?"

Chloe's eyes turned silver. "Beware of Jamie Howard."

Jamie Howard. What the fuck? "What does he have to do with any of this?"

"I have no idea, but he's one scary motherfucker. Don't go near him unless you have no other choice." Jim stood and gathered the remains of their lunch. "I don't want Chloe out in the open right now. Anything else you need us for?"

"Nope." Barney stood, ready to go and speak to some of the other Foxes in Heather's family. Maybe Tiffany was the Fox mentioned?

Damn it, this was going to take all day. "Any clues as to who I should talk to?"

Chloe turned back to him with a grin. "Say hi to Heather for me."

With that, Jim escorted his mate into the building without another word spoken.

"Well. I'm boned." He headed back to his car, wondering if that last part had been a hint, or if she just wanted to say hi to her cousin. Her eyes hadn't been silver, so it must have been the latter.

Still, he couldn't quite shake the feeling that she'd been telling him something. Did she think Heather was the Fox the riddle spoke of? If so, what key did she hold? The key to the riddle?

He'd have to talk to her and find out. It was the only way. But first he'd visit some of her relatives and find out if any of them could give him a clue, because he'd be damned if he had one.

Chapter Eleven

Two becomes one, one becomes three. Bear knows the way, but Fox holds the key.

That riddle was becoming the bane of her mating. Barney was so fixated on it that it was driving him crazy. He was positive that it was the answer to why Chloe was being targeted. If Heather could figure out the answer, then maybe, just maybe, Barney would relent and mate her.

She could hope, right? Besides, it wasn't as if she had anything better to do. She was stuck here until the doctors cleared her of any infection, and the solitude was driving her insane.

It beat the hell out of afternoon talk shows, that was for sure. And the soaps? Blech. Why did humans cheat on each other so much? It was disgusting. If you were in love and happy, couldn't you keep your legs crossed and your panties on? It didn't even have to be in that order either.

Heather tapped the pencil she'd talked her brother into picking up for her against the pad of paper. Perhaps it was best to start at the beginning, with the first part of the riddle. Julian had been the first one to speak the prophecy, but since then Chloe had repeated it several times.

Neither of them was the Bear or Fox spoken of.

So who, or what, was two that had become one?

She began writing, starting with everything that could go from two to one. There was math, of course, with two minus one becomes one, one plus two becoming three. But she doubted it was that simple.

Or…was it?

Two becoming one could be marriage. Most people spoke of two becoming one when two people tied the knot, but the riddle specifically said two *becomes* one. Heather frowned. Wasn't "becomes" present tense? That meant it was happening, not *had* or *would* happen, right? She grunted, wishing she had her tablet PC so she could remember. What was happening right around the time Julian first spoke the prophecy?

She tapped her pencil again on the hospital table. That had to be it. Julian was the first to speak, and something was happening right around then. What was it? She racked her brain, trying to remember.

Wait. No. It wasn't Julian who'd spoken—it had been Chloe! Chloe was the first to receive the message, and had been ordered to give it to Julian. Then all the Kermode had the same damn dream.

She put down Chloe as the speaker, just to make sure she didn't forget. That Fox had spoken in present tense when giving Chloe the prophecy had to mean *something*, but for now she'd just make sure nothing escaped her, not even the tiniest clue.

Chloe gave the message to Julian, who delivered it to Alex and Ryan, as far as she knew. Perhaps she needed to call Julian and confirm?

She picked up the hospital phone and dialed Julian's cell number.

The deep voice of the Kermode Bear filled her ears. "Hello, Heather. I was wondering when you'd call."

"Hey, Super Bear." She wasn't even creeped out anymore by Julian's powers. The guy was just too nice to get upset over a few quirks. Add in the fact that he made Cyn happy, and Heather was all about Team Julian. "Listen, when you got the prophecy from Chloe, who did you tell about it?"

"No one, actually. Bear came to me while I was at work and spoke the prophecy again, and when I woke, Jamie was there. He was the first one to hear it."

Jamie Howard? "Then maybe…" Heather scribbled furiously. "Two becomes one. Jamie lost his mate, and became one person again."

"I thought of that, but then how do you factor in one becomes three?"

Julian sounded as puzzled as she felt.

"Hope, maybe?" Heather jotted down Hope Walsh's name. Hope was the twin sister of Glory Walsh, Ryan's mate. She'd been kidnapped as a teenager and held by a rogue wolf who'd repeatedly done horrible things to Hope.

She was also Jamie Howard's mate, something that had shocked everyone since Jamie's first mate, Marie, had been killed by a rogue who was after Tabby. Ryan and Cyn had rescued Hope, and now the female Wolf was being counseled by Sarah Anderson, the Pride's Omega and an empath who could both feel and influence the emotions of others.

"But then Hope and Jamie become two, right? That's why I dismissed that idea as possible."

"Nope, because Marie still is, and will always be, Jamie's mate. And Hope's, most likely." Heather put Marie and Hope next to Jamie. Hope, as a Wolf, would have been the glue between the three had Marie lived. Pumas didn't get second mates, but Wolves did, though it rarely happened.

There was silence on Julian's end, but when he spoke again he sounded shocked as hell. "But that would mean Marie was *meant* to die that day. That it wasn't a missed shot."

"And that you were meant to save Jamie." Heather shook her head. "It's complex, but it fits."

"But that isn't the only theory that fits, Heather."

True, but she had to consider all the possibilities or they'd never figure this out. "No, but it should get added to the list of theories."

"But why would the spirits be so interested in the mating of a Wolf to a pair of Pumas?" She could practically hear Julian shaking his head, his tone was so dismissive. "Nope. I think it's something else, something that hasn't happened yet."

Perhaps Julian knew more than he was letting on. He had a tendency to be cryptic at the worst possible moments. "Then what do you think it means?"

"I think we need to figure out who the Fox and Bear are. If we can do that, we'll know the answer to the rest of the riddle." His tone was convincing.

"Do you believe Fox and Bear are the two that becomes one?" She noted that, but she wasn't so sure. She was still convinced that the key to the whole thing lay with Jamie, Hope and Marie.

"It's possible." She could hear the disbelief in Julian's voice.

"Then how do they become three?" She threw that at him, thinking there was no way he would have a comeback for her.

"Huh. I'm not sure. Another white shifter, maybe?"

"So you still think Fox and Bear are white? That would make you and Chloe the Fox and Bear, and you've both said you aren't."

"Ah, but there are more white Bears in Canada, remember? One of them could be the Bear the prophecy spoke of."

That was true, but something still didn't seem right. "You don't really believe that. Otherwise there would be more white Foxes around."

He sighed. "No, I don't. Whoever they are, they'd be here, where the prophecy was spoken. But every Kermode had the same damn dream. Bear *really* wanted us to know about this for some reason."

"The Senate would be a good reason." Heather stared at the paper, her mind wandering once more to Barney. "It has to have something to do with that." She wrote down "Senate" and circled it. Twice.

"White shifters and the Senate. We've been over this so many times I'm getting sick of it." Julian sighed. "All right. How about you concentrate on the first half of the riddle. Maybe you can come up with something that will help Barney. I'll see if any of my Kermode cousins can sense anything more than Bear knows the way, yadda yadda blah blah blah."

"I can do that." She wouldn't, but she *could*. The whole riddle needed to be solved as one, not in pieces. *Fox holds the key* might mean that it was a Fox who was supposed to figure it out, so maybe that Fox was Heather herself.

"All right. Call me if you think of anything, and take care of yourself. Don't make me come over there and sit on you."

Heather laughed. "That would go over so well with Cyn, wouldn't it?"

"I'll do it in a heartbeat if I think you're getting worse, you hear me?"

Julian's tone was serious. "I don't want to have to fight off an infection because you're not resting properly."

"Yes, sir, Mr. Nurse sir."

"Talk to you later, brat." Julian hung up, leaving Heather nothing to do but think.

Halle was part of the key, and the people in it. She just knew it. And the only ones who fit the riddle were Jamie and Marie Howard, and Hope Walsh. But with Marie's death, how would they become three?

The white shifters could communicate with spirits, but none of them had ever said they communed with the dead. Kermode spoke to Bear, while Chloe said she mainly spoke to Fox. So it was the spirits of the animals they represented that they spoke to, not spirits in the sense of spooks. So Marie being some kind of ghost that could communicate with them wasn't even a remote possibility.

She crossed that off her list. Making the note and crossing it off was the best way to remind herself that yes, she'd thought of it and yes, she'd dismissed it. Otherwise she'd find herself going in circles.

Okay. So Marie going Casper on them was out. What about pregnancy? One becomes three could mean that Hope might be pregnant when she mated Jamie. But as far as she knew Hope wasn't pregnant when they'd rescued her from Salazar. Julian would have mentioned it when he checked her out for injuries, and she wasn't showing. Which Heather viewed as a relief.

Hmm. Perhaps she'd become pregnant by Jamie, but for some reason their mating would be delayed? Or not. There was always the possibility of pregnancy during a mating bite, something Heather would have to remember for her own circumstances. She put a question mark next to "pregnancy" and moved on.

What about…another mate?

She crossed that one off almost immediately. Wolves had one, rarely two, mates. Three? That would be insane.

Ghosts, mates and babies. What else could turn one into three? And why were the two of them so important that the spirits themselves felt the need to give a riddle that needed solving?

No wonder Barney was going insane with this. She was focusing on her own theory and already she was about to pull her hair out in frustration. Still, she was certain she was on to something. A pregnancy seemed the most logical conclusion, but she felt like she was missing something vital.

Hmm. Did it have to be a person that caused them to become three? Could it be some sort of object? She scratched her head, but nothing specific came to mind. She really needed to go over this with Barney. Maybe he could help her figure out the impossible.

And he'd better remember her burger too.

Chapter Twelve

Heather was staring at a piece of paper with such an intent expression that he had the sudden urge to tiptoe right back out of the room.

"Jamie Howard, Marie Howard and Hope Walsh."

Her soft voice was distant, but it was her words that made Barney take that step into the room. Chloe's warning was still ringing in his ears, and hearing Heather say Dr. Howard's name made shivers run down his spine. It couldn't be a coincidence. "Why did you mention Jamie Howard?"

Heather jumped, her head jerking toward him. "Barney?" Her eyes were huge, her expression startled. "You scared the hell out of me."

He didn't have time to reassure her. "Why did you mention Dr. Howard?"

She blinked and looked back down at the piece of paper. "It's the only thing that makes sense to me."

"How so?" He tried to keep his tone light, but he knew he'd failed when she shot him another fearful glance. "Chloe told me 'Beware of Jamie Howard'."

"Oh." Heather bit her lip. The plump, pink flesh against the whiteness of her teeth tempted him to drop his questions and just kiss her so stupid she never mentioned the name Jamie Howard again. "Are you sure that's what she meant? You know how her words get tangled up."

"Her eyes were silver when she said it. I think it was a direct message from Fox." Barney took the slip of paper from her hospital table, ignoring her faint cry of denial. Instead he handed her the sack of food he'd brought. She tore into the burger wrapper while he glanced over the notes, the simple math, the words "marriage" and "two becomes one" with the "s" underlined three times.

Julian and Chloe's names were written down, but she'd drawn arrows moving Chloe's name above Julian's. Alex and Ryan's names were crossed off, and Jamie Howard's was written several times, along with Marie Howard and Hope Walsh. She'd crossed off the word…"ghost"?

She'd actually written *Jamie and Marie Howard minus Marie Howard equals Jamie Howard*, followed by *Jamie Howard plus Hope Walsh equals???*.

"That's where I get stuck." A pencil eraser tapped the triple question marks. "How do Jamie and Hope make three?"

There was only one thing Barney could think of. "A baby?"

"I thought that could be it." Heather moaned as she bit into her burger. "God, this tastes so good."

He tapped the word "ghost". "I doubt Marie is going to haunt them. From what I hear, she wasn't like that. Besides, I doubt the spirits would want such an arrangement, even if it could be done."

"So you agree that those three together makes the most sense? That they're the ones the prophecy speaks of?" Her hopeful expression belied her calm tone. She wanted someone to believe in her theory, even if it seemed far-fetched.

Barney stared at the paper, debating whether or not her theory had any validity to it. Looking at her notes, he could see how she'd come to the conclusion that Jamie was the key to the whole mess they found themselves in. "It's worth looking into. No one else's theories have panned out, so for all we know you're on the right track."

"Julian thinks it has more to do with the Bear and Fox that are spoken of. He doesn't think Dr. Howard has anything to do with it at all." Heather's expression was determined. "But he's wrong."

He stared at Heather, surprised by her ferocity. "That sure, are you?"

She nodded firmly. "It's the only thing that makes any sense whatsoever." She glared at him as if it was all his fault somehow. "Go talk to Dr. Howard. Find out if he knows anything about this." She tapped the paper again. "Maybe with his help we can finish this."

"And get to our mating?" He leaned forward, touching that tempting bottom lip of hers with the tip of his finger. Her expression immediately softened, her eyes turning the reddish-brown of her Fox. "You know, when this is over and I mate you, I'll be taking you to my home, not your parents. It will be just you—" he stroked her lip, following his fingertip with his gaze, "—and me."

"I'm not a child. I know that."

She was fucking nineteen years old, almost the same age Chloe had been when she met Dr. Woods. He was twenty-seven, and had seen more pain and horror than any grown man should. How could he not want to bundle her up in bubble wrap and keep her safe and sound in his den, far away from the horrors of the world? He had a pretty good idea that was how Dr. Woods saw things too, but Barney wasn't going to wait for Heather to "grow up". He was going to claim his mate sooner rather than later. Her wounds were more than enough to drive home the point that living without her wasn't an option anymore. "You *are* a child still, but you're also my mate."

She blew some of her red hair out of her eyes and glared at him. "Am not."

Her pout was absolutely adorable. "Are too." Before she could argue more, he kissed her, gently parting her lips until she let him inside the sweet warmth of her mouth. He tasted her lips, savoring her unique flavor. He kept the kiss gentle, not ready yet to unleash the full force of his passion on her. She wasn't ready for that. The last thing he wanted to do was frighten her.

When he pulled free she whimpered and chased after him, trying to draw him back into the delicate sensuality he'd been weaving around them both. He gave in to her, kissing her once more, diving into the tenderness she offered like a starving man. God, he wanted her so badly, wanted to touch that smooth, freckled skin, lick each dark mark until he'd relished every single one. Without thought he reached for her breast, brushing his thumb across the nipple. It hardened under his touch, his mate moaning softly as he continued to caress her.

She pulled back with a gasp. "Not here." Her eyes were still foxy brown, her pupils dilated with desire.

"No, not here." He gave her breast one more touch before pulling back with a sigh. His cock was throbbing, his Bear growling to take her, bite her, but the hospital wasn't the right place to take her. She needed to be in his temporary den, in his bed, snuggled safe and warm before they marked her.

She leaned back against the pillows, her lips plump and red, her breath coming in soft pants. Hell. This was pure hell, seeing her red hair against the white sheets, her skin flushed with desire, and being unable to do a damn thing about it. "I want to stay in Halle with my family." She crossed her arms over her chest and tilted her chin up.

As if he'd argue with her. He gave her his best shit-eating grin. "I guess I could think about it."

She blinked, her arms lowering. "Really?"

Damn it. How could he tease her when staying in this town meant so much to her? Her eyes were green again, but so filled with innocent hope there was no way he could tell her anything but yes. "I tell you what. If I give you a budget, do you want to go house hunting while I work on the case?"

She squealed so loudly the nurses at their station probably heard her. She wrapped her good arm around his neck and bounced on the hospital bed. "Yes yes yes!"

"Careful." Her shoulder was doing much better, but not that much. "No pulling your stitches or hurting yourself."

"I won't. I'm not. It's just…" She took a deep breath, her expression so joyful he just had to kiss the tip of her nose. "I thought you'd fight me on this."

"Why? It'll cause a few problems with work, but I was planning on talking to Carl about setting up a Hunter training program here. We have enough of us in the area to pitch in, and frankly it's too big a job for one person. We usually do the training one on one, but Halle is close to the Poconos, to cities…we can train for just about any scenario here without problems."

"And the Pumas would more than likely be thrilled to have more Hunters around, especially now."

"The Pride would be the biggest hurdle, or rather, Max and Emma Cannon, the Alpha and Curana of the Pride." Barney ran his hand down Heather's back. "But I'm pretty sure they'll be all right with it. They have rules for the shifters attending college here. Something can be worked out for the newbie Hunters."

"What about your territory?"

"You let me worry about that. Another Hunter will be assigned there, that's all you need to know."

She frowned for a moment, but it quickly disappeared. "I want a dog."

He blinked, confused. "Okay?"

"Good." She pecked at his lips before settling against the pillows once more. She took a deep breath and let it out with a satisfied smile. "I need a new tattoo."

"Right. So you deal with the house and the dog, I'll deal with the riddle and getting my ass transferred here. Deal?"

"Nope. I'm still going to try and figure out the riddle, but I'm not going to try and fight or anything. Is that a deal?"

"I can live with that." Barney stood and kissed her on the forehead. "Rest, Heather. I'll let you know how things go with Dr. Howard, okay?"

"Okay." She settled back with her pad and pencil, but this time, instead of working on a riddle, she began to draw. Probably her new tattoo, if he were to guess.

He left her to her drawing. He had to go get permission from Max to visit with Dr. Howard, since the man was holed up in his mansion and not speaking with anyone. Chloe had warned him to beware of Dr. Howard, but she'd never said anything about avoiding him. If he had any of the answers Barney needed, or even a direction to point him in, the trip would be worth it.

Since Max had ordered everyone to stay away from Dr. Howard due to his anger issues, Barney would do the polite thing and speak with the Alpha first. One way or another, he was going to speak to Jamie Howard.

Chapter Thirteen

Heather put the paper down and stared at the door he'd just walked out of. She hadn't wanted him to see how nervous she was about his trip to see Dr. Howard. From everything she'd heard, the doctor used to be a good man, but now he was borderline psychotic. So she'd pretended to be drawing, hoping he'd think she was all right when she was anything but.

Barney is a Hunter. He can handle Dr. Howard.

She could tell herself that all she wanted, but the truth was she was always going to worry about him. She couldn't join him when he fought. She had to remain behind, waiting and watching, hoping that he came home safe and sound. Was this how the spouse of a cop felt? If so, she felt like maybe Sarah Anderson, the Pride Omega, might understand how Heather felt. Sarah's husband, Gabe, wasn't just the town sheriff, he was also a Hunter. Maybe she should talk to her, and not just about being the spouse of a Hunter.

Maybe it was time she spoke to someone about her assault when she was younger. Bears didn't have Omegas who could help sort out emotional issues. They had to do it on their own, or with a human psychologist. But how could a human understand what she'd been through? *Doc, they tried to force me into puberty by trying to get my Fox to come out to defend me, and I still don't understand why.* It was a nightmare either way she looked at it.

"Knock knock!" Tiffany entered the room, her high heels clacking on the linoleum. "Bored out of your skull, little sis?"

"You have no idea." None whatsoever. Bored? She wished.

"Did I see Barney earlier? I thought I caught sight of him, but I wasn't sure." Tiff settled in the visitor's chair next to the bed. "I have to admit, you bagged a pretty yummy mate."

Heather bared her teeth at her sister and growled.

Tiffany just laughed. "Oh, scary. I remember changing your diapers, kiddo."

"Just keep your paws to yourself and I won't eat you." Heather stared at Tiffany, wondering if her sister would help her. Maybe Tiffany was just what she needed to take her mind off of her mate. "Barney said I can go house hunting."

Tiffany's eyes lit up. "Shopping trip!" She rubbed her hands together and cackled gleefully. "You'll need furniture and lamps and plates and silverware and sexy underthings—"

"Hey!" Heather could feel the heat rushing to her cheeks. "Knock it off."

Tiffany laughed, the bitch. "He's a big guy. You think he's big like that all over?" Tiffany held her hands up, squinted at them, then gradually widened the gap until they were a good nine inches apart.

"I hate you the most right now." Heather slumped down, embarrassed by the deepening heat of her face. She could see the redness spreading to her chest. She probably looked like a cooked lobster.

Tiffany picked up the tablet Heather had been doodling on and turned it to a blank page. "So, what kind of house are you looking for?"

"It has to suit a Bear and a Fox." Finding a home that appealed to both of them should be easy enough, especially in this community.

"And since he's a Hunter, he'll probably want some sort of security." Tiffany made a quick note. "No bushes or trees close to the windows. He'll need to see if anything is coming for him."

"We might want the house to be near some woods, so I can run." Heather watched as Tiffany made another note. "Maybe we can ask Max if we can use Pride land to run on."

"He lets Tabby and Alex use it, so I don't see why not." Tiffany tilted her head. "But it would be nice to have our own space too."

"Buy your own house." Heather pulled the pad and pencil away from

Tiffany, making her own note. "No. Bitchy. Relatives."

"Damn. You'll never have any visitors." Tiffany chuckled when Heather threw the pencil at her. She picked it up, tossing it back to Heather. "Look, anything you want should be fine, right? I mean, Barney doesn't want a purple and green house or anything weird like that?"

"I swear, I hope your mate is named Yogi." Heather picked up the pencil and began drawing once more. This time she began to draw a simple house with a large front porch and dormered windows on the second floor. "I want something like this."

"Cute." Tiffany pointed toward the trees Heather began to sketch in. "Go for land, you can always expand the house when you have kits."

"True." And it might also prove useful if Barney could get the training program off the ground. They could add some sort of room to the back of the house where Barney and the other Hunters could hold classes. "Wait. Kits?"

"Yup. You're going to have them, right?" Tiffany grinned. "Think about it. A little boy with your hair and Barney's...stubbornness?"

"He's more than just that, you know. He's very affectionate when he's with me."

"Is that right, Frodo?" Tiffany's mocking expression was going to get her smacked.

"Yup, Gimli. He even understands Second Breakfast and my unhealthy obsession with mushrooms." She added a stick-figure Tiffany with lousy hair and Gimli's beard to the picture.

"I don't look like that!"

"Oops. You're right." She put little stilettos on the stick figure.

"Bitch." Tiffany's expression became serious. "You scared?"

"Of you? Hell no." Heather smirked at her sister. "I know your weak point."

"Don't you dare." Tiffany glared at Heather as Heather opened her mouth, ready to sing. "I swear I'll tell Barney all about your naked Barbie orgy."

"They were hot tubbing, you sicko." Heather hummed the opening bars to *The Phantom of the Opera*'s "Think of Me".

Tiffany sighed. "I love that play so much. She should have gone for the Phantom."

"The Phantom was a stalker." Heather had been through this so many times it wasn't even funny anymore. "But...*Raoul*," she sighed, batting her lashes. "He's so *dreamy*."

Tiffany rolled her eyes. "Puh-lease. He shows up, remembers he's always wanted to shag her, and carries her off into the sunset. Pfft. The Phantom loved her for who she was, but Raoul loved the memory of her."

"And she fell for the pretty boy, blah blah blah." Heather closed her eyes. None of this was helping her forget the danger Barney was in.

"Hey." A warm, gentle hand pushed her hair away from her forehead. "He's going to be okay."

"He's tough. So tough he'd been tasked with training other Hunters on how to be a badass."

"Right. So you don't worry over him, all right? If he finds out you're making yourself sick over him."

"I'm not." Heather opened her eyes and scowled. "I'm going to get out of here soon and be claimed by Barney."

Tiffany giggled. "I still can't get over his name."

"Is it that much worse than Bunny?"

"Bunny doesn't have a song."

Oh really? Heather couldn't resist. "Little Bunny Foo Foo hopping through the forest—"

"Don't even bother, we already know he's been turned into a goon." Tiffany picked up the pad of paper. "A house, huh?"

"Yeah." Heather bit her lip. "He's staying."

"Good." Tiffany stood and gave her a hug. "We can start planning your wedding then."

Wedding? "Can we wait on that until he asks me first?"

Tiffany blinked, looking confused. "Why?"

"Because?"

"If that's all you've got, I think you should look at maybe doing a double wedding with Chloe and Jim."

Hell. Barney was going to flip the fuck out.

A soft tap on the door had her looking at her doctor. She sat up, eager to hear the news she'd been waiting for. "I'm being sprung from this joint?"

The doctor laughed. "You're being kicked out. Put some clothes on, get out and give me my bed back."

"Yay!" Heather did a sitting-down booty-dance.

"Remember, you need to see your regular doctor to check your wound, okay?"

"Yes, sir."

"The nurse will be in with your discharge papers. Sign them and you're gone." The doctor winked at her and left.

Heather waved her hands at her sister. "Gimme my pants, woman!"

Tiffany laughed. "Did anyone bring you any?"

"Mom and Dad brought stuff for me to change into once I got discharged, but that stupid fever kept me from leaving." Heather wriggled on the bed in excitement. She'd have to call Barney and let her know she was going home with him today.

She blinked.

Holy fuck.

She was going home with her mate today. Which meant…

"Heather?" Tiffany waved her hands in front of Heather's face. "Yoo-hoo."

Heather finally focused on Tiffany's face. "Does it hurt?"

"Does what hurt?" Tiffany stared at the jeans in her hands. "Well, I suppose it could, but only if you get your short and curlies caught in the zipper. But that's what panties are for."

Heather rolled her eyes. Maybe asking her sister about her first sexual experience wasn't such a good idea after all.

Chapter Fourteen

"You want to do what?" The Alpha's blond brows rose in disbelief. "Fuck no." He turned to walk away, back into his practice, but Barney stopped him by grabbing hold of his arm.

He had to admit, this was probably the first Alpha he'd ever met who was an optometrist. Most of them tended to run organizations or businesses, but nope. Dr. Max Cannon fixed people's eyesight. So did his Marshal, the head of his security, Dr. Adrian Giordano.

Halle was *so* weird. No wonder Heather wanted to stay. He loved it here too.

"Oh, stop snarling, kitty. I just want to have a chat with Dr. Demento, not hurt him or anything." Barney let go and clasped his hands together. "Please?"

Max shook his head. "I can't guarantee you'll be safe if you go see him. He's…different. He used to be warm and funny and now he's a cold-ass killer."

"He took out Salazar, something none of the rest of us managed." As far as Barney was concerned Dr. Howard should have earned a medal for that. Salazar had been a fucking psycho. Unfortunately, he'd been a Hunter psycho, making him Barney's problem. That a non-Hunter took him down was something that still made his butt itch.

"It wasn't that he took him out, it's how he did it." Max ran his fingers through his hair. "He poisoned him with something that worked almost immediately. Jamie is dangerous now, Barney. You need to be wary of him."

Barney nodded. "If he's gone rogue I'll know it. I'll eliminate him, even if it means Hope lives without her mate."

"Hope might be the only reason he hasn't lost it completely, but if he views you as a threat to Hope he'll take you out before you can blink. *That's* what I'm afraid of." Max sighed. "Damn it. Fine. Go talk to him, but if you die I'm not the one who's going to tell Heather."

"Gotcha. On my head be it." He turned, then for shits and giggles stopped. He loved seeing that look on Max's face. "Oh, by the way, I beat your high score on Mario Kart."

"My…did you break into my house again, you asshole?"

Barney sauntered away, ignoring the Alpha's repeated shouts and threats of bodily harm. Man, toying with the big, macho types always made him smile. They all thought they were invincible until someone showed them otherwise.

Of course, that had earned him a few scars, but it was still worth it.

It didn't take long to get to Jamie Howard's house. It was where the Pride had held all of its major events before Marie was murdered, so Barney had known where it was located even before he began investigating Chloe. Now here he was, standing in front of a freaking mansion on the outskirts of town. A mansion that was starting to look run-down instead of like the grand home of the previous Alpha. Marie must have made Jamie her sole beneficiary, as the money he'd made as a doctor would not have allowed him to continue to live in the mansion. Taxes alone would have driven him to try and sell the place.

He stared at the closed gates, noting the rust that was slowly beginning to set in. The vegetation was starting to go wild, the grass uncut, the weeds left to grow wild. Dr. Howard's plush lifestyle with Marie Howard had fallen to pieces, and his home showed it.

Barney pushed the gates open, surprised when they operated smoothly, without a single squeak of protest. Rusty or not, at least the man had oiled the hinges.

Barney rode his motorcycle up the driveway, keeping an eye out for anything unusual. Other than the neglect of the estate, nothing popped out at him. When he turned off his motorcycle the normal sounds of birds filled the air. He set the kickstand and strode to the front door, knocking firmly.

The door opened, but no one was behind it.

"Creepy much?" Barney strode in, not surprised when the door closed silently behind him. The front hall was amazing, with a huge chandelier, marble floors and antique furniture. There was a chill to the air, a sense of disuse as if no one had stood in that hall for quite some time. Barney spoke louder, wondering if Dr. Howard could hear him. "Nice trick. So how did you rig the front door to open?"

Silence. It was starting to freak him out.

"I need to speak to you, Dr. Howard."

A hollow voice sounded just above his head. "Third door on your right, Hunter."

Barney nodded and followed the directions, peeking through the doorways as he went. Each room was elegantly designed, yet the chill followed him. Had Dr. Howard turned the air conditioner to Antarctica?

Third door on the right. Barney reached for the handle, shivering slightly as the cold metal met his palm. This whole place had his senses tingling like mad, but until he actually met Dr. Howard he couldn't say for certain if the man was rogue or not. He opened the door, fully expecting to find a fight on his hands.

Instead what met his gaze was a blond man sitting in one of the chairs, a mug in his hand. From the scent it was coffee. Nothing special about that. The man wore simple jeans and a button-down shirt with sneakers. Again, nothing special.

It was the side table next to him that caught Barney's eye.

The table was loaded with needles, springs, an assortment of cases, and what looked like completed auto-injectors. Barney didn't want to know what drug was being put inside the syringes. He was willing to bet it was the same chemical concoction that killed Salazar.

"Good afternoon, Hunter." Dr. Howard sipped his coffee, his gaze never once landing on Barney. It stayed firmly fixed on some point on the carpet, leaving Barney to wonder if the man was aware of much beyond himself. "I've been expecting you. My Alpha decided I needed to speak with you."

Max must have called Dr. Howard and told him to play nice with the Bear. Yay. Barney loved it when possible prey was forewarned of his arrival.

Not.

The faintly mocking tone sounded eerily familiar. This man was on the edge, barely holding on to the rage riding him. He'd heard it in more than one rogue, but Dr. Howard wasn't setting his instincts on fire. Instead, he felt wary, as if he were around an apex predator and *he* was the prey. It was a sensation Barney wasn't used to.

Fuck. That. Barney would get what he needed and get the hell out of this haunted mansion. "Have you heard the prophecy?"

Dr. Howard's lips quirked. "Two becomes one, one becomes three." He placed his mug next to the needles. "Do I look like a Fox or a Bear to you?"

"It's been theorized that you might be part of it." Barney wasn't about to tell this man who'd come up with the idea. He wanted Dr. Howard far, far away from Heather at all times.

"Oh?" With a quick glance upward, Dr. Howard rendered Barney speechless.

The man's eyes were silver. As silver as Julian DuCharme's or Chloe Williams's. The doctor was the white Puma.

"You think I give two shits about some prophecy?" Dr. Howard stood with all the feline grace his Puma granted him. He strode to the window and looked out, his hand resting on the fabric of the curtains. His claws were out, lightly scratching at the fabric over and over until a small hole appeared, allowing a sliver of light into the room.

There was only one card he could play to get through to the man. The one thing that was probably keeping Jamie Howard from becoming a rogue. "If it involves you, it involves Hope."

Barney was stunned when Dr. Howard turned to face him. There were still threads of silver in the man's eyes, but the expression on his face had gone from disdain to despair. "Hope…Hope's been through enough. The last thing she needs is some tight-ass spirit governing her life when she's just gotten her freedom."

"This could be something that helps you both." Barney remained still, unwilling to do anything to cause Dr. Howard's tone to harden once more. The soft smile when Hope's name was mentioned and the obvious concern was what he expected of a man who had yet to claim his mate. If he could actually get through to the man and bring back a sliver of who he used to be there might be a way to save him. "If Hope's nightmares are eased by finding out the answer to the riddle, wouldn't it make everything worthwhile?"

"No. Not everything." The silver was slowly bleeding back into Dr. Howard's eyes. His demeanor became icy once more. "There are some things that are never worthwhile."

"No, I suppose not." He shuddered at the thought of losing Heather, and they weren't even mated yet. Dr. Howard's heart and mind had been shredded when Marie Howard was pulled away from him. The wounds left behind might never heal, even with a bond to Hope. "It's a shame Julian wasn't able to save your wife."

Dr. Howard's hair turned pure white at the mention of Julian's name. The curtains were shredded in a move so quick Barney didn't even see it happen until the fabric was fluttering to the floor. "Don't say that name." The snarl that curled Dr. Howard's lip showed fangs far larger than the normal Puma's, but it was the calm, precise way he spoke that truly set Barney on edge. It was the complete opposite of the swift, savage rage evident in the fluttering tatters of fabric.

That kind of power, combined with a rogue's mentality, would be devastating. He would have no remorse, no mercy. If it weren't for Hope, Jamie's second mate, Barney would try to kill him right this moment out of sheer terror.

But Barney's Hunter instincts weren't tingling. There was a low hum, a potential threat, but it wasn't fully realized yet. He couldn't kill a man just because he was pissed off. "My apologies." Barney had to keep him calm. "Our main focus right now is on whether or not the riddle will be harmful to Hope." A small lie, but one that he could get away with since that was one of his concerns.

"Hope is safe." Dr. Howard turned to gaze out the window, giving Barney his back. "I've made sure of it."

Shit. That didn't sound suspicious *at all.* "How?"

Dr. Howard glanced at the hypodermic needles. "It's best you don't know."

"You killed her rapist with one of those, didn't you?" Barney had heard about it from Ryan and Glory. "Good job."

"Considering he was your fucking responsibility, you're welcome."

"Yeah. We fucked up. Hope suffered. But he was a Hunter gone rogue, so he knew how to elude us." Barney wasn't going to apologize to Jamie Howard. If anyone deserved that it was Hope. "But that's not what I'm here about, and you know it."

Dr. Howard shook his head, chuckling mirthlessly. "There is nothing more I have to say." He shot Barney a silver-tinted glance. "Keep Hope out of this."

"That may not be something I can promise, and you know that."

Dr. Howard's eyes narrowed. "Try."

"If my sources are correct, there won't be anything I can do. If you and Hope are somehow a part of this, keeping either of you out won't be possible." Barney took a step toward the hallway, not happy with the way Dr. Howard was staring at him. The man looked ready to jump across the room and rip his throat out if Barney didn't backtrack immediately. "I'd rather you knew and could protect her than be in the dark and get side-swiped by this."

Dr. Howard's expression turned blank for a moment before a smile curved his lips. "Thank you for that, at least."

Barney stepped through the door and headed for the front. Fully aware Dr. Howard could somehow hear him, he added, "And for the record, you aren't the only one hoping that Hope pulls through."

The silence of the door shutting behind him was his only answer.

Chapter Fifteen

Heather sat on the edge of the hospital bed, her nerves completely on edge. Barney was on his way from Dr. Howard's estate. He was going to bring her home.

His home.

She didn't know if she wanted to do a fist pump and squeal like a little girl in excitement, or shift into her Fox and run for Mommy and Daddy. This being grown-up shit sucked balls.

She bit her lip as she studied her fingernails. Should she tell him she was a virgin? The trauma she'd suffered in her childhood had kept her from wanting to have a boyfriend, let alone have sex. But Barney…Barney wasn't someone she could run away from. For one thing, she actually *wanted* to have sex with the man. She'd been eager for it, right up until she realized she'd be having it that day.

For another, he'd hunt her down and drag her little Hobbit ass back before she could yell *Freedom!*

She knew this was the way it was supposed to go. Meet mate, fuck mate, bite mate, boom. Mated. But now that it was about to actually happen, she wasn't certain she'd be able to stop shaking long enough to unlock her jaw and give him the mating bite she'd been dreaming about.

Worse, the mating dreams were giving her all sorts of ideas on what would happen once she and Barney got down to the naked and nasty. While it felt incredible in the dreams, she was worried it would hurt once Barney started to enter her. She was a Fox who was not into pain, so the idea of having sex for the first time was kind of scary. Tiffany would just make jokes, so talking to her wasn't an option. That meant calling her mom.

She reached for her cell phone, only to find a big hand blocking her way. She screeched, scrambling back on the bed.

"Whoa!" Barney grabbed hold of her and kept her from scrambling right off the other side and onto the cold linoleum. "What the hell?"

"Momma." Heather winced. "Ah. Hi, Barney?"

He blinked, his expression amused. "I'm almost afraid to ask why that was phrased as a question." He eased her upright, holding her arms, probably in case she acted like a lunatic again. "Why did you call for your mommy, Heather?"

"Um…" She couldn't tell him that she was freaking out over fucking… well, fucking.

"Well?" He scowled. "No one bothered you while I was gone, did they?"

"No!" Her shout startled them both. "I mean, I'm good. I'm fine." She smiled, praying it looked natural. "I'm getting sprung, remember?"

"Uh-huh." He pulled away from her, releasing her arms. "So. Ready to go?"

Nope. She took a deep, bracing breath. This was it. She was going to mate Barney, the stubborn Bear who haunted her nights and annoyed the hell out of her during the day. "Yeah."

His brows rose. "You look like you're going to the gallows."

"Nah, just your be—I mean apartment." She stood, her knees all wobbly with nerves. "I can do this."

He put his arm around her. "You know, I want to tell you I'm willing to hold off until you're ready, but I'm not that nice a person."

"That's a hell of a turnaround from you pushing me away." She desperately wanted to go back to her uncomfy hospital bed. She was having a heart attack, right? No one's heart could beat this fast without it being fatal.

"Breathe, Heather." He was frowning, holding her even closer as they edged out the door. "I lied. Nothing will happen until you give me the okay."

She hid her face in his chest. "I've gotta tell you something."

"If it makes you that red you can tell me in the car." He waved to the nurses as they passed the station. Heather was too embarrassed to do more than smile as he guided them to the elevator. "I don't want anyone else hearing your secrets."

Ah, there was her overprotective Bear. "It's not bad. I hope."

"Doesn't matter. It's yours, and that's enough for me."

That was sweet of him. She was about to press a kiss to his shoulder when a nurse came running up, pushing a wheelchair. "Ma'am, you can't walk out."

"I'm fine, really." Heather held up her arm. "Look, it moves and everything."

The nurse smiled. "That's nice, but it's hospital policy that you get wheeled out by one of our staff. Once you're at the front door, your friend can take over."

"I could push her out now." Barney was eyeing the wheelchair with a sly expression. "Bet I could get her to do wheelies."

The nurse rolled her eyes. "Ms. Allen, have a seat, please."

Heather eased out from under Barney's arm and sat in the wheelchair. "Onward, ho!"

The nurse didn't laugh, but Barney did, so maybe that lame line was worth it. She bet the nurse had heard it more than once.

Barney punched the button and waited silently beside her until the elevator arrived. The nurse gently pushed her in the empty car. Barney stepped in front of her, blocking the exit. While he doubted anything would happen, she would be vulnerable when the doors opened. If anything came at them, Barney would face it, not her.

The nurse chatted quietly the entire ride down, talking about Heather's discharge and reminding her about physical therapy. When the doors opened Heather was ready to leap out of the wheelchair and run for the front door, but with Barney's ass blocking the way it wasn't happening.

Barney stepped out of the elevator and out of the way so the nurse could lead. He walked behind, his footsteps damn near silent for such a big guy. Then it was out the door, and the nurse was saying good-bye while Barney helped Heather into his car. He gave her a hand with her seatbelt and shut the door, waving to the nurse as he walked around the front of the car. He slid into the driver's seat and started the car before putting on his own seatbelt. "Let's get the fuck out of here."

"Amen." She stared out the passenger window as he pulled out onto the street. She'd calmed a little, but her nerves were still trying to get the better of her. "I'm a virgin."

"I figured, what with your fear of men."

She glanced toward him, surprised to see him smiling. "Really?"

He shrugged. "You were never afraid of me, though."

"You're my mate." It was instinct. She felt no fear when she stared at him. Rather, she wanted to climb him like a monkey and do wild things to him.

"I freaked a bit when I found out that you'd been attacked."

"They went after Chloe, not me."

"No. Not that attack." He passed by Max and Emma's home. There were several cars in the drive and parked along the curb. It looked like the Alphas were having a meeting with the Pride. "The one when you were young. I wasn't certain you'd ever be able to accept me."

Heather bit her lip. How to explain the moment she'd first seen him? He'd strolled through Glory's front door, talking about protecting Glory from her stalker, but the moment he'd caught her scent… "You said *crap*."

"I told you before that I didn't want a mate." Barney pulled into his apartment building's parking lot. He parked the car and turned it off, but sat still for a moment. "And you know why now."

"Yeah." But still. That moment she'd seen him, caught his scent, no one else in the world would do for her.

"And besides, you called me butt munch." He smirked at her. "You were adorable."

She stuck her tongue out at him, making him laugh. "You're still a butt munch."

"I know you can come up with something better than that. You have some pretty good sarcasm genes running through your family."

"True." She tilted her head and began humming the Barney theme song, giggling like crazy when he covered up her mouth with his hand.

"Anything but that." His tone was pained. "I'll forgive anything else, just…" He shuddered and pulled his hand away.

"It could be worse."

"How?" He stared at her, his expression daring her to come up with something worse than what she'd already hummed.

"I could ask where your buddy Fred is. And you really need to introduce me to Betty, Mr. Rubble."

"Hmph." He cupped her cheek. "Still nervous?"

Oh hell yes. She nodded, but closed her eyes and leaned into his touch. "It's not as bad, though."

"Good." His thumb caressed her cheek. "I'm going to make it a little less scary."

She frowned, opening her eyes. "How?"

His fangs extended as he smiled. "Trust me."

"Oh shit," she breathed as his teeth penetrated the skin of her neck. He'd given her the mating bite, binding them together for all time.

That was her last clear thought before the orgasm ripped through her, the pleasure so intense she was left half-blind and shuddering in his arms.

Chapter Sixteen

Heather convulsed against him as the spasm rocked her. She was exquisite in her pleasure, her features taut has her nails dug into his biceps, drawing blood. Barney's eyes changed, enhancing his vision. And what a vision she was. He couldn't take his gaze from her face as she came down from the orgasm. Her cheeks were flushed, the green of her eyes turning golden as her Fox came to the fore. Her fangs descended as she licked her lips, her gaze glued to his neck where she would mark him. He had no doubt her mark would be on him before the end of the night.

He was hoping for sooner rather than later. He wanted to experience the high of having his mate's fangs in his flesh. For all his earlier protests, he needed that mark more than he needed to breathe.

His Bear needed her inside, in his den, naked against his sheets. She still wasn't safe. He hadn't caught the shooter or managed to invade the Senate archives. Having her out in the open, vulnerable, was making his Bear growly as hell.

"C'mon, sweetheart. Let's get inside."

She nodded, still panting from the bite. All females experienced orgasm at the bite of their mate, while males, from what he'd heard, wound up feeling the urge to make love to their mate. He was certain it was some sort of animalistic need to continue the species, but honestly he didn't care that much. Not when Heather was hanging on his arm as he helped her out of the car, her legs too wobbly to hold her up.

He got her up the steps and held on to her waist as he dug for his keys. His hands were steady as he opened the door. "In you go," he murmured, guiding her into his tiny, one bedroom apartment.

She sniffed, wrinkling her nose. "Smells like two-day old burritos in here."

"Bachelor pad chic at its finest." He kicked the door shut and led her toward the bedroom. She could get the two-dollar tour tomorrow. Tonight, she was getting a first-class view of the bedroom. "In you go."

"Wait." She twirled out of his hold, almost tripping over a pair of jeans he'd left on the floor. She held up her hand. "Um, can we eat first?"

He blinked, then sighed. "Have a seat, Frodo."

She rolled her eyes, but she sat gingerly on the edge of his bed. Her hands grabbed the edge of his mattress so tightly he was sure her claws had pierced it. "Sitting."

He knelt in front of her and put his hands on her knees, ignoring the way she twitched under his touch. "Calm down, sweetheart. We're going to do this at your pace. There's no rush, okay?"

She took a deep breath and blew it out. "Okay." She unclenched her hands and placed them over his. Her nails were still claws, but she was careful not to prick him. "What do we do first?"

He smiled. "We curl up on the bed and kiss."

She stared at him for a moment. "That's it?"

"I like to linger over my appetizers." Her eyes grew wide as he tipped her back. "Scoot up, little Fox. Put your head on one of the pillows."

She did as told, kicking her shoes off in the process. "Now what?"

Heather was so pale he thought she'd pass out if she stood. "Let me get my shoes off too." He kicked off his sneakers and sauntered over to his side of the bed. He flopped onto the bed, laughing when she yipped. Her Fox was close to the surface, drawing his Bear to her. He rolled over onto his side and rested his head on his hand. "Hi."

"Hi." She tentatively reached out and touched his arm. "I'm sorry I'm such a wreck."

He wanted to sigh, not because he was frustrated, but because she was.

"Would you rather I show you my video game collection?"

She smiled, thank God. "Are they anything like etchings?"

"Only if you want to murder them."

Heather choked out a laugh. "Hello, artist here. So not killing the pretty."

"Hmm." He leaned forward, planting a soft kiss on her tempting lips. "That's good to know."

Her cheeks flamed bright red as brown bled away the green of her eyes. "Will it hurt?"

"I don't know, but I promise I'll do my best to make sure it doesn't."

She gulped. "I heard the first time hurts."

He couldn't shrug her fear away. Besides, he knew nothing about virgins other than there might be some blood. "It could. I'm not sure. I've never made love to a virgin before."

Heather snarled. "You've never made love before."

"Yes, ma'am." Those cute little teeth she bared at him were going to bite him soon, hopefully in a good way. "I want to touch you."

The snarl went away, but her red cheeks only got brighter. She nodded once, sharply, but the hand she'd left on his arm started to tremble.

"Thank you." He wanted her to know he appreciated the precious gift she was giving him. He would be her first, and her last. The idea that his mate came to him untouched turned him on so much he was afraid he wouldn't be able to slow down at the proper moments.

His Bear growled low, letting him know that if Barney had issues, his Bear would be more than happy to remind him not to harm their fragile mate.

Barney kept his gaze on his mate's face as he lifted the hem of her shirt. For now, he'd keep his hand on her stomach, waiting until she became comfortable with his caress. The feel of her soft skin under his palm tempted him to move higher to feel her breasts resting in his palm and tease her nipples until they hardened, but he held back. For one, she looked like a prisoner facing execution. For another, his Bear was already growling, reminding him to go slow.

She gasped when his fingers brushed across her side. He pulled her closer, kissing her closed mouth, waiting patiently for her to respond to his lips grazing hers.

With a shiver she opened her mouth, accepting him so easily he was awed. He kissed her, not passionately, not yet. No, he wanted to keep this sweet. Her fear was still there in her trembling lips, her shivers against his palm. This wasn't the time to rush, but to savor everything she gave him without pushing for more. This was her time, not his, and he would follow her pace.

She kissed him, getting bolder the more he allowed her to move on her own. He'd said he wanted to touch her, but reality was he needed her to touch him. To want him. Without that, this would go no further than a petting session. He'd bitten her, claimed her, but she had yet to do the same. When it was time, when she finally claimed him, he would be ecstatic. But for now...

Her hand left his arm and caressed his stomach, carefully pushing up his T-shirt. He moaned into her mouth, careful to do no more than that, but God it felt so good. Even that tiny caress was enough to make him rock hard and eager.

He dared to move his hand, pushing her shirt slightly higher, to just under her breasts. His thumb caressed her ribs as the kiss grew hungrier, but still he restrained himself. He wanted to roll her onto her back and take control, but she wasn't ready.

He was going to blow in his pants like a goddamn teenager, and there was nothing he could do about it.

"Barney," she sighed against his mouth. He opened his eyes, watching with increasing hunger as she arched into his hand. The kiss was broken, her head tilted back as desperation contorted her features. He bit his lip, drawing blood. He had to touch her breasts, *had to*, like he would die if he didn't get to taste her sweetness. He inched his hand upward, keeping her bra in place. Perhaps that would help her feel safer in his hold.

Her moan of pleasure was his reward. Her face was filled with a yearning he'd seen before, but never before had it been so glorious. He cupped her breast, caressing her nipple with his thumb. The hardness of her nipple enticed him, but until she was as desperate as he was he wouldn't do anything more.

She lunged for him, taking his mouth, kissing him with clumsy earnestness. His mate was perfect in her demands, pushing him and tugging at him until he lay on his back. She was on top, straddling his waist, his hand still at her breast when she broke the kiss. "Now what?"

"Anything you want." He lifted his hands from her skin, smiling when she whimpered. He put his arms behind his head. "You're in charge."

Her caresses were tentative, running up and down his torso with feather-light touches. The fascination in her gaze was slowly overcoming her trepidation. She kept glancing at his hands, as if he'd move them at any moment and put an end to her explorations.

As if.

The only thing he did was whip his shirt off, tossing it over the side of the bed. "You tell me what comes off next."

She blushed so brightly he was afraid she'd faint from all the blood rushing to her head. "Um. Fair is fair, right?" She slowly lifted her own shirt off, revealing a simple, silky black bra. Her breasts looked so pale and creamy against the dark material that he couldn't stop himself from licking them, tasting to see if they were as sweet as they looked.

Heather gasped, her head falling back. Barney grabbed her around the waist, keeping her from falling backward as she ground against him. God, she was going to kill him. He nibbled her neck, delighting in her soft cries.

She whimpered and put her head on his shoulder. "Off. Take off my bra."

The words were so softly spoken he barely heard them. He did as she requested, unhooking her bra while he continued to pepper her neck with soft kisses and nips. His fangs were still extended, scratching at her skin. He could almost taste her blood on his tongue again, but now wasn't the time to bite. No. He'd bite her again as he tried to enter her, to help ease some of the pain of making love for the first time.

He cupped her bared breast in his hand, stroking over the hardening nipple, taking it between his fingers and pinching it until she was gasping again. Their jeans were beginning to irritate him, keeping him from the warm paradise he knew awaited him if he could just get her to undress completely.

Patience, Bear. We'll get there. But first he had to get her consent. If she told him to stop here, his dick might fall off in protest but he'd obey. She was his mate, his most precious person, the only one born for him. He could wait.

"What now, sweetheart?"

She clenched her hands on his shoulders. "I…I don't know."

He smiled. "Want me to show you something?"

She nodded shyly. "Please?"

He'd figured she wouldn't be able to go too far. It would be a while before his innocent mate began making demands of him in bed. So instead of doing what he really wanted to do, which was push her down and devour her, he spoke, telling her what was about to happen. "Sit back a bit."

She did as asked, pulling away until only the tips of her breasts touched the hair on his chest. "Now what?"

He bent and took one of those hard tips into his mouth.

Heather cried out, arching her back and pushing herself farther into his mouth. He sucked on her, barely able to keep himself in check as she began riding his jeans-clad cock. The friction wasn't enough to do anything more than torture him, but Heather's reaction was spectacular.

She writhed in his lap, almost pulling her breast from his mouth more than once. He switched, desperate to see if her right breast was as sensitive as her left.

It was.

"Jeans off?" he whispered against her skin.

Again she nodded, but didn't move. So Barney unbuttoned and unzipped her jeans for her. "You have to do the rest, sweetheart."

He kept his hands on her as she struggled to remove her jeans, eventually laying her back down on the comforter as she shoved the pants and her underwear off.

"Holy fuck," he breathed. This was his mate, this pale, ethereal creature who gazed at him with trust and longing.

"Barney?"

That wouldn't do. She was starting to get nervous again. "I have something else to show you."

"Oh?"

He nodded. He'd leave his jeans on for the moment. First, he was going to taste his mate, explore every nook and cranny until she came for him again.

Chapter Seventeen

She was naked, exposed, vulnerable to whatever he planned on doing. And from the look on his face, the pirate planned on looting her booty.

"Barney?" she asked again. She was getting more and more nervous as he stared at her, licking his lips like he was deciding what to do first.

God, she hoped he'd suck on her breasts again. That had felt…wow.

He bent down and did exactly what she'd hoped he would, taking her nipple into his mouth. His fang drew blood, sending chills down her spine and right to her clit.

Her hips arched, her pussy reacting to the sensation, desperate for a touch or something that would ignite the inferno she could feel building inside her.

His hand drifted down her body, cupping her, giving her that needed edge to start the tumble. When his fingers began to stroke her clit she cried out, clutching at his hair, his arm, his shoulders, anything that would make him hurry up and make her come.

His response was to suck more strongly. His fingers moved more insistently, as if demanding she come for him, and she obliged, crying out with pleasure as her body was racked with shudders.

She'd barely finished when she realized his fingers had been replaced with his tongue. Moist, hot heat enveloped her clit, sucking on her with a fierce intensity. Instinctively she cupped her breasts, toying with them, doing the same things to them that he had. It ramped up the pleasure.

Dear God, why hadn't she done this before? She should have jumped his bones the moment she saw him rather than being afraid. Her gentle giant was keeping to his word, asking her what she wanted and then giving it to her with an enthusiasm that couldn't be faked.

She cried out as something entered her. A finger? His tongue? She didn't care. All she wanted was more. The slight burning sensation meant nothing to her, only the way he continued to eat her with a hunger that had her riding whatever it was that had invaded her.

It had to be a finger, because Barney lifted away from her pussy with one final lick. His gaze turned to her breasts, and she noticed that his eyes had gone completely brown. His Bear was in charge now, both of them seeking to give her ecstasy beyond her wildest dreams.

He licked his lips and zeroed in on her breasts as he continued to fuck her with his finger. Just his eyes on her was enough to make her want to do more, to make him hungrier, so she called to him. "Barney."

Her voice was breathless, her body shuddering under his touch.

His name seemed to spur him on, because with a low growl he practically attacked her mouth, kissing her and moving his hand until somehow he was stroking her clit as well as fucking her. His tongue invaded her mouth, and she could taste herself in a way she never had before.

Close. She was so close to coming again, but she needed something more, something…she couldn't define it, didn't want to. All she knew was she needed it.

She pulled free of the kiss and struck, digging her fangs into Barney's neck with a fierceness that surprised even her. His blood entered her mouth, the mating enzyme she released through her fangs causing her to ache even more.

"Fuck." Barney's groan was low and almost mean-sounding. His body left hers, leaving her reeling in surprise until the sound of ripping cloth filled her ears. She got on her elbows to see what he'd done.

He'd ripped off his jeans with his bare hands.

She tilted her head, curious even as her body continued to throb with need. "How do you not have the biggest wedgie in the history of underwear?"

He stared at her for a moment before tilting his head to the side. "Bad jeans?"

"Ouch." She lay back down, crossing her legs, making the delicious throb even worse.

"Sorry." He licked her mating spot, the one he'd made on her skin, making her moan. "I've got this sudden need to feel you writhing on my cock."

"Oh," she breathed. She arched up against him and felt the hard flesh of his cock slip across her stomach. "Soon?"

"Soon," he crooned. "How many times do you want to come before I do?"

She whimpered, unsure if she should uncross her legs or not. He was going to kill her with orgasms before he finally took her. "Can you do that finger thing again?" Maybe if he stretched her out a little more, it would ease the way.

"Of course." His tone had softened, her gentle giant back in control once more. At least she thought so until he was nose to nose with her, those huge brown eyes staring right at her. "And then I'm going to fuck you."

She nodded slowly, spreading her legs for him. "I trust you."

Barney shuddered. "You have no idea how much that turns me on."

"Now?"

"Now." His hand moved, brushing her hip, sliding along her stomach until he was once more caressing her clit. He kissed her again as he slipped his finger inside her, but the burn was a bit brighter this time, the sting a little bit sharper.

"Hurts," she muttered, clinging to his biceps.

"I know." Barney lapped at her mating mark, and the sting practically vanished under a wash of sensation. "I'm sorry it's hurting you."

"No no no, don't you dare stop," she breathed. He'd started to withdraw his hand, but she managed to grab his wrist before he could pull away completely. "Keep doing that thing with my neck. It makes the sting stop."

"Then hold on. I'm going to try three fingers now."

She gasped as she was stretched, but once again he licked her mating mark, sending pain and pleasure tumbling together through her body. "Oh God." Her hand clenched around his wrist. "Coming."

"Go," he muttered, sinking his fangs into her skin.

Heather screamed, clamping down on his hand as she shuddered in an ecstasy so fierce her vision blanked out.

"Yes, baby, come for me." Barney's hand was still moving, still fucking her. She could hear the sounds of him moving in and out of her, the wetness and the stretch driving her insane. His lips continued to caress her mating mark, stretching out the pleasure he wrung from her, almost bringing her to the point of exhaustion. She was panting as she came down from the high, sweating and still throbbing.

"I've never had a lover so sensitive before." He kissed her cheek.

Her claws came out and he hissed. She still had hold of his wrist, which meant she must have drawn blood. Good. Her Fox didn't like hearing about any other lovers but herself.

"Right. You're the only one for me. Now let go of my wrist, baby, so I can fuck you properly."

She did as asked, removing her claws from his flesh. He held up his wrist and showed her the damage, but she didn't care. She licked the wounds she'd caused. He'd remember not to say something like that to her again.

"Shit. You're a possessive little vixen, aren't you?" The pride in his tone didn't stop her from lapping at the wounds. "How do you want this?"

"Want what?" She stared up at him, the blood forgotten.

"Fucking, sweetheart." His brows rose. "There's more than one way to do this, so what's your preference?"

"Tell me what you like." She found she liked it when he spoke to her. It fired her imagination and made the desire that much stronger.

He nipped at her chin. "Missionary. On your back, me on top, my cock inside you." He bit at her shoulder. "Doggie. You on hands and knees, I'm behind you, fucking you." Heather shivered as he continued to describe positions. "You, draped over the bed, your ass in the air."

She could feel his cock nudging at her pussy and had the feeling she didn't have long to decide before he decided for her.

"You, riding me as I touch you all over."

Oh. That one. "Me on top." She could just picture him touching her breasts as they fucked.

He rolled over, taking her with him. She wound up draped over him, her legs on either side of his. His cock was almost where she needed it to be, but not quite. "This is your show, sweetheart. Sitting up, laying down, either way I can fuck you like this."

She sat up, straddling him like she'd done earlier. "How?"

He smiled. "Lift up on your knees."

She did as instructed.

"Now, take me in your hand and guide me where you want me. If…" He shuddered as she gripped him. "If you need to, scoot back."

Before too long she'd maneuvered and wiggled until she had him at her entrance. She took a deep breath—

"Slowly." His hands landed on her hips, stopping her from plunging down. "Take your time."

She felt the tip of him slip inside her, stretching her. This time he wasn't licking her mark, so the sting was fierce. She stopped, letting herself adjust to the pressure.

"Good girl. I won't break. Do what you need to."

She nodded, biting her lip and sliding a little farther down. She whimpered, needing him to do something, make the sting go away.

Barney's fingers stroked over her mark. Over and over he caressed it, watching her with those intense brown eyes, his gaze glued to her face rather than where they were joined.

Heather smiled sweetly and plunged down on him, gasping at the strain.

Barney groaned, but it wasn't in pain. "Why did you do that?"

She could feel her clit touching the thick curls at the base of his cock. Curious, she rotated her hips.

Oh.

Oh.

Mama likey.

Heather continued to move, dragging her clit over his curls over and over again, tantalizing herself with what was coming.

"Oh, fuck." Barney's hands were on her hips, guiding her. "Just like that, baby."

She put her hands on his stomach. The stretch and burn were fading in the throbbing of her body, the need rolling through her once more. Experimentally she lifted up, plopping down on him again.

Barney's claws extended, his teeth elongating even further. Her Bear liked that.

She did it again, and again, her mind on one thing only. She needed to come in the worst possible way, and having him inside her made that need an all-consuming flame. She whimpered as she rode him, digging her fingers into his sides, scratching him with her claws.

True to his word his hands glided over her skin. He palmed her breasts, squeezing them, toying with her nipples over and over again, driving her insane. He stroked her mating mark, making her shiver. He spread his palm over her stomach and caressed her clit with his thumb, sometimes brushing just the curls hiding it, sometimes rubbing it with fierce intent.

But it still wasn't quite enough to send her over the edge.

Barney planted his feet on the mattress, forcing her to bend a little closer to him. Now he was doing the fucking, plunging in and out of her with fierce intent. "What do you need?"

She could see the strain on his face. He was holding back, waiting for her to come first before he tumbled over the edge. So she told him what she thought would end both their torment. "Bite me."

"With pleasure." He reared up, sinking his fangs into her mark once more.

Heather couldn't even cry out. Her whole body began shuddering in the best orgasm she'd ever had. She could feel herself clenching his cock as the spasms rocked her body. She was certain she was going to die here, and she wasn't sure she cared. If this was bliss, she god-damn needed more of it. His muffled cry against her neck told her he'd found his release as well.

The shudders began to subside, leaving her limp in his arms, tired beyond belief. She rested her head on his shoulder. "So. That's sex, huh?"

Barney chuckled. "Pretty much."

She bit her lip. "That wasn't so bad."

He tilted her chin up so her gaze met his. His expression was full of warmth and affection and something she couldn't quite put a name to. "No. Not bad at all."

She bit her lip, wondering if she was about to be too forward, but hell. This was her mate. "Round two after pizza?"

"Mmm. A girl after my own heart."

As he lay back down and pulled her tightly to him she thought he had no idea how very accurate that statement was. She just hoped she'd manage to steal his heart before too much longer, because hers was already in his large, capable hands.

Chapter Eighteen

Barney stared at the woman wrapped in his arms. He'd claimed his mate, made her his, and now the consequences would be his as well to deal with. Her scent was all over his skin, her essence inside him, her mark there for all to see. There was no way he could keep her out of sight. Anyone who looked at him would know he was a mated man, and her scent could easily be tracked right back to Halle.

So. How did he keep her safe? He could leave her here, assign Artemis or Apollonia to guard her, and head back to Arizona.

"Don't even think about it."

Barney started. "What?"

She stirred, and it was then that he realized she was staring right back at him. He'd been so completely caught up in his own thoughts he hadn't seen her awaken. "Whatever it was that had you scowling so fiercely."

"That would be your safety, little Hobbit."

She whined in the back of her throat. "That again?"

"Now that you're out of the hospital I need to go back to Arizona." There was no way around it. Casey Lee and Derrick were getting the run-around wherever they went. They needed him if they were going to get any further with the case.

"Oh." She pushed up on one elbow. "I could stay with my parents and have Ryan take me back and forth to work with him."

He'd thought she'd put up more of a fight. "You're okay with this?"

"Nope, but we don't have a choice." Heather pressed a kiss to his chest.

"It's your job. Just like inking male behinds is mine." She winked at him as she reminded him of their lunchtime conversation and how little he'd liked hearing about her client that day. Had that only been a couple of weeks ago?

"I was thinking of asking Artemis to keep an eye on you." If anyone could protect her it would be the white Tiger. He doubted even Apollonia stood a chance against Artemis if he got serious.

She bit her lip. "I don't want to be separated from you."

"I know." He cupped the back of her head. "The last thing I want is to be away from you. But it's the life of a Hunter. I take out the bad guys, and sometimes that means leaving home for a while."

"I could come with you." She traced the edges of his nipple with her nail. "I could stay in the hotel while you work."

"Hell no." He stopped her roaming hand before he became too distracted. "You're not getting anywhere near this."

"Barney—"

"No." Just the thought of her anywhere near the Senate gave him hives. "If you're there, all I'll be able to think about is you. I need to know you're here and safe, or I'll get my ass killed."

"I know." She put her head back on his chest with a pout. "It's just…I don't want to be away from you yet."

"We both knew I'd have to go back." He didn't like it any more than she did, but what else was he supposed to do? Allow Chloe to die? "While I'm gone, start house hunting, stay close to Ryan, Artemis or Alex, and don't leave home alone."

She nodded, her hair brushing against his skin. "When do you leave?"

He grunted. "Haven't made the plane reservation yet." He tangled his fingers in her hair. "I haven't wanted to move all morning."

She eased up, pulling free of his hold. "I hate to say this, but the sooner you go the sooner you'll be back."

"Eager to have this over and done with?" He felt the same.

"More than." She stood, stretching. She seemed so nonchalant and easy in her nakedness, but he could see how red the tips of her ears were turning. Without looking at him she headed for the bathroom. "I'm taking a shower first. You relax, or better yet, book a flight. I'll make breakfast when I'm done."

The door shut behind her, blocking the best view he'd ever woken to. "Damn." He got up and headed for the tiny kitchenette table where his laptop was. He busied himself with booking a flight out that day, choosing to take the red-eye. He made a quick call to Casey Lee to inform him of his impending arrival.

"Hey, boss." Casey Lee's drawl sounded strained. "Your gal out of the pokey?"

Barney shook his head, even though Casey Lee couldn't see it. "She's out, and claimed."

Casey Lee whistled low. "Thought you were gonna wait on that until after this mess was cleared up."

"My Bear wouldn't stand for it." And neither would he, but he didn't need to tell Casey Lee that. "I'll be in town late tonight. I'll expect a status report when I arrive."

"Can do. Mr. Barnwell has been more than accommodating, but he's the only one we can say that of. Everyone else is avoiding us."

"Well, they won't avoid me." He leaned back in his chair, listening for the sound of his mate moving about as he contemplated his next move. "I tell you what. Let me think on the plane, and we'll discuss what we've come up with once I get back. I have a lot to tell you two as well."

"Will do. Want us to pick you up?"

"It would be appreciated." He could hear the shower turning off. Heather would be out any moment. "Time for me to go. I have a wet, naked redhead to play with."

Casey Lee groaned. "Man, I want a mate too."

"Be careful what you wish for, buddy." Heather had his full attention. Talking to Casey Lee was no longer an option. "Bye."

He barely heard the other shifter's farewell. Heather was coming into the room, wearing yesterday's jeans and one of his T-shirts. It was so big on her it fell to her knees. Her damp hair made parts of the T-shirt transparent.

He slipped sideways in his chair and tapped his thigh. "Come sit for a minute."

She walked over to him, eyeing him warily. "I'm kinda sore."

That made him want her to sit even more. "I'll heal it, sweetheart."

She bit her lip but sat, curling her arms around his neck. "Good morning, Barney," she whispered.

"Good morning, Heather." He kissed the tip of her nose and sent tendrils of healing energy toward her. The tissues of her pussy were inflamed from their lovemaking, so he healed the overly stretched muscles, redirecting the excess blood flow. He soothed away the pain, and her soft sigh was his reward.

"Thank you." She snuggled in, her head against his shoulder. "Do you have your flight booked?"

"Yeah, and Casey Lee and Derrick are picking me up at the airport." He ran his hand down her back. "I'm going to take a shower. You want to cook here or go out for breakfast?" He wasn't sure what was in his fridge or even if it was edible.

"I'll take a look." She sat up with a smile. "If I find something alive in your fridge we're going out."

"Make sure you slam the door shut. We wouldn't want it creeping under the bed."

She shuddered in horror. "Thanks for that image, you butt munch."

He patted her rear as she stood. "Keep saying that, and it might come true." He grinned at her, making sure she could see his fangs.

She shook her finger at him. "Be a good boy, Boo-Boo, or no more honey for you. I'll lock the picnic basket so tight not even Houdini could get in."

He threw his head back and laughed as he made his way into the bedroom. Man, he'd never thought to have a mate like her. She was feisty as hell.

He showered quickly, not wanting to leave her alone any longer than possible. Once dressed he headed back into the kitchen to find her leaning against the refrigerator door. "What's wrong?"

"Do you have a flamethrower?"

He tilted his head, curious. "Why?"

"Because the fungus on your...cheese, I think? Tried to eat me." She looked utterly horrified. "And there was something kinda orangish in there."

"Orangish? As in an orange?" It wasn't like he'd been eating here a lot recently. Several of Frank's waitresses knew him on a first-name basis.

"Nope. It wasn't round. It was kind of..." She waved her hands around. "That shaped."

"Oh." That made absolutely no sense. "So. IHOP?"

"Works for me." She glanced behind her. "After we chain the door shut."

He shook his head, amused at her antics. "Get your shoes on. I'm going to call Artemis and make sure he can keep an eye on your wandering Hobbit ass while I'm out of town."

She stuck her tongue out at him and made her way back to the bedroom. He picked up his cell and called Artemis.

Before he even got a chance to say hello, Artemis spoke. "I can do it."

"Do what?"

"Watch your mate."

Fucking smart-ass Tiger. "How the hell did you know I was calling you about that?"

"Don't worry about it. She'll be safe. I won't leave her side. Drop her off at her parents after breakfast." Artemis hung up before Barney could question him any further.

"So? Do I have a bodyguard?"

Barney nodded. "An extremely freaky one."

She started to laugh. "He'll fit right in."

"Good point." He put his arm around her and led her to the front door. "C'mon. I hear some pancakes calling my name."

Chapter Nineteen

Barney had left her at her parents' just as he'd been told to do by Artemis. Now the white Tiger was lounging on her parents' couch, complaining that he was hungry. Her mother was busy making sandwiches for the walking stomach, while Heather sat in the recliner, desperate for something to do. "Ugh."

"Bored?"

"I feel like I should be doing something to help Barney." And not shopping for a house, no matter how fun that sounded. The riddle was an itch under her skin now that her mate was out of sight. "I know he didn't get a lot out of Dr. Howard, but what about Hope?"

Artemis's head turned toward her. "Hope Walsh?"

Heather nodded. "Has anyone spoken to her?" She was pretty sure Hope was so far out of the loop she didn't even know it existed. "She might have an insight the rest of us don't."

"Wanna go chat with her?" Artemis sat up and gave Heather's mom a huge smile as she carried in the plate of sandwiches. "Thank you, Mrs. Allen. This looks great."

"You're welcome, Artemis." Stacey Allen ruffled his dark hair. "You eat up now. You're going to visit Hope and Sarah today?"

He blinked up at her in that lazy, cat way he had. "Yes, ma'am."

"Good. That girl could use some friends." Mom pointed to the platter of sandwiches. One was already in Artemis's mouth. "Eat, before the Tiger gets them all."

"Yes, Mom." Heather grabbed a sandwich and began nibbling. "Can we go after lunch?"

Artemis nodded, not even pausing before he stuffed another sandwich in his mouth. He muttered something that was utterly garbled by meat and bread.

"Ew." Heather wrinkled her nose. "Happy to know you like salami."

Artemis winked at her and swallowed. "I wanna move in here."

"Sorry, I'm taken." Heather giggled. "But I can introduce you to my sister Tiffany." Tiffany would kick his lazy butt from here to Sunday and back again.

"Is she a cute little redhead like you?" Artemis looked hopeful.

"Nope. Short dark hair, blue-green eyes and an attitude that makes Rambo look like a Mouseketeer."

"Oh, a challenge. I like those." Artemis winked and grabbed one more sandwich before standing. "Let's get out of here and go see Hope."

"Thanks, Arty."

He growled, the sound utterly feline. "Don't even go there."

"It's okay." She patted his arm. "Everyone knows you're a total BAMF."

"Bamf? What's that?" Mom was carrying two travel mugs, probably full of her homemade iced tea.

"Bad-ass em ef'er." She wasn't going to say the whole thing in front of her mom. That was just asking for an ass-kicking.

"Hmph." Mom shooed them out the door with their mugs. "Be safe, both of you."

"Yes, Mom," they echoed.

Artemis pulled her over to his car, a cherry red sports convertible. "Climb in."

"Thanks." He held open the door for her. "What kind of car is it?"

He beamed with pride. "A vintage 1969 Firebird."

"Oh. Sweet." She didn't know much about vintage cars, but this one looked oh so pretty.

"It's my baby." He slid behind the wheel and put on his seatbelt. "I had to fit it out with a three-point harness so it's legal, but otherwise I've tried to keep everything the way it was in '69."

When he started the car the engine freakin' purred. "I see why you like it."
He laughed. "It's why I borrow my sister's car whenever I go on a date. I
don't want anyone messing with my baby." He slid the car into gear and roared
out of the driveway.

Heather held on to the seatbelt for dear life. So much for keeping her
Hobbit ass safe. Artemis Smith was an insane man behind the wheel. Any second
now her brains were going to be splattered all over Main Street.

Usually it took fifteen, but with Artemis behind the wheel, blithely
ignoring things like speed limits and red lights, it had been more like ten. She
got out of the car on shaky legs, eager to be on solid, non-moving ground. "I
think I'll take the bus back."

Artemis shrugged. "I'd say it's your loss, but I'm just going to toss your ass
into my car anyway." He patted her head. "So enjoy the ride. Pretend you're at
an amusement park."

"That can kill me." Heather strode past him and to the Alpha's front door.
"I hope Sarah's here."

"Why? You need to talk to her?" Artemis reached over her head and
knocked on the door.

"Not for me, for Hope." She plastered a smile on her face as the door
cracked open. "Hi, Emma."

Emma nodded, patting the baby she was holding on the back. Little Felix
could lift his head now, and was staring at them with curiosity. "I was wondering
when either you or Barney would show up here."

"Heard he'd talked to Dr. Howard?" Heather accepted Emma's silent
invitation to enter the house.

"And that means someone needs to talk to Hope as well." Emma led the
way into the family room, with the great stone fireplace. Hope was there, seated
on the sofa, sipping something that smelled like chamomile tea. Sarah was on a
chair opposite her. "Hope, Heather's here to talk to you."

Hope nodded. "Jamie warned me you'd be by."

Sarah gasped.

Heather blinked, confused as to why Sarah looked so shocked. It sounded good to her. Mates should talk to one another, even if Hope wasn't quite ready for her mate to claim her. "Oh. I'm glad the two of you are talking."

Hope smiled secretly. "It was a shock to me, but…he makes me feel safe."

"Good. Your mate should do that for you." Heather settled on the sofa next to Hope. "So did he tell you why I'd be by to talk to you?"

Hope nodded. "I don't know anything about the riddle, or prophecy, or whatever it is."

Artemis slid his hands in his pockets and stood behind Sarah's chair. He could see the front and back doors from there, so he'd probably positioned himself that way to protect Heather.

The effect on Hope, however, was astonishing. The smiling woman began to quiver, the scent of fear strong in the air. She seemed to shrink in on herself, her shoulders tightening, her hands shaking around the tea cup.

Sarah stood and put her arm on Artemis's biceps. "Artemis, would you mind going to the kitchen and getting us something to drink?"

The Tiger didn't say a word, simply sauntered past them, ignoring Hope completely.

Once he was out of sight, Hope relaxed. "I'm sorry. I still have trouble with men around me."

She sounded so sad, so defeated, Heather couldn't help herself. She hugged Hope tightly. "I felt the same way for the longest time, but my mate helped me a lot."

Hope sagged in her hold. "What happened to you?"

Heather bit her lip. "When I was young, around ten, I was attacked by a group of men who tried to force me to shift."

"Oh."

Heather could tell Hope had no idea what that meant, but before she could inform her Sarah stepped forward and took Hope's hands between her own, cup and all. "A shifter doesn't experience their first shift until after puberty starts. So they tried to force Heather into puberty so they could…" Sarah left the rest out of her explanation.

"Oh my God." Hope shuddered. "I was sixteen when I was taken. At ten? That must have been horrible."

"My cousin Alex saved me. He's a gentle giant, but when he's pissed, he's a killing machine." Heather could still remember the rage on Alex's face as he decimated the other Bears. "I wound up more afraid of him than my attackers for a while, and I still have nightmares where they manage to finish what they'd started."

"I'm surprised you can allow men around you at all." Hope put her head on Heather's shoulder. "That's why I'm not with my mate now. I can barely stand Max, and I know he'd never hurt me."

"Because I'd hurt him," Emma replied. She'd been a silent witness to everything.

Hope's shoulders shook on a silent laugh. "I think he's safe."

"We're working on reducing her fear." Sarah squeezed Hope's hands. "She'll never be fully rid of it, but if we can lessen it, that would be wonderful."

Heather stared at Sarah's hold on Hope. "What about the nightmares?"

Sarah sighed. "I think someone else is helping with those. Right, Hope?"

Hope simply smiled, a light blush appearing on her pale cheeks. "He keeps the monsters at bay."

Heather jolted. "The mate dreams? You actually talk to Jamie through the mate dreams?"

Hope nodded. "Isn't that how it works?"

"Not most of the time, no." Sarah patted Hope's hand and pulled back. "It does for me and Gabe, though. We thought we were the only ones until we met you."

"Does he mention Marie at all?" Heather was hoping that Jamie had told Hope something that he wouldn't tell Barney.

Hope nodded, her expression full of sorrow. "We've discussed her. We both believe that Marie was... She was supposed to be..." Hope closed her eyes. "She was ours."

"Marie would have been Hope's mate as well. It was meant to be a tri-mating." Sarah thanked Artemis for the cup of tea he handed her. "If Jamie had died as well, she'd never have even a chance of becoming well. She'd never be able to endure the touch of a man again."

Hope chuckled, but it lacked humor. "But I would still have had the option of women." Her words were bitter. "I'm glad the man who killed my mate is dead."

"I'll let Ryan know. He's the one who killed him." Heather leaned her head against the top of Hope's. "He'll be happy to know he helped even a little bit."

Hope sighed. "That's not why you're here, though." She was watching Artemis, distrust all over her face. "You want to know about the riddle."

"Yeah." Heather sat up. "Do you know how it goes?"

"No, and I'm not sure I care." Hope held up her hand, stopping Heather's next words. "It can't have anything to do with me. I wasn't even around, remember?"

"Two becomes one, one becomes three." Heather took a deep breath. "I think two becomes one is Marie dying."

"Then how does one become three?" Hope scowled, still watching Artemis rather than Heather.

"I'm not sure, but I'm positive it involves you and Jamie somehow. He doesn't want to hear it, but…" Heather shrugged. "Nothing else fits."

Hope's shoulders sagged, her short blonde hair barely long enough to cover her temples. "I'm so tired of everything. I just want it all to end."

Sarah immediately focused on Hope. Heather watched as Hope's shoulders slowly straightened, the despair sliding away. "You're going to be all right. Jamie would tell you the same, and you know you can rely on him."

"I do," Hope whispered. "I just wish things had been different."

"I hate to ask this but…" Sarah glanced between Heather and Hope. "Could you have another mate?"

Hope shook her head. "No."

Artemis spoke softly, as if trying to keep Hope from being even more frightened than she already was. "Wolves will have one, maybe two mates. Never more. That's not the answer."

And since he was the white Tiger, Heather was inclined to believe him. He knew something he wasn't telling, either because he was an ass, or because he couldn't.

So maybe she could test her theory out while Artemis was there to hear it. "Could the answer be pregnancy?"

Hope grimaced. "I never got pregnant with Salazar. I'm not sure I'm capable."

Artemis said nothing, his expression remaining blank.

Hope patted Heather's arm. "If I think of anything that might help, I promise I'll tell you." She bit her lip. "Are you certain the first half of the riddle is me and Jamie?"

Heather nodded. "Yeah, I am. No one else does, except maybe Barney, but I'm positive."

Hope smiled, and for once it looked like a happy expression. "Then maybe you're the key mentioned in the rhyme."

"I guess so." Huh. Maybe she *was* the Fox. "Then Barney knows what to do." And his obsession with the white shifters, Hope and Jamie's bond...it was all tied together after all. "We'll have to trust in him."

"If you don't mind, I'll trust in Jamie." Hope's smile faded. "He's all I have."

"No." Heather hugged Hope hard. "You have Halle now. We protect our own."

"Amen," Emma whispered. "Preach it, sistah."

Hope's soft laugh was all the reward Heather needed.

Chapter Twenty

"Are you sure you can get in there?" Casey Lee had his back to a wall as Barney picked the lock to the one area even Hunters were banned from.

"Trust me." The lock gave way, and Barney grinned. "I'm an expert." He'd already disabled the alarms and the motion sensors. Cutting the power wasn't an option. A generator would automatically kick in and alert everyone still in the area. He'd triple-checked for any back-up alarms, but hadn't been able to find any. Picking the lock to the back door had been the final thing needed to get inside.

"Derrick is with Carl?" He needed to make certain Carl was still being protected, as well as Darien. Darien had agreed to move in with Carl and his mate until all of this blew over, giving Casey Lee and Derrick fewer places to protect and patrol.

"Yup. He's still pissed he lost rock-paper-scissors." Casey Lee chuckled. "He always picks rock-rock-paper."

Barney carefully pushed the door open. "Got it." He tuned to Casey Lee. "Keep an eye out for me. Find a good perch, stay out of sight, and if things start to look bad you get your ass out of here. I have a legal reason to be doing this. You don't." If necessary, Barney would pull the Leo card and let Sebastian Lowe save his ass. He wouldn't sit in shifter jail while the Senate went after his mate.

"I think I can get up to a good spot where I can see the building." Casey Lee hefted a pair of binoculars. "I wanted to take my sniper rifle but Derrick talked me out of it."

"We're not here to kill, we're here to gather intel." Barney pushed Casey

Lee's shoulder. "Get in place, and remember the plan."

"Right. You get the supposed hit list of white shifters, I keep watch on your furry ass." Casey Lee saluted and ran off, his scent disappearing. He was using his Fox powers to hide his trail. Only Barney's scent would remain in the area.

"Good boy," Barney whispered. He snuck into the building and lit the small flashlight he'd brought with him. His night sight was the same whether he was using his human eyes or his Bear's, so the flashlight was necessary in the dark building.

There was not a sound as Barney began walking through the room. The information desk was in front of him, a place where Senators went to find the materials they needed, whether it was paperwork or microfiche. There was library shelving everywhere, desks with computers and microfiche readers, and a small area with vending machines for when the Senators needed to take a break from researching the laws of the shifter world. Barney wasn't certain what all was contained in the room, but this wasn't the area he was looking for.

No. According to what Casey Lee and Derrick were able to discover, there was another part to the building, the basement. It was there the oldest records were kept, and it was there he'd find the lists of shifters who'd lost their lives. If Casey Lee and Derrick were right, not only would he find the death records, he'd find a list of special deaths, hidden away from the normal everyday records. It would take some time to find them, so he ignored everything on this floor in favor of making his way to the basement.

He eventually found the stairs hidden away at the back of the stacks. It wasn't a secret entrance, but it was tucked into an alcove away from the rest of the room. He checked the knob, not surprised to find it locked.

Out came his lock picks, and in seconds he was on his way down. It was even darker down here, without the windows allowing the moonlight in. Once down, the layout of the room was similar to the one upstairs, but without the information desk.

This couldn't be where the list was kept. It was too open, too obvious. No, it had to be somewhere else, where only the Senators involved could access it.

He searched the room, looking for hidden rooms or floor safes, but after two hours his search was fruitless. He stood in the middle of the room, scanning the shelves with his flashlight, ready to curse up a storm. This couldn't have been for nothing, damn it. It had to be here. Casey Lee had assured him that his source was certain the list was here, safe behind locked doors.

Wait. Behind locked doors? Did that mean that one of the small offices in the room might have the list? Could it be that simple?

He began going around to the small offices he'd ignored earlier, finding all of them unlocked. Just in case he searched each, checking the desks for false bottoms, looking in filing cabinets and tapping the floor for any hollow areas where documents could be hidden.

Nothing. He was boned, and not in the good way.

If the documents weren't here, they must be somewhere nearby. There had to be a place where no one would think to look, where they'd…

He blinked as his flashlight roamed across…

No. That couldn't be it. But it was the only place he hadn't checked.

Barney pushed open the door to the men's room. He checked each urinal, flushing them, wiggling them to see if they moved. Nothing. The sinks hid nothing from him, and the soap dispensers and paper towel dispensers all acted normal. Nothing was out of the ordinary. Each stall had a toilet, but none of them had a tank he could inspect. There was nothing under the seats, or under the toilets themselves.

"They really need to clean in here more often," he muttered as he inspected the last stall. When he was done he leaned against the tile wall, utterly exhausted. "One last place to check."

He strode out of the men's room and into the women's.

Here there were no urinals, but more stalls to check. Again, there were no surprises around the sinks or dispensers, so he began to check the stalls.

In the last stall, the handicapped one, he found what he'd been searching for. One tile, when wiggled, slid aside to reveal a button. Barney pressed the button and stepped back as a three-foot-wide portion of the tile wall silently slid back and to the side.

A secret entrance, just as he'd thought.

It had been so cleverly hidden that unless you knew what to look for you'd never see the slight crack in the "grout". Curious, he turned slightly and flushed the toilet.

Yup. It was a working stall. That meant that whoever used the room had to go in and out at night or risk being seen. Either that or so few people used it that there was no risk whatsoever.

He strode into the room, wondering what he'd find.

There was a single desk, a small filing cabinet, a bookcase and printer. A state of the art computer sat on the desk. He strode around the desk, hoping to see something that would indicate who used this room, but it was almost sterile in its lack of personal touches. There was nothing that would show who'd been there.

Barney grabbed the Scotch tape dispenser and some index cards. He might not be able to find out who used the room from pictures, but sure as hell there'd be fingerprints on almost everything. He began using the tape to try and lift prints, attaching the tape to an index card when he found one. He noted on the card where it had been found and the date and time.

He managed to lift about four partial prints before he realized he was running out of time. He needed to be out of here before whoever used the room discovered him hiding down here. The last thing he wanted was for the Senators to realize the archive building had been broken into. It would put the Leo in a very bad position, pitting him against the Senators before he had proof that some of them were conspiring against the shifter world.

He began to dig through the rest of the desk, finding orders with Vaughn's signature on them. Vaughn was the Hunter liaison, and had been missing for weeks, but there was an order with his signature from days ago, ordering Casey Lee and Derrick back to the Senate for questioning by the Lion Senator, Holmes. There were other orders for other mercenaries, orders that made Barney's blood run cold.

Other shifters were being hunted, killed in cold blood, without explanation. Just orders to do as told and not question. Whoever had set this up was a rat bastard of the first order, and Barney was going to kill the son of a bitch when he caught him.

He finished going through the desk and went to the filing cabinet, checking out the first drawer marked A-B. In the drawer he found names. Lots of names. Wren Bunsun was listed, with a special mark next to her name shaped like a star. Artemis Smith, Jamie Howard, and Chloe Williams-Woods all had the same mark, but it had been changed, almost erased. Ryan Williams, Keith Allen, Tiffany Allen and Heather Allen…

Fuck. A. Motherfucking. Duck.

Heather's name was on the list, and she had the goddamn star next to her name.

His hands shook with rage. His mate's name was listed amongst those who were targeted by the Senate. Could her attack at the age of ten have been an attempt to kill her rather than rape her? How far back did this go? And why those of mixed blood?

He had to focus. Heather would want that. He needed to figure this fucking puzzle out before he let his Bear loose on the entire Senate and simply removed the threat by force. Heather might not want that, but at least her little Hobbit ass would be as safe as he could make it. He'd sacrifice almost anything to make sure she was never hurt again.

Julian's entire tribe of Kermode was also listed, as were those few Polars who still lived, but their stars had been erased just like Chloe's.

He rifled through, noting the number of names with *.d* next to them. Deceased shifters? All of them had the star, and all of them were of mixed lineage. Almost all of them were children or teens. All of their deaths were listed as "accidental".

There was nothing accidental about any of them. They'd been systematically destroyed for years, and from what he could see it had been going on for longer than Barney had been alive. Some of the records dated back to the Revolutionary era, when America was fighting for independence from the British.

White shifters had to come from those of mixed blood, from indirect lines. It was the only explanation that made any sense whatsoever. From the lost Arctic Foxes, to the almost extinct Polars and the Kermode Bears, there must have been far more white shifters before this purge began. Why did the Senate want them dead so badly?

It had to be the connection the white shifters had with the spirit world, but why would the Senate want that connection cut off? Had the spirits said or done something that the Senate didn't approve of, and so they wanted to cut off the shifter world's communication with them?

Or was there something more sinister going on? In the drawer he found the list of Lowes who'd ruled the American shifters since 1776.

Each Leo had an erased star, just like Chloe. Was it because they were confirmed white shifters? Was that what the erased star meant?

None of the Leos had been killed the way the other white shifters had been. They'd all lived normal, happy lives. The direct line of the Lowe family had wound up diverging a few times as the Leo wound up being born by a sibling or a cousin, but they always carried the name Lowe.

Was it because killing a Lowe would be too obvi—

Pain, the scent of blood, and darkness.

Chapter Twenty-One

Heather stared at the plane ticket that had been sent to her email address early that morning. The return address was Barney's. The plane tickets were for her and Artemis to fly to Flagstaff, Arizona, on the noon flight.

Something wasn't right. Hadn't he told her to stay in Halle? So why was he sending her plane tickets? And why hadn't he called to let her know he was sending them?

She tried calling his cell for answers, but it went straight to voicemail. She left a message telling him that she was on her and way to call back.

"Artemis?" She called the Tiger over to take a look. "What do you think?"

He leaned over her shoulder and pointed at the truncated address. "Expand that." She did as told, and Artemis cocked his head. "That's definitely his email address. Did you call him?"

"Yup. Went straight to voicemail." He was right, that was definitely Barney's email address. "You think someone else could have mailed this out?"

"A hacker? It's possible." Artemis studied the tickets. "They look legit, though. Want to check the airline?"

She did, and their flight was definitely legitimate. Someone had bought them tickets. "Are your freaky Tiger powers giving you any heebee-jeebies?"

He stared at her like she'd just grown a second head. "My what, now?"

She huffed out a breath. Getting responses from him was harder than getting them from… Oh, that was a good idea. "Should I call Julian?"

"Nah, don't worry about it. Sorry, but my Tiger senses aren't tingling." Artemis yawned. "If we're leaving, we should go soon." He tilted his head, a flash of silver crossing his irises. "What are *your* senses telling you?"

She stood. "That something's gone wrong, and this is some sort of trap."

He nodded approvingly. "And?"

The thought of leaving Barney to the mercy of whoever had hacked his email and sent her those tickets was unbearable. "I think we're heading to Arizona. But first, we have to take care of something."

The tickets were for the noon plane, so they didn't have a lot of time. She raced to pack a bag. While packing she called Chloe. "I'm headed to Sedona."

"Barney?"

"The email address the tickets came from was his, but no phone call, no nothing. Just the tickets."

"Trap." Chloe wasn't using a lot of words.

"Are you all right?" If Chloe wasn't using a lot of words, she was worried about something.

Chloe sighed. "I'm fine. At work. Cleaning a Chinese Crested's ears."

"Anything Fox thinks I need to know?" Heather slammed some T-shirts and jeans into her overnight bag and began to pack her makeup.

"Not right now. Just be careful, and make sure your bomb knows you're going."

"Will do." Bomb? Could she mean mom? "Keep an ear out for the cavalry charge."

Chloe giggled. "I'll come running if it sounds."

Heather hung up and headed into her bathroom, grabbing her toothbrush, toothpaste, shampoo, conditioner and body lotion. She carried them back to her bed where she carefully packed them in her bag.

"Heather?" Mom stuck her head in Heather's room, eyeing her curiously. "What are you doing?"

"Barney sent me plane tickets to Flagstaff. I think we get a rental car from there and drive to Sedona." She wasn't going to tell her mother about her concerns. It was best to let her think everything was all right.

Mom crossed her arms over her chest and scowled. "You're not going alone, young lady."

Heather winced at her mother's tone. "No, Artemis is going too."

Her mother stared at her for a moment. "All right. Call me when you get there, and then every night after, or I'm coming to bring you home."

"Mom—"

Stacey Allen's expression turned stern. "Don't argue with me, or I'll bring the entire clan."

Hell. She would, too. "Yes, ma'am."

"You don't want to see what will happen if I'm forced to call them all."

No, Heather did not. Her mother was a scary woman when she thought her kits were in danger. "Yes, ma'am."

Mom nodded firmly, seemingly satisfied. "Good." She smiled sweetly. "Don't forget your toothbrush and extra underwear."

"Already packed." She looked around the room as her mother stomped down the stairs. Was she forgetting anything? She didn't think so, and she didn't have time to check.

Heather ran down the stairs, her bag packed, only to find her mother giving Artemis a lecture. "If I find one single hair on my daughter's head out of place I'll rip out your whiskers one by one."

Artemis backed up a step. "Yes, ma'am."

"And you too. You're protecting my daughter, and I don't take that lightly. I expect you to come back in one piece, understood?"

He nodded warily. "Yes, ma'am."

"Now give me a kiss and get out of here." Mom tapped her cheek and waited expectantly.

Heather was nearly dying of laughter by the time Artemis gingerly gave the expected kiss. "Good boy." Her mother patted his cheek. "I'll make the meatloaf you like when you get back."

Artemis looked flummoxed. "Yes, ma'am."

"You're welcome." Mom turned to Heather. "Give me a hug, sweetie."

Heather hugged her mom tight. "I'll see you soon, okay? We have to go house hunting, remember?"

Her mother hugged her back just as tightly. "I remember."

"I'll call when I get there, okay?" Heather pulled back. "The safe word is…?"

Her mother smiled. "Bunny."

Heather laughed. "Got it." She adjusted the bag on her shoulder and waved to Artemis. "Let's get this party started."

Once in the car, Artemis asked the question she'd been waiting for. "Safe word?"

"When we were kids, when we went out we always had a safe word. If something was wrong and we couldn't say what it was we would say the safe word and the whole clan would come running to the rescue. But it only works if we have access to a phone."

He nodded. "Makes sense, I suppose."

"It was also for if anyone tried to tell us that our parents sent them to pick us up. If they didn't know the safe word, we were supposed to kick them in the nuts and run."

"Try the side of the knee as hard as you can. A guy can absorb nut pain if his adrenaline is high enough. Take out his knee and he isn't going anywhere."

"Thanks, Artie." She giggled at his glare. "I'll remember that."

He grunted and drove off, taking them straight to the airport.

Once they were in the air, she turned to Artemis and asked the question that had been bothering her since she received the email. "If these tickets really do turn out to have been sent by one of Barney's enemies, what should we do when we arrive?"

Artemis shot her a toothy grin, his eyes turning silver. "You leave it to me. We need to do this, though, so don't worry your pretty red head over it."

Okay. Well. "So my job is to hide while you play?"

"Damn straight. You get hurt on my watch and Barney will rip my balls off, and your mom will rip out my whiskers." He sighed sadly. "Also, she won't make that meatloaf anymore, or comb my fur when I'm itchy."

It sounded like her mother had pretty much adopted poor Artemis. She wondered what his mother would think of that.

"So relax, I've got you covered. Read or something." He put his head back and promptly fell asleep for the rest of the flight.

Read or something, huh? She pulled out her tablet PC and began researching Sedona. It was a small city in the northeastern region of Arizona, known for its red rock hills and history of Hollywood movies.

It was a little over a seven-hour flight from Philadelphia to Flagstaff, and Artemis napped the entire way. The only time he woke was when they had to switch planes in Phoenix. Heather was far too nervous to sleep, so she read instead, trying to learn as much as she could about Sedona, the Leo and the Senate.

She tried emailing Barney back, but she'd received no reply by the time they landed. Artemis kept her behind him as they disembarked, making sure no one got too close to her. Since they'd only packed overnight bags they didn't need to head to baggage claim, so Artemis led her toward the area where he could rent a car. They didn't know where Barney's hotel was, but since she planned on calling him again while Artemis took care of the car that shouldn't be an issue.

"Ms. Allen?" A deep voice called her name. She turned to find a tall, dark-haired man with pale, jade-green eyes standing there. He wore a charcoal-gray business suit with a white button-down shirt and a green tie.

He smelled of Lion.

She exchanged a quick glance with Artemis, who shrugged. "I'm Heather Allen."

The man smiled, but it didn't reach his eyes. "I'm Ian Holmes, and I've come to pick you up." He nodded to Artemis. "And Mr. Smith as well."

"I see." She tried to remain calm, but this was exactly what she'd been afraid of. "You don't mind if we take our own car, do you?"

Mr. Holmes gestured, and two Lions, also in dark suits and green ties, stepped up from behind him. "I'm afraid that won't be necessary, Ms. Allen. I assure you, however, that you're perfectly safe with me."

"Did Barney send you?" If he couldn't come himself it would make sense he'd send someone, but there was something about Ian Holmes that had her stepping slightly closer to Artemis.

"I'm afraid not, Ms. Allen." For just a moment, a flash of real concern showed on his face before it disappeared behind a façade of disinterest.

Artemis shrugged. "Good enough for me." He sauntered up to the Lion and held out his hand. "Nice to meet you."

Was he insane? He had to be. He was just accepting this.

But when he glanced back at her, Heather could see a flash of silver in his gaze. He winked and shook Mr. Holmes's hand.

Mr. Holmes's brows rose in surprise. "And you as well, Mr. Smith." He shook Heather's hand next. "If you and Ms. Allen will follow me." He gestured toward the doors, where Heather saw a black SUV at the curb. "We have little time to talk before we reach our destination."

"All right." Heather kept Artemis between her and the men. She didn't trust them, not even a little. But that glint of silver in Artemis's eyes…

He must have something up his sleeve, so she'd follow and see where he led.

Artemis stopped her just as one of the men opened the back door. "You go first."

She nodded and hopped into the car, Artemis following right behind her. This put her at the other door as one of the men settled next to Artemis. One of the men took their bags and put them in the back of the SUV. Holmes got into the front passenger seat while the other two men flanked him, one driving, the other staring out the window intently.

Once the car started moving, Artemis poked Holmes on the shoulder. "Can I ask a question?"

Holmes waved his hand. "Please do, Mr. Smith."

Artemis blinked in that cat-like way of his, as if he was debating whether or not to be fascinated or bored by the whole situation. "Why is the Lion Senator picking us up at the airport?"

Heather blinked. This man was a Senator? Fuck. The pile of shit she'd landed in was higher than she'd thought.

"Hm. That would be because of Ms. Allen." Holmes turned to stare at her. "I believe you, or one of your family members, may be the key to finding out what is happening to the white shifters."

She took a deep breath, suddenly scared out of her wits. "Are you one of the Senators who's hunting them?"

"Not at all, Ms. Allen." He put his hand over his heart. "I'm one of the Senators trying to save them."

"How do we know we can trust you?" Heather ignored his soft chuckle. "This is my family on the line, Mr. Holmes."

"There is more than just your family at stake, Ms. Allen." He waved toward Artemis. "Mr. Smith, for instance, is endangered as well."

"How did you find out about them?" Heather watched where they were going. She might not know Sedona, but she wanted to be able to trace her route back to the airport if she had to run for it.

"I'd imagine the same way you did." Holmes turned back toward the front. "Now, if you don't mind, I need to text someone."

That really didn't work for her. "But—"

"I believe all of your questions will be answered shortly, Ms. Allen. For now, please enjoy the view. Sedona is quite lovely this time of year."

"Mr. Holmes—"

The man beside Artemis held up his hand. "I'm sorry, Ms. Allen. Senator Holmes is busy. Please hold all questions until we arrive at our destination."

Heather began to softly sing the most annoying song she could think of.

Artemis winced. One of the bodyguards groaned, and the Lion Senator's left eye began to twitch.

The bodyguard who'd asked her to be quiet was the only one who laughed. "What does the Fox say, indeed."

"Hatee-hatee-hatee-ho!"

Chapter Twenty-Two

Jesus God, his head was killing him. Barney slowly opened his eyes, squinting into the darkness. Where the fuck was he? What had he done, or hadn't done? He tried to sit up, but the sound of rattling chains stopped him cold.

He stared at his wrist, feeling the weight of the cold metal surrounding it. It was thick, the chains equally so. Both wrists and ankles were bound by the metal.

Looking around, he wasn't all that surprised to find himself lying on a hard cot placed against a cold, concrete wall. Ahead of him was a metal door with a square window covered in thick glass. A toilet and a sink were against another wall.

He sat up, gingerly holding his head. There was a lump back there, and the scent of dried blood. Someone had hit him hard enough to knock him out.

How long had he been here? Looking down, his clothing had been removed, leaving him naked other than the thick steel cuffs. He took a deep breath, trying to sort out the scents around him.

Lion. Definitely Lion, and in the room recently. He sniffed his arm, wondering if it was the Lion who'd removed his clothing, but instead of feline he got the distinct odor of Hyena. It was a Hyena who'd set his chains.

He sniffed again, catching a faint whiff of Ocelot. There was also something else, another shifter, but he couldn't quite identify who or what it might be. Worse, all he was getting was the shifter type, not the individual shifters. He had no idea who the Hyena or Lion might be, only that they'd been in the room. Had they figured out a way to scrub their scents, or were they messing with him by piping scents into the room? Was the Hyena the only one he could be certain of?

Fuck this shit. Barney focused, sending healing energy to the lump on the back of his head. His headache eased as he dealt with the inflammation and tissue damage. Before long all he had to worry about was the dried blood.

He stood and stretched, finding yet another bit of damage. A small pinprick on his arm told him that the blow might have knocked him out, but a drug had kept him out. He could be anywhere now. And if the person who had created the bathroom office knew Barney had intel on them, then Heather was in danger.

Just that thought made his Grizzly insane. He roared, breaking the chains as he shifted, his Grizzly ready to tear apart anything that got between Barney and his mate. The steel bands broke at the latch, freeing him from the shackles.

He lumbered to the door and wrenched it open, the screech of tortured metal filling the hallway beyond.

Pfft.

He felt a pricking sensation in his neck. There must have been an automatic sedative, similar to the one in the shifter jail, for those who attempted to break free.

But Barney was a Hunter, and he was in his Grizzly form. The Bear easily shook off what the unconscious man had not been able to. He roared his challenge, ready to fight his way out of wherever he was. He knew now that this wasn't the Senate's jail, where they housed rogues. No. This was someplace else, a private jail. The question was, whom did it belong to?

Now that he was free of his cell he could scent things more easily. There were all types of shifters here, some in cells, their scents muted. The guards were easier to scent, most of them being Lions, a few being Hyenas. He thought he caught the scent of Fox and possibly Wolf as well.

Barney lumbered out, shoving past the guard racing toward him. He bared his teeth and let loose a primal scream, determined to get free.

The guards attacked, and Barney held his ground, using his weight and size to his advantage. He swiped at them, his claws digging deep into their flesh, taking two of them out of the fight.

He couldn't let them get control over him. If the Lions began to try and order him around, there was a chance, thanks to their unique abilities, that he'd be forced to obey. Lions could, as kings of the jungle, order others to do their bidding. Only their Alphas were stronger, able to control crowds of shifters, but together there might be enough Lions here to command one pissed-off Grizzly.

The corridor was far too narrow for him to fight as he'd like, but returning to his human form would mean losing the thick pelt of fur and skin that kept him safe from their claws and teeth, both bared in the cat shifters. One of them pulled a gun, trying to shoot him down. If they shot into his body, his largest target, the bullet would penetrate and do damage, but the odds of it killing him were negligible unless they got a lucky shot. There was a slim possibility that a bullet fired at his head would glance off his thick Grizzly skull, but at such close range he wasn't willing to take that chance. Barney managed to get one of the other guards between him and the gunman before the shot went off.

The Lion went down, a dart sticking out of his neck.

So. The orders were to recapture, not to kill. Good to know. It meant he could act without fear of death. He'd try not to kill too many of them. They'd need to be questioned once he was out of here.

Damn. He was not looking forward to giving *this* report to the Leo.

He roared again as another guard went down under his claws. He could hear other shifters, those behind the metal doors, begging to be released, but he had no time to worry about them. He'd come back for them once he determined whether or not they deserved to be there. He reared, forcing the guard in front of him to back up before the full weight of a Grizzly landed on his shoulders. Barney lumbered after him, forcing him back even farther. He could see the doorway beyond the guards, one that hopefully led to the way out of here. Even if the corridor were wider, that would be good for him, giving him more maneuverability. That door became his target, getting there his only goal.

He could see some of the guards taking off their clothes, preparing to fight him in their shifted form. Fuck. If that happened, if they dog-piled him, he'd have no chance of coming out of this intact. He needed to think fast. He didn't have enough room to set up a charge, but—

A scream off to his left caught his attention. Yes. That could work.

He turned, ripping another door off its hinges and using it as a shield. The *pfft* of a sedative dart being deployed was barely audible against the pleas of the shifter inside the cell. Barney ignored him, kind of hoping he'd shift and get free of his bonds on his own. Maybe the shifter would even help him get the fuck out of there. While he didn't want a rogue on the loose, this wasn't the rogue jail, so Barney was willing to take that chance.

The Lions had completed their shift. Barney used the door to block their initial leap, but the weight of the door plus the Lions was too much for him. He was forced onto his back, his belly exposed to the claws and jaws of the Lions. Only the door that landed just above his pelvis prevented them from eviscerating him.

Still, having Lion claws trying to dig into his junk wasn't making his life any easier. He roared and managed to get his feet up under the bottom of the door. Using all his strength he managed to thrust both the door and the Lions off of him. Twisting, he got up, facing the Lions who now snarled back at him.

They were at the same disadvantage he was, but their slightly smaller bodies and twisty spines gave them more maneuverability than his bulky frame did. And the manes on the males protected them the same way Barney's fur did. He'd have to aim for their bodies and limbs if he hoped to stop them.

One of them leapt again, gaining his feet more quickly than Barney had thought possible. He instinctively swiped at the Lion, slamming him into the wall with a horrible crushing sound.

The Lion hit the ground, unmoving.

The guards stared at the fallen Lion in horror. Almost as one, they all turned on Barney and snarled.

So much for not killing.

The Lions attacked him with a ferocity that would have surprised him if he hadn't fought Pride animals before. They were trying to avenge a fallen brother, and Barney, without the freedom to move as he wished, was going to go down under them unless something happened quickly. Even the shifters who weren't Lions were quickly shifting, joining the other guards in their attack on him. The

Hyenas danced in and out of the Lion Pride's attacks, nipping at his joints. A Fox managed to get under him, nipping at his belly. A Wolf almost got his neck between its jaws as the Lions dog-piled on him, biting and clawing at his back.

He reared, managing to toss some of the Lions off of him, but with so many of the attacking he couldn't keep track of them. The Fox got in a good bite, sinking its fangs into his thigh. The Wolf got his leg, knocking him off balance.

The Lions were on him as he went down, and for the first time Barney considered that he might not survive this.

A deep voice filled the room, one that Barney knew well. One that scared the shit out of him. "Stand down."

The shifters surrounding Barney paused in their attack.

"Now."

With low growls and yips, the shifters pulled back, leaving Barney to stare at a pair of dark boots coming his way. He lifted his head and stared up at the head of the Leo's security team and Sebastian Lowe's most trusted ally.

"You really know how to have fun, don't you, Barnwell?" Kincade Lowe tilted his head, his brown eyes filled with anger. "You want to tell me why you're fucking with my guards?"

Barney lowered his head with a groan.

"Shift."

Barney obeyed. You didn't flip Kincade Lowe the bird if you wanted to live to see another day.

"Follow me." Kincade turned, muttering to his guards to shift and dress once more. Barney followed, limping and bleeding from multiple wounds.

Kincade opened the door Barney had been focused on reaching. "Why the fuck were you in my jail?"

Barney glanced back, staring at the concrete hallway. "I have no idea."

Chapter Twenty-Three

They'd driven about an hour outside of Sedona when the driver made a right turn. Another ten minutes, and they were pulling up in front of large metal gates flanked by adobe walls topped with sandstone. Carriage lights flanked the gates, and the drive had gone from tarmac to paving stones. In the distance she could see mountains, and on either side was sand, cacti and desert grasses. "Where are we?"

No one answered. The driver leaned out of the window and waved a card at an electronic reader. Within moments the gates swung open, allowing them entry.

As they pulled down the stone driveway, she began to get glimpses of the home they were approaching. With adobe walls and a clay tile roof, the building was truly a desert beauty. The greenery was sparse, but what there was of it blended beautifully with the desert backdrop. The home was a mish-mash of angles and wrought iron, with lighting everywhere she looked and a simple fountain by the front door.

The car stopped, and the Leo Senator got out. "Please, Mr. Smith, Ms. Allen. Follow me. There's someone I'd like you both to meet."

She exchanged a glance with Artemis, who shrugged. He looked as confused as she felt, but they followed anyway. Whatever was going on, whoever they'd been brought to see, had to be big in the shifter world to own such a home.

Lions braced either side of the large, ornately carved double doors that led to the interior of the home. The scents of the desert perfumed the air, making her nose twitch. Fox and coyote, unknown trees and bushes, owls and other creatures lived close to this mansion by the mountain.

Mr. Holmes rang the doorbell and waited, his hands clasped loosely behind his back.

When the door opened, a woman answered. She was dressed in a black suit, her blonde hair pulled back in a French twist. Her makeup was minimal, as was her jewelry. "Mr. Holmes. Mr. Lowe is expecting you."

Shock raced through Heather's system. Everyone knew that name. "Mr. Lowe? As in the Leo?"

The woman looked at her and smiled softly. "Ms. Allen." She tipped her head in greeting. "A pleasure to meet you. I'm Mr. Lowe's assistant, Savannah Harper." She stepped back and waved toward the interior of the home. "Please, come in."

Heather followed Mr. Holmes into the house. Light wooden floors, scarred from years of claws and paws, gave the room a homier look than she'd thought possible from the outside. A stairway off to the left led to a balcony that overlooked the entryway, while a set of glass doors on the right showed off a gorgeous office filled with bookshelves and showcasing a partner's desk. Beyond the entryway, she could see light wooden floors taking over where the marble let off. "It's beautiful."

"Thank you. The Leo is very proud of his family home." Savannah Harper led them under the balcony to a large great room.

Where the front of the home was smaller windows with wrought iron cages over them, the back was nothing but windows overlooking the mountains and the pool area. Two couches faced one another, both overstuffed leather. Between them was a battered-looking coffee table that could probably handle a full-grown Lion pouncing on it in play. Matching end tables had lamps with stone bases that matched the huge fucking fireplace on the right side of the room.

"Please, have a seat. Sebastian will be with you in a moment." Savannah Harper left the room, ostensibly to fetch the goddamn ruler of the entire shifter fucking world.

Heather fucking sat.

Artemis picked her up off the floor and put her on the sofa. "Barney might ask me some uncomfortable questions if he finds bruises on your ass."

"Guh." They were about to meet the *Leo*. Wasn't she supposed to be at least a little freaked out?

Mr. Holmes took a seat next to her, his bodyguards standing behind them. "The Leo will—" He squawked indignantly as Artemis shoved him down one seat. "Mr. Smith!"

"What?" Artemis slumped into the seat between Heather and Mr. Holmes.

The bodyguards did nothing, just stood there with their hands clasped in front of them. When Mr. Holmes glared at them, the one who'd spoken to Heather and laughed at her song shrugged his shoulders. "He's her bodyguard, sir."

He said it as if Mr. Holmes should have understood that and automatically seated himself somewhere else. Instead, Mr. Holmes glowered at Artemis. "You could stand with my men."

Artemis stared at Mr. Holmes as if he were a moron. "Then what would I do if you and your men turn against her?" He shook his head and turned to Heather. "When the Leo gets here, stay calm. He's a nice guy, or so I've heard."

"Thank you, Mr. Smith. It's nice to know someone out there likes me." A tall, blond man with striking hazel eyes and a wide, open smile sauntered into the room. Behind him was a dark-haired man, with dark, cold eyes, and behind him—

"Barney!" Heather darted past both men to her mate, who grunted in pain when she hit him. "What happened?" She could smell blood, his blood, all over him, and her Fox started going nuts. She began crying in distress, the sounds pouring out of her as she instinctively tried to soothe her wounded mate.

Hard hands landed on her shoulders. She was pushed back, Barney's blue eyes riddled with the brown of his Bear. "Why are you here?"

"Huh." Artemis replied before she could. "I'm guessing he didn't send us those plane tickets after all."

Artemis was going to get himself killed if he kept taunting the Bear.

"Heather?" More brown seeped into Barney's gaze.

She took the deepest breath she could. "Your email address was legitimate and we couldn't decide if it was a trap or not and Mom gave me a safe word and if I say it the cavalry charge starts and Mr. Holmes took us here even though he was kinda douchey to me and he knows about the white shifters but he wouldn't tell us anything so I sang the Fox song, the really annoying one, and Artemis has been really protective so don't skin him please?" She panted, all out of breath. "How did you get hurt?"

Barney's mouth hung open in shock. Good. While he was processing, he couldn't yell at her.

The Leo, on the other hand, began to laugh. "Did you just call the Lion Senator a douche?"

The douche stood and cleared his throat. "You've mated, Barnwell."

Barney shifted his gaze to the Lion Senator. "Yes."

Mr. Holmes scowled. "You know Hunters aren't supposed to mate until near retirement. You yourself preached this to all of your trainees. Why did you break protocol?"

Barney growled, the sound almost subsonic.

Mr. Holmes acted as if he didn't hear a thing. "You should be in Montana, protecting your territory, not chasing some teenager across the country so you could mate her."

The growl wasn't so subsonic now. The blue was completely gone from his eyes too. Heather had to do something before Barney obliterated a Senator for being an asshole. "Barney." He kept his eyes on the Senator but tightened his hold on her, pulling her against his chest. "Someone sent me plane tickets to come here."

"Did you send them, Holmes?" Barney's tone was silky smooth, deadly in its calm.

Mr. Holmes sighed. "Of course I did. She's part of this and needs to be here, under guard."

"Not Chloe?" If Holmes knew about the white shifters, then he must know about her cousin.

"We tried that, but she resisted. You were our second choice, as you were the second most vulnerable."

"So you planned to kidnap my mate all along?" Barney snarled, his hands flexing across her back. She could feel his claws scraping at the cloth of her shirt.

"Are you the one who sent that bounty hunter after Chloe?" If he said yes he'd have to fend off a rabid Fox.

Mr. Holmes stared at her blankly before returning his gaze to Barney. "Well, Barnwell?"

"I think that's enough, Holmes." The Leo's tone was commanding, forcing Mr. Holmes to shut up.

The Lion Senator glared at Barney once more before sitting down.

Artemis stood and bowed to the Leo. "Sire."

"Artemis Smith." The Leo smiled and held out his hand. "It's good to finally meet you."

Artemis shook the Leo's hand. "It's a pleasure, sire."

"I understand you have a sister who's a Hunter?" The Leo took a seat across from Mr. Holmes, the other, dark-haired man sitting right next to him. "Oh, by the way, this is my cousin, and head of my security, Kincade Lowe."

Kincade nodded. "Speaking of security, Sebastian, I found Barnwell in our jail."

Sebastian looked shocked. "*Our* jail?"

Kincade nodded grimly. "Seems someone put his furry ass in there after tranquilizing it."

"Shit." Sebastian rubbed his chin as he stared at Barney. "Find out if anyone else in our jail is an accidental guest, Kin. I want to know ASAP."

"Done." Kincade stood and stepped to the side, speaking softly into something strapped to his wrist.

Sebastian turned back to Artemis. "As I was saying, your sister is a Hunter?"

Artemis nodded. "She's currently guarding Chloe Williams, sire."

"Good." Sebastian shot a hard look at Mr. Holmes. "She stays in Halle, along with the Hunters already there."

Mr. Holmes's cheeks flushed and his eyes narrowed. It looked like he didn't care for the Leo's words. "But, Leo, there's—"

"That's an order, Ian."

Heather bowed her head, along with every other shifter in the room. The power that flowed from the Leo in that moment was so overwhelming her sight began to dim. She'd do anything she could to obey that order and keep the Hunters in Halle. She'd never felt anything like it in her life.

The power continued to flow through the room until Holmes muttered, "Yes, sire." Then it was gone, and Heather found herself being held up by Barney because her knees had completely given out. She felt like a weight had been lifted off of her shoulders, but the need to keep the Hunters in Halle was still strong. If magic existed, this was what she imagined a *geas* must feel like. "Damn. Remind me to kick my brother's ass."

Barney titled her chin up, forcing her to look up at him. "Why?"

She grimaced. "When we played D&D he put a *geas*, a magical compulsion, on me to always protect his cleric. Now I know what that feels like. You *really* need to get back to Halle."

He chuckled. "It wasn't directed at you, so it will ease in a couple of hours."

Hours? Shit. "Can I sit, please? I can't feel my feet." Barney scooped her up in his arms, ignoring her protests. "Put me down, Boo-Boo."

"Boo-Boo?" the Leo muttered.

"Why?" Barney demanded, refusing to move even when she poked his shoulder.

She showed him the blood on her finger. "You're hurt, dumbass!"

"Nothing I can't handle." Barney turned to the now seated Leo. "Can we stay the night? My mate and I need to have a little chat."

Sebastian waved his hand. "Take the guest room you used last time. We'll talk more in the morning."

"Yes, sire." Barney walked out of the great room and headed for the stairs at the front of the house. "You've got some explaining to do, young lady."

"Hmph."

Chapter Twenty-Four

"You scared the fuck out of me," Barney growled. He led his wayward mate into the bedroom they'd been assigned. He was ready to paddle her ass for coming to Sedona. "I know the email came from my email address, but why didn't you call and make sure I'd sent it?"

"I did. I even left you a voicemail message, but you never called back." She flopped down on the bed, her arms spread, her legs dangling over the edge. "Oh, this is comfy."

"Heather." He crossed his arms over his chest and glared at her, trying to ignore how cute she was being. She was acting like a kitten, rolling on the bed and practically purring in happiness.

"What?" She was now curled up in the middle of the bed. She'd managed to kick off her shoes, so her bare toes were peeking out from beneath the hem of her jeans.

She was so adorable, so innocent, he couldn't imagine anyone taking that away from her. He'd fight to the death to keep her the way she was. He'd lose, he knew. Life did that to people, made them wary, even cynical. But he'd try and keep it to a minimum with his precious little Hobbit.

"You should have stayed home."

"You too!" She winced. "Sorry. You said this would wear off in an hour or two?"

"Yes." He ran his fingers through his hair as everything that could have happened to her ran in a loop behind his eyes. He'd seen some pretty horrific things in his time as a Hunter, and he was picturing his mate in each and every one of them. "I don't care how many ways you checked things out or that Artemis was with you, or that everything turned out okay in the end."

"Whoa." She sat up, her expression serious, finally. "Calm down, big guy."

"Your job is not to protect me." He could feel his Bear rising, determined to make her understand that it would be him, not her, who did the protection thing.

"You better not say my job is to be barefoot and pregnant." She glared at him, her eyes turning Foxy brown.

"Hell no." He was the last person who'd say something like that. "But I'm trained to Hunt." He stepped toward the bed, trying desperately to get her to understand. "I've killed when I've been forced to. I know how to protect myself." He lifted his shirt and showed a small scar. "This? This is the worst damage I've ever sustained, and I healed it. It took me two days, but I did it." He lowered his shirt again. "But if something happened to you, there's no way I could heal it." He held out his hand, letting her see him shaking, showing her his vulnerability. "I still have nightmares about you being shot."

She closed her eyes and leaned her forehead against his stomach. "I'm so sorry. I didn't mean to make you worry like this."

"Tell me it was stupid." He needed to hear her acknowledge that.

"I knew it might be a trap, and I took precautions, but yeah. I'll tell you it was stupid."

She was placating him. "You'd do it again."

She looked up at him and grinned. "Fuck yes."

He pulled her against him, lifting her until she was held against his chest. "Stupid Hobbitses."

"If you call me your Precious, I'm gonna—" she squinted up at him as his hold on her tightened, "—be extremely flattered."

She looked so irritated at the thought that he had to laugh. His Bear had begun to settle down now that she was in their arms, safe and secure. It might not be his den, but with Kincade and Sebastian Lowe in bedrooms near them, it was almost as good.

He brushed his chin over the spot where her mark was. The sensation would be muffled by her T-shirt, but she'd still feel something.

She moaned, hiding her face against his chest.

The scent of desire began to fill the air around her. He breathed it in, letting it fill his senses. The need to fuck her, to prove that she was alive and well, filled him.

He pushed her down on the bed, ignoring her squawk of surprise. She had to move her legs so that her feet were on the mattress. He took hold of her knees and spread her thighs, kissing each fabric-covered knee in turn.

"Barney?" Her eyes were wide, but he could see the building desire in her.

"You make me crazy, you know that?" He took hold of her wrists and held her down. "You always have."

"I figure it's my job to make you nuts." She gave him a cheeky grin. "Right, Gandalf?"

He coughed. "Aragorn. I'm definitely Aragorn."

She tilted her head, still grinning at him. "Hmm. You've got that pretty blond hair."

His brows rose. "Pretty?"

"And dazzling blue eyes."

Oh hell no. "I'm not Legolas, damn it."

"But Legolas was a Hunter too, remember?" She was barely holding back her laughter.

He pressed down against her so she wouldn't accidentally knee him when he blew a raspberry on her neck.

She squealed, wiggling under him, her body rubbing against him in all the right ways. "Stop that!"

"Stop trying to give me a heart attack." He stared down at her, hoping she'd pick up on how serious he was. "Nobody asked you to throw the ring in the volcano, Frodo."

"He volunteered," she pointed out. "Besides, I had Samwise with me, remember?"

Uh-huh. Speaking of which, he had a bone to pick with Artemis the next time he saw him. "And why didn't he try to stop you?"

She looked away for a moment. "His eyes. They turned silver. Then he was shaking hands with Mr. Holmes like they were long lost buddies."

Barney froze. "Tiger told him to go."

"I think so." She cupped his cheek. "We really didn't plan on scaring you. We took every precaution we could think of." Suddenly, she scowled. "And I have to call my mom."

"What?" She was pushing at his shoulders, trying to get him off of her.

"I told her I'd call when I arrived. For all I know, she's already—why are you dialing?"

He smiled down at her. There was no way in hell he was going to allow the Bunsun-Allen clan to descend on the Leo's home. The man would never be the same. "Hello, Mrs. Allen?"

"Oh, hello, Barney. Is my daughter there?"

He heard the edge in Stacey Allen's voice. "She got distracted by meeting the Leo."

"That's no exc— Who? My baby met the *Leo*?"

He chuckled softly as Heather glared at him and her mother damn near choked to death.

"She's here, safe and sound, and I'll have her call you tomorrow. All right?"

"All right. Tell her I said good-night."

He said his good-byes and hung up the phone. "Now. Where were we?"

She looked anywhere but at him. "I have no idea."

"Mm." He kissed her chin. "Then let's get ready for bed."

Her cheeks started to turn red. "We can do that."

He hadn't had a second chance to make love to her before returning to Sedona. Perhaps now was his chance to taste her again.

He let her up, watching her wander around the bedroom. Someone, probably Sebastian's assistant, had seen to it that her luggage was brought upstairs to his room. She began unpacking, watching him out of the corner of her eye as he sat and watched her. "Need help?"

"I've got this, thanks." She turned, smiling, holding a pair of flimsy panties.

"That's…good." He could feel his Bear. Both of them were fascinated by the emerald underwear. How would it look against her pale, freckled skin?

"Um." Her eyes went wide as she shoved the panties behind her. "Yeah. I'll just put these away." She turned and nearly fell over the open suitcase. "Fucker."

"Who, me or your carry-on?"

She glared at him.

He smiled. "Guess I'll start getting ready, then." He stood and yawned, stretching his arms over his head. He swore he could hear her gulp as he reached for the hem of his T-shirt. "You need to finish unpacking," he added as nonchalantly as he could.

"Yes. Unpacking." Her gaze moved to his groin. "Definitely unpacking."

He had to bite his lip as she turned around and put her underwear on top of the bureau.

He pulled off the T-shirt. When it was right around his head he heard a distinct thud. She must have tripped over the suitcase again, because when he whipped it off she was righting herself, one hand on the bureau, the other clutching that same pair of green panties.

"Having trouble finding places to put your stuff?" He reached for the button of his jeans.

"Gah." She turned around and opened a drawer. "Nope. I can put them next to your undies." She shoved them in, no doubt making a mess out of his orderly pile of tighty-whities.

"Okay." He unzipped his jeans. "You have pajamas?"

She nodded, digging in the suitcase and holding up a black Pokémon tank top and matching shorts. Those shorts would barely cover her butt.

"Cute." He kicked off his shoes and pulled off his socks. "Finish unpacking, sweetheart. We have to go to sleep, right?" He began sliding his jeans off his legs.

She whimpered. Before his jeans were kicked off she'd gotten almost everything unpacked except her bathroom stuff. "Bed?"

He nodded. "Want to change in here, or the bathroom?" He knew which one he was hoping for, but he'd understand if…

If…

Sweet mother of mercy. Her T-shirt hit the floor before he could restart his brain, but who'd want to? Skin. She was showing him her beautiful freckled skin, and he was reaching for her before she'd managed to kick off her shoes. "I think we can skip the pajamas."

She nodded, molding her hand to his cock. The head was already peeking out of the top of his underwear, weeping and ready for her. "I can do that."

"Guh." He shuddered as her hand moved, tracing him oh so delicately. Her touch was barely felt, but his skin tingled in the wake of her fingers. "Naked?"

She laughed, and with that won their little round of teasing. "Naked sounds good too."

"Now?" He pushed into her hand, desperate to make that light touch harder, stronger.

She nodded, giving him permission. "Now."

No matter how much he needed, he wouldn't hurt her. He carefully unhooked her bra, her breasts freed from the silken material. Pink perfection, dotted with little brown spots he wanted to touch and lick. Someday he'd do just that. He'd lay her out and kiss every freckle he could find. Hopefully it would drive her as crazy as he already was.

She held still as he pressed a kiss to each breast before unbuttoning her jeans. He slid them down her legs, taking her panties with them, and set them aside.

Heather was staring at him, her pupils expanding, her eyes turning brown. "Now yours."

He stood, shoving his underwear off as quickly as he could. "Bed." His voice was gravelly, full of want.

With a sweet smile she took his hand and led him to the bed. She turned down the sheets and climbed in. "Now you."

He crawled on top of her and kissed her before she could say anything else.

What else was he supposed to do? She was there, bare and waiting. He stroked his hand up her thigh, tracing the length with his hand, feeling her muscles move as she reacted to him. She wrapped her arms around his neck, somehow managing to smile even as he kissed her.

"Why are you smiling?" He had to know.

"It's just…" She bit her lip, her expression suddenly shy. "I never thought we could laugh together like this, you know?"

No, he didn't. "You mean while naked?"

"Yes, Barney. While naked." She shook her head, her expression full of amused affection. "I'll explain it once your brain cells migrate back north, okay?"

"Sure." Whatever worked for her, he was all on board for. He licked her mark, bringing her back to where he really wanted her to be. She arched up against him with a gasp. Her legs wrapped around him, her heels digging into his back.

"Heather?"

"Do that more."

His eyes narrowed as he gazed at the mark. "You want me to fuck you while I lick your mark?"

She quivered. "Can you? I mean, will that work?"

He smiled. "Let's find out."

He slipped inside her slowly, carefully, letting her get used to him again. He lapped at her mark, keeping his hips still while she rocked herself against him. Those tiny little motions of hers were driving him crazy, but he kept still, using up all his willpower.

Her breathing began to change as she panted. She was reacting the same way she had when he'd licked her pussy, sipping at her until she came.

Shit. Was she about to come? Just from this?

He couldn't hold back any longer. He began fucking her, harder than he'd planned, deeper, but she took it, riding the waves with him. He licked at the mark, waiting for that first hitched breath, the first quiver of an orgasm before sinking his fangs deep inside her.

She screamed, clenching around him so hard he saw stars. His own roar drowned her out as he poured into her, filling her with his seed.

He remembered just in time to flop down next to her, not on her. Squishing her was not on his agenda that day. "Fuck, that was good."

She nodded, rolling over to wrap herself around him.

He pulled her close, putting his hand just above her ass. Her leg entwined with his, he fell asleep, content that, for now, his little Hobbit's ass was safe.

Chapter Twenty-Five

Heather moved gingerly down the stairs, her thighs still sore from her night with her mate. Who knew being a cowgirl could be so deliciously painful?

Suddenly she was grabbed from behind, a familiar, sexy scent surrounding her. Barney's scruffy cheek grazed against her neck, sending tingles down her spine. She loved a little morning fuzz on her mate's cheeks. Something else she'd learned that surprised her. "Good morning, mate."

"Good morning." She tilted her neck, granting him access to the mark he'd given her.

He pressed a soft kiss to her neck, right above her mark. "Let's go get some food. I think you're late for second breakfast."

She jabbed her elbow into his stomach. "Because someone decided to keep me up late."

"You're young, you'll get over it." He patted her bottom and stepped past her. "C'mon. Let's find out what the Leo has to tell us this morning."

Heather shook her head and followed her mate down the stairs. Barney seemed to know his way around the Leo's home, taking her directly to the dining room.

Sebastian and Kincade stood when Barney and Heather entered. Artemis was busy filling a plate from a buffet filled with eggs, sausages, bacon, Belgian waffles and fruit.

"Good morning, Ms. Allen." Sebastian waved to the seat next to him. "Please, have a seat."

"Thank you, sire." She poked Barney's arm. "I'll take the waffles with some fruit, please."

His brows rose, but he moved to the buffet. "Yes, ma'am."

"Can we drop the formalities, please?" Sebastian looked pained. "Your mate has been a friend to me, and I'd like the same with you, if that's possible."

Possible? The Leo wanted to be friends with her? "I can do that."

Sebastian and Kincade settled back down as Heather joined them. Sebastian leaned his elbows on the table and put his head on his hands. "So. A number of people in my jail weren't placed there by me."

"Who the fuck were they?" Barney continued filling Heather's plate, his back to the room, but Heather could sense the tension in her mate.

"Some were Hunters, like you. Some were…" Sebastian glanced at Kincade.

"Mercs, like your friends Casey Lee and Derrick." Kincade shoved a whole piece of sausage in his mouth. "Ah kupuh ruh clurks err wurkfurs fuh luh fennet."

Heather turned to Sebastian. "That was disgusting."

The Leo chuckled. "He said that a couple were clerks or workers for the Senate. People who had access to certain areas that normal shifters don't, people often overlooked by their higher-ups. We're still questioning them to find out what it was that they knew, and how they arrived in my private jail."

She tilted her head. "Do I want to know why the Leo has a private jail?"

Sebastian patted her on the head. "Nope."

"Okay." She smiled up at Barney as he placed a loaded waffle in front of her. "Thanks."

"You're welcome."

"You mentioned last night that there was a list in that office you found." Sebastian's gaze followed Barney as he went back to the buffet. "I want you and Kincade to fetch it for me."

Barney nodded, grabbed two slices of bread, and put some eggs between them. "Let's go, Lowe. The sooner we have that list the better."

Kincade stood. "You guys stay inside the house. I find out either of you left and you'll find out why I'm head of security." Heather thought he was talking to her and Artemis until Kincade turned to Artemis. "Sit on them if you have to, but Sebastian and Heather remain here."

Artemis nodded.

Barney bent and kissed Heather. "Mm. Strawberries." He winked and strode from the room, and Heather thoroughly enjoyed the view.

Kincade followed, stopping only once to point at Sebastian. "Sit. Stay."

"Woof." The Leo put his hands up like paws and panted. "Grr. Argh."

Kincade rolled his eyes and followed after Barney.

Heather heard the front door close and took a huge bite of her waffle. Barney would be fine. Kincade was with him, so he wouldn't disappear on her.

"How is your cousin, Ms. Allen?"

Heather turned back to Sebastian to find him staring at her with what appeared to be genuine concern. "She's...as good as she's going to get."

"I understand she was jumped and almost died." Sebastian shook his head. "I can't understand what the hell is going on. There are white shifters who live their lives in peace, like the Kermode, yet someone attacks Chloe Williams."

Heather held up her hand. "I think you misunderstood something, sir. Chloe wasn't born a white shifter. She was a red Fox before she was attacked."

Sebastian blinked. "That's...odd."

Heather nodded. "We were surprised too."

Artemis, who'd taken Kincade's chair, piped up. "I wasn't born white either." He sighed, lowering his head. "I...died."

"What?" Heather leaned forward. This. This was part of it, she just knew it.

"It was a long time ago, and something I don't like to talk about." Artemis stared at Heather before turning to Sebastian. "But after I was brought back I could speak to the spirits."

Sebastian made a face. "I was born white, but I can't speak to them." He looked intrigued and wistful at the same time. "What's it like?"

Artemis laughed. "It's like talking to a really annoying older brother who wants you to figure out something for yourself but won't give you enough clues to do it." He shook his head. "Hunting with him is cool though."

"Did Tiger give you the riddle?" Heather was dying to know what Artemis did.

Artemis shook his head. "Nah. He just told me to hightail it to Halle. He said I'd have one hell of a time there."

"Huh." Heather turned to the Leo. "So you're the only white shifter who can't talk to the spirits."

"Yeah. It's awesome." Sebastian stood and grabbed the coffee pot, pouring himself another cup. "Anyone else want some?"

Artemis held up his cup. "Hit me."

The Leo poured. "Perhaps I should visit Halle. It sounds…interesting."

The Puma Alpha would probably welcome a visit from the Leo. Not. She had no idea what sort of protocol would be required for a visit from the Leo. She wasn't certain the Leo visited *anybody*. Didn't they usually come to him? Senators visited Packs and Prides when a new Alpha was inducted, but the Leo never left Sedona unless it was for personal reasons.

Wait. "Isn't your sister part of the Poconos Pack?" Charlie Lowe worked for the Luna, Belinda Lowell.

He sat back with a happy smile. "So she is. Maybe I should go see how she's doing."

"Sounds like a good idea. I know I miss my family when they're not around."

"So do I." Sebastian sat back down and stared at his empty plate with a pensive expression that he quickly shook off. "So death seems to be the trigger for the white shifters."

"Except the Kermode, right?" Heather might not be a Bear, but her family was full of them. "They actually go on some sort of spirit journey to see if they are chosen as Kermode or not."

The Leo blinked, looking confused. "A spirit journey?" He sat back, staring at nothing. "Is that the answer? Not death, but touching the spirit world?"

"Maybe? All I know is, Julian bit Cyn, but she *didn't* become a Kermode. She's a Grizzly. And I heard some mated by Kermode don't even become Bears, but other types of shifters. Very few become Kermode." She'd learned a lot from Julian when he visited Cynful. He'd been willing to answer most of her questions, probably because he knew if he didn't Cyn would.

"Interesting. I'd like to meet this Julian, find out more about him." Sebastian sipped his coffee. "Their leader is really tight-lipped about his people. Even Carl can't get anything out of him."

"Julian is...interesting." Heather didn't have any other way to describe Super Bear. "He's the one who saved Chloe, but he almost died doing it. Kermode have super healing powers, but it costs them to use them."

"Maybe that's why their leader is so quiet," Artemis added. "If it was generally known that we had Bears who could heal near-death wounds and speak to the spirit world, they'd be the target of every greedy Alpha or family that wanted their own personal white Bear."

"Other Bears are really protective of them too." Heather had seen it firsthand. "They're just as reluctant to speak about a Kermode's powers as the Kermode themselves are. And Julian's family, so—"

"I didn't realize he'd mated into your family," Sebastian interrupted.

"Not exactly. We declared him family when he saved Chloe. His mate is my boss, Cynthia Reyes."

"Ah, I see. What do you do?"

Heather grinned. "I'm a tattoo artist. Apprentice, but still." She turned around to show off her two-tailed kitsune tattoo. "I designed this one, and many others."

She felt a soft touch against her skin. "Very nice."

"Thank you." She put her shirt back in place, covering the kitsune.

"Do you think, if you killed me and brought me back, that I'd be able to speak to the spirits?"

Heather spit out the water she'd just started to drink. "Oh *hell* no we are not killing the damn Leo." She shrugged, hunching her shoulders as Sebastian began to laugh. "Sire."

"Okay, no killing me. Got it." Sebastian rubbed his chin thoughtfully.

"Hmm, I wonder. Artemis, could you talk to the spirits and ask them why I can't?"

Artemis shook his head. "I think this is one of the things we're supposed to figure out ourselves."

"Then taking killing me off the table, there's no chance I'll ever hear their voices, huh?" Sebastian grimaced. "I've heard tales of how, long ago, the spirits let their desires be known. I was told that long ago the Leo could hear them all, but now?"

"You have spiritual cooties?"

The Leo blinked at Heather, then began laughing again. "I *really* like you."

She pointed to her mark. "Happily mated, but thank you."

He smiled coyly. "Do you have a sister?"

This time it was Heather who started to laugh. "Yup, and she's hell in heels too."

"Sounds more like Kin's type than mine." He rubbed his hands together. "We'll have to introduce them to one another."

Heather thought about her sister and the intense Kincade meeting. "Nuclear war" were the only words that came to mind. "I look forward to it."

Chapter Twenty-Six

Barney followed Kincade into the archive building, nodding to the few Senators who were in the place. None of them seemed surprised to see Kincade, but Barney got more than one shocked look. A Hunter in the archives was practically unheard of.

"Stay close, note expressions." Kincade led the way to the basement archives door.

"Teaching Grandma how to suck eggs here." Barney had already noted three people he'd love to chat with later. All three had looked more than surprised; they'd looked frightened. He'd recognized the Ocelot and Lynx Senators, but he had no idea who the third one might be. One of the Senators suddenly pulled out his cell phone with a scowl.

"Wonder who he's calling."

Kincade glanced over his shoulder as he started down the stairs. "That's the Wolf Senator."

"Huh." A fourth person was added to his speak-to list. "Think he's one of the partygoers?"

Kincade frowned for a second before rolling his eyes. "The Wolf Senator is a friend of mine. If he's involved in our little party, I'm going to rip his spleen out through his anus."

Barney shuddered. "I'd hate to hear what you'd do to him if he was an enemy."

Kincade grunted and led the way down the stairs. "You really don't."

Barney led Kincade to the ladies' room. "In there. Last stall."

Kincade nodded and pushed open the door, ignoring the squawk of indignation from a woman currently washing her hands.

Barney nodded to the lady. "Sorry. There's a rat." He held his hands two feet apart. "A New York sewer-sized one."

She blinked, her mouth hanging open.

"Don't wanna get bit, do you?" He winked and held the door open. "Don't worry. Kincade and I can handle a big, nasty, rabid rat."

She gagged, her eyes going wide. She covered her mouth with her hand. "Jesus. In here?"

He nodded, watching out of the corner of his eye as Kincade headed toward the last stall. "Didn't you hear the scratching? We think it's in the walls."

"Thanks." She scooted past him, staring back at the bathroom in horror before making her way over to the other Senators. As she passed him, the scent of Jackal hit him. She must be the Jackal Senator. Jackals were a strange lot, neither Coyote, Wolf or African Wild Dog, but somewhere in-between. They didn't move in Packs like the others, but in family groups or pairs, more like the Foxes. Because of this, they were lower on the canine totem pole than any other canid shifter. Barney didn't give a shit about whose balls were bigger in the pecking order, but the Jackals didn't deserve the shit they got from the Wolves and Coyotes. Just because they could be a little freaky didn't mean—

Kincade's sharp whistle broke his train of thought. "Which tile?"

Barney walked over to the last stall and leaned in, moving the tile. Kincade pressed the button, hissing like a wet cat when he saw the office.

"Yeah, that was my reaction. Without the spit."

Kincade shot him a glare as he stepped into the office. "Where's the list?"

Barney led the way, opening the file cabinet. "It was right here." He pulled it out, handing it to Kincade. "You might want to have your men go over the other documents. There's more going on here than just a play for the white shifters."

"Hmm." Kincade looked around, studying the desk. "Should have brought some with me."

"So I see." Barney glanced out the door to find three men entering the ladies' room. "Gents, you're in the wrong space. Unless you're wearing skirts, get out."

The one on the left growled, marking him Wolf.

Barney turned to look at Kincade. "I think he wants to play."

Kincade cracked his knuckles. "I think I can handle a game of kickball."

Barney shivered and looked at the three thugs. "You hear that? He's coming to kick you in the balls."

The Wolf leapt, the other two following him.

Barney backed into the office, wanting more room to fight than the bathroom afforded him. You'd think a Senate-only women's bathroom would be large and luxurious. Hell, he'd seen better setups in airports.

Kincade grabbed the Wolf by the throat and slammed him into the ground.

Shit. Dude was *strong*. Barney focused on the other two, leaving the Wolf to Captain America. He managed to dodge the swipe of claws from a feline, a Puma from the scent. An uppercut to the kitty's jaw had him reeling back, leaving the third to throw a roundhouse punch at Barney.

Barney saw stars. That one was going to leave a mark.

Kitty was back in Barney's face again, trying to claw his eyes out. Barney kicked his attacker in the knee, taking him down. He then lashed out with his foot, hitting the Puma in the back of his head. The Puma groaned, but stayed down, at least for now.

His attention turned back to the third guy. This one had Jackal written all over him, damn it. He hated fighting fucking Jackals. They always seemed to know what moves Barney was going to make. The only time he'd ever been beaten one on one was against a Jackal rogue. He still thanked God the rogue chose to run rather than finish Barney off. Something had spooked it, but Barney never found out what.

This time, the Jackal was looking back and forth between Barney and Kincade. The Wolf was down, unconscious from what Barney could tell in a quick glance. Kincade was glaring at the Jackal and making come-hither gestures that would have turned Barney's insides to jelly. He'd rather face a Jackal family than a pissed-off Kincade.

Barney turned back to the Jackal. "Let's do this."

"Can we not and say we did?" The Jackal threw his hands in the air. "I'd rather live, thanks."

"Who hired you?" Kincade growled.

The Jackal frowned. "The Senate did."

Kincade and Barney shared a quick glance.

The Puma slowly got up. "Fuck, Cole, why not tell him we're—"

A second after the Puma stopped speaking Barney heard the gunshot. The Puma went down, his face completely obliterated.

The Jackal dove left, narrowly avoiding the same fate. "Fuckity fuck fuck."

"Ditto." Barney swerved right, flanking the doorway with the Jackal. "Mercenary?"

The Jackal nodded. "Yeah. Name's Cole, Cole Miller. We were hired by Kris Jennings to protect this place. We've done work for her before."

Barney glared at him. "Killing other shifters?"

The Jackal made a face as he pulled out a Kimber 1911. "No one's ever breached security here before you, so no. At least I haven't. Don't know about the other two."

"Then who the fuck is that?" Kincade gestured toward the door where the gunman was hiding.

"I have no fucking clue, but he took down Dean without a second thought." Cole stared toward the door. "Something tells me we've been terminated."

Barney almost felt sorry for the guy. This was one hell of a way to get fired. "Nine mil?" Barney pulled his own Sig Sauer out of his jacket. He rarely had to resort to it, but today it was needed.

".45." Cole stuck his head out and pulled back quickly as another shot was fired.

The desk was overturned with a cracking crash that startled Barney. Kincade had his own handgun out, a Glock 31. "What did you see?"

Cole responded. "One shooter at the doorway. Didn't catch anything else." He closed his eyes, muttering under his breath. "No way out except to kill him."

And that was the freaky part of Jackals. They could assess a life or death situation in seconds and come up with a solution that would keep their asses alive. In a fistfight it made them practically Spider-Man. In a firefight, it let them determine the best positions to be in with barely a second's thought.

Something proven when the gunman fired right at Kincade, winging him. Kincade ducked back behind the desk with a curse. "Any ideas, gentlemen?"

"Other than arresting the Ocelot Senator?" Barney fired blindly into the bathroom, hoping to startle the gunman. "Live."

"That's always my number one priority," Cole muttered.

"Ha. Ha." The scent of Kincade's blood slowly began to fill the room. "If there's only one gunman we could rush him."

"And die in a hail of gunfire? No thanks." Barney peeped around the doorway and fired on the man he saw standing there. The man ducked out of the stall. The fucker had been trying to sneak into the room, damn it.

"He's on the other side of the goddamn stall door. We should be able to take him." Kincade glanced at Cole, who was shaking his head frantically. "Or not."

"Fire," Cole whispered. He lined up a shot at the stall door and pulled the trigger.

A cry erupted from behind the stall door. Cole's shot had punched through the stall's door and struck their opponent.

"Sweet." Barney fired as well, hoping to either hit the gunman or drive him off. Either would work in his book.

Kincade pulled out his cell phone. "I'm calling for backup," he whispered. "Try and pin him down."

Cole nodded. "Gotcha." He fired again, edging into the stall.

Barney eased in front of him. "Me first."

Cole nodded.

Barney kicked down the door, knocking it right off its hinges. He let out a

Grizzly growl as the gunman went down under his weight. "Fucker."

Cole leaned back into the office. "Is that pinned enough for you?"

Kincade shook his head, his lips quirking in amusement. "Yeah, that works." He stood, going back to his conversation.

Barney let Cole check for more gunmen, keeping his weight on the downed man. "Who hired you?"

"Senator Kris Jennings," the man wheezed.

Barney exchanged a look with Kincade, who was picking up the unconscious Wolf. He slung the man over his shoulder fireman style. "I sense a theme here."

"Me too." One that said Kris Jennings was about to meet the claws of Kincade Lowe. He hoped she'd kept up on her life insurance. Her heirs were gonna need it.

The grim look on Kincade's face did not bode well for the Ocelot Senator. "Let's get these guys in jail." He glanced at the dead Puma. "I'll send someone in for the body."

"Works for me." He gestured toward Cole. "I suggest you let this one go, but question him."

"I'll cooperate." Cole shuddered. "They didn't tell me that they were sending me in after Kincade fucking Lowe."

Barney's brows rose. "They?"

Cole nodded. "I'll tell you everything once we're out of here. It's not safe." His gaze darted around. "We need to go, like, now."

Kincade grabbed the list in his damaged hand and followed Cole and Barney out of the bathroom.

Barney saw the crowd surrounding the area and shrugged. "Sorry. Bathroom's out of order."

He wished he had his cell phone's camera out. The looks on the Senators' faces were priceless.

Chapter Twenty-Seven

Heather was pacing in the Leo's library. It was taking longer to get the list than she'd thought, and her nerves were on edge. "Should I call them?"

The Leo looked up from his book. "No. Let them do their job. They'll return soon."

"What if something happened to them?" She began biting on her nail. "I mean, you could get us in the building, right? Just so we could check things out."

The Leo's eyes gleamed with mischief. "Hell yes."

"Then what are we waiting for? Let me grab my purse and we can go." Heather started for the door.

"Can you shoot a gun?"

The Leo's question sounded casual, but she was willing to bet it was anything but. "No."

"Can you fight in hand-to-hand?"

Damn it. His point was made. "No." Her shoulders slumped. "I ink a mean tattoo, though."

Sebastian snorted out a laugh. "I bet you do." He turned the page in his book. "As I said, they'll be here soon."

"Not soon enough." She flopped down onto the sofa, moving Artemis's feet out of her way. The Tiger had decided it was time for an afternoon siesta and promptly passed out on the velvet couch. She glanced around at the expansive library the Leo had. "Maybe we could do some research on our own."

He glanced up from his book. "What do you mean?"

Heather stood and began looking at the titles of some of the books. "We have a lot of shifter lore here."

"I've read a lot of these, and I can tell you there's very little on white shifters." The Leo stood, staring at the bookshelves, his brows furrowed. His voice was thoughtful as he glanced upward. "But some of them I haven't." He reached for the library ladder and began pulling it along the shelves. "There's a book my father never wanted me to read. My uncle agreed with him. Dad said it was outdated, like a number of books on the upper shelves. He wanted me to concentrate on the more modern problems of the Leo." He scowled. "In fact, he wondered why the book was even in the library, but after that it was never mentioned again."

"Your father was the previous Leo?" Heather held the ladder steady as the Leo began to climb.

"Nope. My dad was the Leo's brother. The Leo wanted me to study every single book in here, but no one could do that and have a life." He stopped climbing and looked down. "My teen years were hell."

She chuckled. "I bet."

"Work, work, work." The Leo sighed as he resumed climbing. "I was just glad there were books I didn't have to study. Ah, here it is." He pulled a dusty, yellowed book off the shelf. "Coming down."

"Gotcha." Although she could admit, the view going up was pretty stunning. She was mated, not dead, and the Leo had one fine booty.

"All right." He stepped onto the floor and let go of the ladder. "Let's see what this book has for us."

Heather followed him back to his chair, where he settled down and cracked open the book, careful of its aged exterior.

"What in the fuckity fuck?" Sebastian was staring at the book like it housed bees instead of words.

"What is it?" She glanced over his shoulder to find that, hidden inside one book was another, smaller one. "Huh. I wasn't expecting that."

"Neither was I." The Leo lifted the second book out. "Someone went to a lot of trouble to hide this from me."

"From you, or from all Leos?" Heather stroked the cover of the new book. "There's no title."

"If it was hidden from all of us, why put it in our private library?" He glanced up at where the book had been on the shelf. "Hidden in plain sight, where any of us could accidentally stumble on it."

"It doesn't make sense, unless someone did want you to find it." She could only think of one person. "Ian Holmes?" The Lion Senator was knee deep in this, but she wasn't certain whose side he was on. If he'd hidden the book in plain sight, maybe he wanted the white shifters to survive.

"You think he knew of it?" Sebastian opened the cover. "How out of touch with my Senate am I?"

Barney and Kincade entered without knocking. She stood with her hands on her hips and glared at her mate. "You're late."

He smirked. "We had to dance a little before we could leave."

Kincade headed right for the Leo, and she could smell the blood on him. He'd been hurt, and recently. "Here's the list."

Heather ignored him and began searching her mate for injuries. "Are you hurt?"

"No, sweetheart. Kincade's the only one."

"And he healed me on the way back." Kincade gave his attention back to Sebastian. "The perp is in our jail, ready for interrogation."

"Thank you." The Leo carefully placed the old book down before taking the papers from Kincade. Heather watched as he stood, rifling through the pages, and headed over to a large desk in the back of the library. "This is…all of these?" He sat abruptly, looking horrified.

"Yeah." Barney walked over to Heather and casually put his arm around her waist. She wasn't sure why, but she got the feeling he needed the contact with her in that moment. "Heather's name is on that list too."

"What?" She took a step forward, or at least tried to. Barney's hold on her tightened, keeping her next to him. "I'm not in danger right now, Boo."

"Boo?"

She shrugged. "Boo-Boo's getting too long to say." She turned her attention back to the Leo. "What does the list say?"

"It's names, lineages, dates of death and birth with some markings next to the names." Sebastian put the papers down on the desk and began shuffling them. "These marks, any idea what they mean?"

"Chloe's mark was erased, as was Artemis's." Barney led Heather over to the desk and bent to point to the names he'd mentioned. "Here and here."

Kincade stood on the Leo's other side. "And look. Each is listed as being of mixed parentage, either in the first or second degree."

"Meaning?" Heather had no idea what he'd just said.

"Parents or grandparents," Barney translated.

"Ah." She frowned as she spotted a familiar name. "James Howard? Jamie? *He's* the white Puma?"

"Oops," Barney muttered.

"You knew?" Why was she even surprised?

"I found out when I visited him." Barney turned back to the list. "He's got his mark erased as well."

"And it was his grandparents who were different shifters. Puma and Wolf, from the looks of it." Sebastian sat back, reading the list. "Too many have a deceased marker next to their names. Far too many." He dragged his finger down the list. "Some of these died before puberty."

"Meaning they never got the chance to shift and find out what they'd be." Heather remembered her own attack and shivered. "They were trying to kill me too, weren't they? They wanted me to shift to see if I was the white Fox, but Alex got to them before they could finish the job. Either that or they wanted it to *look* like an attempted rape gone wrong."

"I think so." Barney kissed the top of her head. He hugged her tight, pulling her back against his front, his chin on her shoulder. "Thank God Alex made sure that particular group would never do anything like it again."

"I owe him more than I thought," she whispered.

"Bake him a cake." Kincade's brows rose when she stared at him, dumbfounded. "What?"

She rolled her eyes at him. "Seriously. Not the time."

"There's always time for cake," Kincade muttered back.

"Look how far back this goes," Sebastian whispered. "Jesus. They've been killing off people since the Revolutionary War?"

"It's more than just the Ocelot Senator, then." Kincade tapped his fingers on the desk, his claws coming out. "We're looking at a really long-term conspiracy."

"Thank you, Captain Obvious." Heather had heard Emma call her mate that more than once, and she couldn't think of anything better to call Kincade.

"Better obvious than oblivious," Kincade replied. "Take a look here. The Kermode all have the mark, and all of them have been erased."

"But not all of the parents of Kermode were Kermode themselves." Sebastian traced the line of white Bears. "Meaning the entire bloodline is made up of different shifters."

"That's true for all the ones who had the mark and were killed before their first shift." Barney pointed to several names. "All of them were of mixed blood, like Chloe Williams. Artemis's mother wasn't a Tiger, but a Lynx. So it's the mixed blood that marks a white shifter."

"That is *so* weird. That can't be all of it, just having mixed blood, or every shifter with mixed blood would be white, right?"

"Not true. Only the Polars bred true. Most, if not all, Kermode have mixed blood, but not all Kermode give birth to Kermode. Even among the Lowe family there's only one white Lion born into the family at a time, and he's the *only* white Lion ever." Sebastian rubbed his hand over his head. "I just don't understand how one becomes a white shifter."

"You were always white?" Barney asked.

Sebastian nodded. "Since my first shift."

"Bloodlines." Kincade started to pace. "It must have something to do not only with mixed blood, but the bloodlines themselves."

"So if we traced ancestry, we might be able to predict that a white shifter would pop up in a certain family, but not necessarily which person would become a white shifter." Barney stared at Heather. "That explains the attack on you, but not the attack on Chloe. She didn't become a white shifter until she nearly died."

"Same thing with Jamie Howard, right? He died and Julian brought him back." They exchanged a horrified glance. "Why does near-death result in a red Fox turning white?"

"I'm not sure, but it must have something to do with the spirits. Reconnecting, maybe?"

There was a loud snort from the sofa before Artemis's snoring resumed.

Heather picked up one of the pages. "Here it says that the Polars were the same as the Lowe family, white shifters from birth, but look. This is a new mark." The line at the bottom of the list of Polars had an *e.* next to it.

"E for extinct." Sebastian threw the page he'd been holding onto his desk. "There are no more Polars in the world."

"Could...could this be about extinction?" Heather bit her lip and frowned. "Could they be trying to exterminate any possibility of white shifters?"

Both Sebastian and Kincade looked at her like she'd lost her mind, but Barney's hold on her tightened. "It's a possibility. If they keep the white shifter population down, what do they gain?"

"Or what do we lose?" Kincade stared at the list again. "Seb, maybe it's time to bring the white shifters here."

"No." Sebastian stood. "The whites are gathering in Halle for a reason. I say we go to them."

"You're out of your fucking gourd if you think I'm letting you go to Halle, Seb." Kincade crossed his arms over his chest. "It's so dangerous I'm inclined to keep Barney and Heather here on indefinite hold."

"No can do." Barney hitched his thumb toward Sebastian. "The Leo has me investigating the white shifters, remember? And I'm not one to go against orders."

Kincade stared at him. "I love how you said that with a straight face."

"Thank you." Barney chuckled, his breath warm against Heather's ear. "I try."

"We need to figure out who is involved in this and why." Sebastian put his hands on his hips. "Kincade?"

"We start by arresting Kris Jennings."

"Excellent. Sign me up." Sebastian nodded. "All right. You and Barney deal with that. Barney."

"Sir?" Barney lifted his head off her shoulder.

"I want you to work with Kincade. Heather and I will continue to go over this paperwork and see if anything else stands out. We'll also see if we can get Artemis to help us."

A large snore erupted from the sofa.

"Don't worry. I'll make him help." Sebastian smiled, showing fangs. "He won't know what hit him."

The whimper from the sofa quickly turned into a snort, then more snoring.

"We know a lot already, thanks to Cole. He already told us he was working for Kris Jennings. My men are questioning the gunman to find out if there's anyone else involved." Kincade stared at Barney. "There's a chance that Jennings knows we're on to her. She saw us go into her office. She could be on the run."

"Wonderful." Barney rubbed his hands together. "I love a good Hunt."

Sebastian sat back at his desk with a sigh. "I'm going to go over that book Heather and I found. Maybe there are some answers in that."

"Yes, sire." Barney bowed, which was awkward as hell considering he was still holding her.

"Text me if you find anything." Kincade walked out of the library,

"Will do," Sebastian shouted after him. "It's not like I don't know whom I report to," he muttered under his breath. He glanced at Barney. "You still here?"

"Nope." Barney picked Heather up and put her in the chair across from Sebastian. "We're gone." He kissed the top of her head. "Keep your Hobbit ass—"

"Safe, I know." She reached up and stroked his cheek. "You too."

"I will." He winked. "I've got backup this time." He strolled past the sofa and smacked Artemis on the head. "Wakey wakey, little flakey."

"Ugh." Artemis sat up, rubbing the top of his head. "Asshole."

"Sorry, mine's spoken for." Barney strutted out of the room, patting his rear, singing something about Artemis shoulda put a ring on it.

"Oh my God." Heather put her face in her hands. "I signed up for a lifetime of—" she waved her hand toward the door, "—that."

Sebastian was too busy laughing to answer.

Chapter Twenty-Eight

"Check your ammo," Kincade shouted. He strode down the line of men, all of them suited in black and dark blue. On their arms was the symbol of the Leo, a stylized roaring lion's head. This was the Leo's personal guard, the men and women completely loyal to no one but the Leo himself. Some were armed with handguns similar to Kincade's Glock, others with M4 carbines, and almost all of them had Remington 870 shotguns strapped somewhere on their person. All of them carried tactical batons. Those who didn't have retractable claws wore gloves reinforced with steel. In their pockets were pepper spray grenades and flash bangs.

Wait. Was that an RPG strapped to the back of one of the SUVs? What the hell was Kincade expecting? World War III?

Each of the team did as told, hollering out when they reaffirmed they were locked and loaded. Two turned away for more ammo, earning the good-natured jeering of their fellows.

Kincade looked on with an expression close to boredom until all of his team was ready. "You know the drill. We're apprehending Kris Jennings, Ocelot Senator and traitor to the Leo." He glanced at one man in particular. "Any problem with this, you are free to stand down."

The man, probably an Ocelot, shook his head. "No, sir! No problem here."

"Good." Kincade patted the man's shoulder. "We go in, take her *alive*, and we bring her to the Leo in chains. Tape her mouth shut, people. Ocelots can manipulate your emotions, so don't let her talk you into loosening her chains." He strode up and down the line, personally checking each man as Barney looked on. "We run into more than we can handle, we call in the specialists."

All of them winced at that.

"Specialists?" Barney muttered.

"And none of us want that, do we?" Kincade ignored Barney's comment.

"No, sir!" The team shouted back.

Barney checked his own equipment. He'd kept his Sig Sauer rather than take the Glock Kincade had offered him, as well as the steel gloves. His own five-inch Grizzly claws were more than enough in hand-to-hand. He had, however, accepted the shotgun and the baton. He'd chosen to wear his Hunter garb rather than the elite uniform, making him stand out in the crowd. His cowboy hat was firmly on his head, his feet in his favorite pair of boots. His beat to hell duster was reinforced in the chest and abdomen with ballistic cloth. On his forearms were a pair of thick leather bracers, designed to deflect claws and knives.

He was ready for the Hunt to begin.

"Let's get this party started, ladies and gentlemen." Kincade hustled his crew into three SUVs, each capable of holding eight people. He took hold of Barney's arm and led him to the first vehicle, putting him in the front passenger seat. Kincade took the wheel, leading the convoy out. "The specialists are snipers. If we have to call them in, Kris Jennings will die."

"Ah." Barney understood. "Sometimes the Hunt goes badly, and the mark dies."

Kincade nodded. "We need her alive so she can answer to Sebastian. He's the only one likely to get anything out of her. She'll be able to manipulate anyone else."

"He's immune to her power?" That surprised Barney. Even the Leo had his limits, or so he'd thought.

Kincade smiled. "More like he doesn't listen to anyone's bullshit. Besides, he can order her not to use her powers on him, and she'll be forced to comply."

"Good point." He watched the desert landscape roll by. "He's right, you know."

"About?"

"Going to Halle."

Kincade scowled, his tone turning dark. "I don't think so."

Barney didn't reply. He'd thought, once upon a time, that he'd never leave Montana. Now look at him. Mated, ready to move to a small college town and eager to get his life started for real. "I want to start a school for Hunters in Halle."

Kincade grunted. "I figured you would. You've been training them for a while now. Why not centralize it?"

"And it can teach us to work together rather than as single Hunters. We're dying out there, or worse, turning rogue. We need to be able to help one another."

"I don't think Sebastian will object." Kincade turned down a long driveway not far from where they'd started. "It's the Senate you'll have to convince."

"Carl is behind it, but Ian is too old-school to accept it."

"I'll put out some feelers and see where they lead. You may get your wish sooner than you think."

"Thanks." They pulled up to the Ocelot Senator's house, surprised to find the area loaded with cars. "Fuck me stupid."

Kincade picked up the radio mic. "We have company, people. Play it low until we get inside, then nab the Senator."

"What if these aren't party guests, but *party guests*?" Barney gestured toward the front door, where two men could be seen talking into their own mics.

"Then we end it." Kincade pulled around the circular driveway, forming a half moon with the vehicles. He got out, gesturing to Barney go get out on the driver's side rather than the passenger's. "You do what we tell you. This is a raid, not a Hunt."

"Aye, sir." Barney knew full well he was there solely because Sebastian wanted him to be. "Where do you want me?"

"Stay by my side unless your instincts go off."

Staring at the mansion, Barney couldn't sense anything. "This is politics, not Hunter business. She's not rogue, not that I can sense."

"Hmm. I think your definition of rogue shifter and mine are different." Kincade moved to the back of his vehicle and cupped his hands. "Stand down.

We're here for Senator Kris Jennings. She's under arrest for—"

He was forced to duck back behind the SUV as gunfire erupted from the mansion windows. The two men who'd been guarding the front door immediately ducked inside, closing it behind them.

"Shit. Welcome to World War III." Barney pulled out his Sig Sauer. "We're pinned."

"I noticed," Kincade responded sourly. He had his M4 out and pointed at the house. "I need you to sneak around the back, see if there's a way in."

Barney nodded. He'd never been in quite this position before, but he could handle what was being asked of him. He glanced around, wondering what he could use as cover.

He stuck his head out from behind the SUV, shooting his Sig Sauer toward the windows. The answering hail of gunfire forced him back behind cover. "Yeah. Not gonna happen. We need to take a few of these guys out before I can do that."

Kincade yelled, "Watch your sixes and sevens!"

Two of the enforcers turned, their backs to the SUVs. Both of them had their M4s pointed at the driveway.

"We can't stay here. We need to figure out how to advance." Barney fired over the hood of the SUV. A faint cry of pain was his reward. "We could get in the SUV and drive into the door."

"You watch too many movies," Kincade replied as he too fired over the hood. The gunfire was damn near deafening at such close range. "We hit the steps, not drive up them."

"You need a stuntman on your team." Barney got on his stomach and looked at the mansion from under the SUV. "Looks like they've got the main floor windows all knocked out. Not seeing any of the upper windows broken."

"Good. Hopefully they're all on the main floor."

"Jennings is probably somewhere else, guarded in case we breach the house." Barney had faced that sort of situation with one rogue who'd made enough money to hire bodyguards. "That I can handle."

"See any way in?" Kincade fired again, keeping up the barrage until

Barney's ears rang.

"Not yet. We need to thin their ranks some more."

One of the men with Kincade whispered in his ear. Kincade nodded, pointing twice at the third vehicle. The man nodded and raced off between the SUVs.

"RPG?" Barney asked, his eyes still trained on the house.

"RPG." Kincade stuck his head under the SUV. "We're aiming for the first window on the left."

A rocket propelled grenade, possibly filled with tear gas, would take down a number of them. Especially shifters with sensitive noses or eyes. That would get them the time they needed to get into the house and find Kris Jennings. "I'll go in that way, then. One man might slip by from the back."

"While we storm the front." Kincade glanced to the right, where the RPG was located. "We'll fire on the left once you've moved."

"Give me a three count once the first grenade's gone off." Barney readied himself to move. His adrenaline was pumping, his Grizzly ready to head out of this no-win situation and nab their target. This, grabbing the bad guy and bringing him or her to justice, was what he was born to do.

He heard the telltale *pop-fwoosh* of the grenade being launched, then Kincade's soft three count. He rolled out from under the SUV and crawled along the driveway, keeping as low as he could. He could hear the coughing and screaming as the pepper spray took effect.

He'd just made it around the corner of the mansion when the second *pop/ fwoosh* went off, undoubtedly making the gunmen's lives miserable. Barney had been on the receiving end of pepper spray before.

Personally, he wasn't a fan, but in this case? He loved it so much he wanted make babies with it.

He made it to the back of the house without incident, surprising the hell out of himself. Were all the guards at the front? Surely there had to be—

Damn it. He rolled under a bush as a bullet impacted the dirt right next to where his head had been. He got to his hands and knees, his gun still in his hand,

and searched for the man who'd tried to blow his brains out.

He caught movement out of the corner of his eye and lashed out, his claws digging into someone's ankle. The scream that followed was barely heard over the charge of Kincade and his men bringing down the front door of the mansion.

Barney pulled, practically severing the foot of his attacker. The man fell with a grunt, and Barney finished him off, shoving his claws into the man's throat. The man gurgled for a moment before he died, his eyes wide and horrified before their life drained out.

Barney pushed away from the body and pressed his back to the stucco and stone of the house wall. He glanced up, seeing a window above him. Going in that way might work, but if someone on the other side heard the window opening, Barney would be screwed.

No. He'd stick to the original plan and head around to the back. If there were more guards he'd deal with them.

He slid along the wall, keeping his coat from getting too scratched up by the stucco. God, he hated that shit. It looked pretty, but it could grow mold, crack, and worse, scratch the crap out of you.

He reached the back of the house without another encounter. He checked the yard, finding no one there. All of them must have been in the house, dealing with Kincade. Or so he hoped. There could be a sniper in the trees, guarding the back of the house. If there was, he was fucked. He'd just have to risk it. So he ran for the back door and rammed it open, hoping the sounds of Kincade and his men would keep him from being found out.

Turned out he was right about that sniper. The bullet barely missed his head, singeing the top of his ear and some of the hair away. He dove once more to the floor and used his foot to slam the door shut.

He was inside. Now all he had to do was find the Ocelot Senator.

Chapter Twenty-Nine

Now it was Sebastian's turn to pace. He was holding the yellowed book in his hands, reading random passages out loud while Heather compiled a list of deceased shifters versus those who had lived and become white shifters. "I can't fucking believe it. Listen to this: 'And the white shifters will stand at the side of the Leo and be his advisors in all things.' What the hell? That's the fucking Senate!" He turned another page. "Ah. Here we go. 'But should no white shifter be born of a line, then the line shall elect an advisor to be approved by the Leo.'"

"Wait. So the Senate was made up of white shifters once upon a time?" Heather looked up from her notes, astonished at what the Leo was revealing. "So that means that the white shifters *were* killed over power?"

"And then all mention of them was suppressed so that no Leo would ever know that he was missing his link to the spirit world. We had our own fucking bible here all along, and we ignored it because it wasn't 'relevant'." He carefully turned another page, grimacing as he read. "It seems like there was this whole other universe I knew nothing about. And my father hid it from me." He looked like he wanted to throw the book across the room, but luckily he refrained.

"Why hasn't the Leo ever looked into this before?" Heather glanced at the book, but the list she was writing wouldn't handle itself. She went back to it, keeping one ear on the Leo's reply.

"I think you were right. It was hidden from us. The Kermode became something of a legend, the Arctic Fox became extinct because of predators, and the Polars' demise was blamed on global warming."

"Seriously?" Heather scowled. "Polars lived anywhere they wanted to."

After all, who would stop them?

"I know," he grunted in response. "It's just so damn stupid."

"Did your uncle know about this?" Heather added another name to the deceased list.

"I don't think so. He agreed way too easily with my father." He sat down heavily on the sofa, jarring Artemis, who'd nodded back off once Barney and Kincade left. "My father was the Lion Senator."

"Fuck," Heather breathed.

"He was voted out after I became the Leo. The Lions believed he would be prejudiced toward my ideas, and they wanted someone more neutral. Even now, he tries to tell me what I should or shouldn't do." Sebastian closed his eyes, rubbing his forehead wearily. "I may have to bring him in for questioning." Sadness infused his tone, his expression falling as he opened his eyes. "This sucks."

"Yeah." She couldn't imagine her father turning out to be a traitor, not only to the family but to all Foxes. Before she could say anything about it, something caught her eye. "My brother and sister both have the mark, but it's been crossed out instead of erased."

"Meaning they never did whatever it was to become a white shifter." The Leo scratched his head. "Or maybe they thought that once they hit adulthood they were no longer eligible?"

"But Jamie Howard became a white Puma at the age of—" she double-checked the paperwork, "—twenty-seven."

"Which just means they were wrong."

"True." She added three more names to the deceased list. The list she was compiling was only during the current Leo's reign. So far, twenty possible white shifters had been killed before puberty struck, while ten had died while in their teens or late twenties. And she was only on page one. Everything in the book was confirming what they'd theorized, that only one white shifter existed for a species except under special circumstances.

"Artemis?" The Leo poked him with his toe. Artemis was sprawled out on the carpet, his arms and legs askew, his eyes closed. A single silver strand marred the darkness of his hair.

"I think he's communing with the spirits." Heather had seen Julian do something similar, except he hadn't been all sprawled out like that. He'd been cross-legged, his back straight, his shoulders relaxed. "See the white stripe? He's using his powers, but he's not in his man-Tiger form."

"Really?" The Leo leaned down and breathed in Artemis's ear. "Hello, Artemis."

Nothing, not even a twitch of Artemis's lips. He didn't even pretend to snore.

"He'll come out of it when Tiger releases him." The spirits could be demanding of the ones they chose.

"I wonder what it's like to talk to your spirit animal." He stared at Artemis for a moment before shaking his head. "Ah. Never mind. I need to read more of this book, figure out what else my dear old daddy was hiding from me."

"Why didn't you read it?" She glanced up, asking the question that had been bothering her since the moment he told her of the book. "The Leo wanted you to."

"My father is a very strict man." Sebastian shivered. "I didn't say no to him, not until I became the Leo. Then I kicked his ass out of my house when he tried to get Kincade replaced with a Beta of *his* choosing."

"You and Kincade are close, huh?" No more deceased on the first page. She started the next list, of those who'd actually become white shifters. That would be the shortest.

"He saved my life once," Sebastian said softly. His voice was full of affection for his Beta. "He's also my best friend."

"You had to use your Leo voice, didn't you? To get your dad to leave, I mean." She added Jamie Howard, Chloe Williams, Artemis Smith and someone named Bianca Flores, a Jackal, to the white shifter list.

Four. Only four had survived. Shit.

Time to start the list of those who'd lived and hadn't become white. That, also, would be a short list.

"Fuck." There was horror in the Leo's voice, catching her attention once more.

"What?"

His expression was equally horrified. "Listen to this: 'Should all white shifters cease to exist, so too shall the Leo, for his life is tied to theirs.'"

Her jaw dropped. "Fuck," she breathed. "No wonder they've been hunting them down."

"Power." He carefully put the book back down on the table, but she could see the way his hands shook. "It all comes down to power."

"And who has it." She tapped her finger on the table. "They'd not only gain control of their own species, with no oversight, but they'd be able to rule the entire shifter world without having to worry about someone stepping in and stopping them from whatever abuses they wished to heap on us."

"They could rule as they wished." He picked up his coffee mug and studied it for a moment before throwing it at a wall, shattering it. "Fuckers think that they can kill me? We'll see about that." He turned on her, his eyes the gold of his cat. "New priority," he said, his Leo voice in full force. "Get me a list of every living white shifter. Name, address, number of people they've fucked, I don't care. I want them."

She bowed her head. "Yes, sire." She immediately began going through the other pages, barely listening in when he got a phone call. Tiger, check. Jackal, check. Puma, check. Fox, check. Bear…well. She supposed Julian would do, so she wrote his name down. Jaguar…nope. Not yet, anyway. There was no Hyena either, but down near the bottom of the second page she found a white Lynx named Darren Perkins. No Cheetahs, Wolves, Coyotes or Ocelots had survived to become white, but the Cheetah and Wolf at least had some with marks next to their names. She jotted them down with question marks.

"Heather!"

"What?" Why was the Leo shouting at her? She was doing as asked, wasn't she?

"Sorry. I called your name three times and…" He sighed. "We have an update from Kincade."

"Did they get her?" She *really* wanted to know what Kris Jennings had to say.

"They're under heavy fire, but they've managed to breach the mansion."

"Heavy fire?" Her heart sank. "Barney?"

Sebastian smiled. "He's fine. Kincade says he went through the back door, so he wasn't in the line of fire."

"Good." Her heart could start beating again. She put her hand to her chest to make sure it was. "Good."

"You have the list?" He held out his hand and it was no longer shaking. His eyes were still mottled with gold, his Lion very evident in the way his claws kept extending and retracting.

"Yes, sire." She held up the list. "It's as complete as I can make it. Any white shifters past page two are already dead."

"Shit." He glanced at the list and grimaced. "Possibilities?"

"Huh?"

"Like yourself, or your cousin Wren. Since Chloe's the white Fox, that means that there are others in your family who could have been rather than her. Possible white shifters, if you will." The Leo handed the list back to her. "Give me them as well."

"That will take longer." She bit her lip. "Wren is a baby."

"And these assholes will target her, just as they did you. Just as they did Chloe." He snapped his fingers. "Names, Heather."

"Yes, sire."

She jotted down what she could find, including ages of the children who were listed as potentials. "Here."

Sebastian grunted as he read it. "All the ones who are missing. Wolf, Ocelot, all of them. And multiples of each." He sighed wearily. "I can't keep all of them safe."

"There might be a way." She stood, tapping the computer monitor. "We could spread the word of what we've learned. Secrecy is what has been killing them. If we get the word out about white shifters and where they come from, you declaw the Senators attempting to kill them."

He stared at her for a moment before smiling. "I'll leave you in charge of the newsletter."

"Hell no." She waved her hands. "I've got a job I love, and a mate I'm returning to. Get someone else." She frowned at the computer. "Someone who knows codes and how to break them."

"Huh?"

"Think about it. They have to communicate with each other somehow. Get someone tracking Kris Jennings's emails and you'll find a trail to other Senators."

"I think I love you." The Leo kissed her on the cheek. "You're officially my favorite Fox of all time." He rubbed his hands together. "And I know just the person for the job, too."

"Who?"

He laughed. "My guardian Angel."

Chapter Thirty

Barney rubbed his ear, healing the damage the sniper rifle's bullet had done. Fuckity fuck. He'd have to stay down, avoid windows until he was out of the…

He glanced around. Right. Kitchen. Big fucker too. Looked like something out of a magazine, all distressed white cabinets and thick granite countertops with gleaming stainless steel appliances meant for a chef.

He pocketed his gun and crawled across the hardwood floors, ducking behind the island when another bullet came whizzing past him, sending splinters up as it hit the wooden floor. Barney flinched when one of the splinters hit his hand, but held still behind the island, watching the two entrances he could see for any signs of activity. Nothing appeared to be coming his way, so Kincade must have them thoroughly pinned down at the front of the house.

Barney calculated the distance between himself and the set of stairs he could see off to his right. It led both up and down, which meant this place had a basement, most likely one meant for entertaining. He had to decide quickly whether or not she was upstairs or down.

Upstairs could have an escape route if she chose to go out a window. Otherwise, she was blocked in until Kincade got to her. Downstairs, there might be a panic room or a secret passage that would grant her an escape route.

He closed his eyes and tried to listen to his instincts. Up, down, up down, eenie, meanie, miney, mo.

Downstairs it was.

Barney raced for the stairway, ducking when he heard gunfire. The wooden rail was hit, taking a good chunk out of it. He turned the corner of the stairs, making his way down into the basement.

It was lit from the windows that had been installed all around the basement, nice-sized ones meant for not only light but as an escape should the house catch fire or some other disaster befall it, like a pissed-off Kincade Lowe. None of the windows appeared to be open, but that didn't mean anything. He pulled out his cell and sent a quick text to Kincade, giving him his status and location. He didn't wait for a return text. He could tell from the shouting and the gunfire where Kincade and his men were.

He began to case the basement, using all of his enhanced senses. The Ocelot Senator's scent was strong down here, especially around the bar and the pool table. There were other scents as well, including his cousin Carl's and Darien Shields's. Both men had been here, but their scents were faint. Other Senators and their aides could also be scented around the room. She must have held a party at some point, roughly two weeks ago from the age of the smells.

Two others were particularly strong, but he didn't recognize them at all. He made a mental note of them, prepared to show Kincade where he'd scented them. These two had been here as recently as two hours ago, and were frequent visitors. He'd know them if he ran across their scent again.

Barney looked around the edges of the room, searching the bookcases in a small reading nook for "special" books, books that were actually levers. He found nothing, other than the Senator really enjoyed political novels written by human senators, representatives and presidents.

If she was pulling from human politics, the shifters were screwed. The humans couldn't agree on whether or not peanut butter worked better with jelly or jam.

The pool table came under scrutiny, but no James Bond crap happened when he toyed with the inlay, the balls or the pockets. He could find no hidden buttons or levers, so he moved on to the bar, where the scents were also strong.

He found a beer keg, so he checked that out. Nothing, other than a nice, foamy stream of golden goodness. He hated to waste the beer, but he was on the job. Drinking wasn't an option.

After, however, he could get as hammered as he wanted.

Hmm. No hidden buttons under the bar, no loose tiles behind the bar, either on the wall or on the floor.

Barney stepped away from the bar, trying to clear his nose of all the scents around it. He had to focus more on Kris Jennings's scent than anyone else's. He'd met her before, knew what she smelled like. Finding her shouldn't be this hard, not for a Hunter.

There. Another spot where her scent was strong, over by a sofa, loveseat and chair set. Oddly enough, her scent was strongest at the edges of the television mounted to the wall on a decorative panel.

He smiled, searched the TV, and found a button that shouldn't have been there. He pulled out his gun and pressed the button, standing to one side as the wall the panel was mounted on slid the other way.

A gasp sounded. A shot rang out, right where Barney would have been standing had he not moved to cover.

Then it was Barney's turn. He entered the room, finding two men guarding the Ocelot Senator. The man on the left screamed as Barney swiped his off-hand upward, knocking the gun—and the man's pinky finger—to the floor. The second man was covering Ms. Jennings, his body over hers while she cowered on the ground.

Barney finished off the first guy with a side-kick to the knee before he could recover from the pain of losing a finger. The bodyguard covering Ms. Jennings lifted his head and pointed his gun at Barney.

Barney pointed his gun at the bodyguard. "Standoff."

The first bodyguard moaned, clutching at his knee and his hand, or at least trying to.

"Now." Barney held out his hand. "Give me your gun and I won't tell Kincade Lowe that you tried to fuck over the Leo."

The bodyguard's eyes went wide. "What does the Leo have to do with this?"

Barney smiled, and the man paled. "Who do you think ordered the

Senator's arrest?"

The man put the gun down and got on his knees, his hands above his head. "No job is worth getting on the Leo's bad side."

"My sentiments exactly." Barney walked past him cautiously, just in case this was all a ruse.

The bodyguard didn't move. The other bodyguard stayed on the floor, watching through pain-filled eyes.

He'd recover, eventually. He pressed his gun to the forehead of the Ocelot Senator, who still looked startled to see him standing in her safe room. "Hello, Ms. Jennings."

"Do I know you?" She tried to give him big, innocent eyes, but he wasn't buying it.

He pulled her to her feet, not even trying to be a gentleman about it. This bitch had his mate on a fucking hit list. She could rot in hell. "Nuh-uh. You're not going to get me with your freaky Ocelot powers." He slapped his hand over her mouth and, the gun at her temple, began frog-marching her out of the safe room. He kept her between himself and the bodyguards. Just to make things official, he repeated himself. "Kris Jennings, you are under arrest on the orders of the Leo. I'd suggest you take any complaints to him, via Kincade Lowe, PO Box—"

"Barnwell!" Kincade's irritated shout echoed through the basement.

"Yes, Lowe?" Barney replied languidly.

"You have her? Good work." Kincade slapped him on the shoulder. "I should hire you for my team."

"Get me the duct tape and let's get her in the car." He nodded toward the bodyguards. "Might want to do something about those two as well."

Kincade's brows rose. "You took off his finger?"

"Only the pinky." Barney sighed dramatically. "He'll never have high tea again."

Kincade snorted out a laugh. He pulled out his phone and texted. "We're getting some ice and a plastic baggie. Maybe we can save it."

"Better make up a good excuse as to how he lost it then." Barney flicked the blood off his claw. "Can't exactly tell the authorities at the hospital that he was attacked by a Grizzly."

Kincade took the duct tape one of his men brought him and used it on Jennings's mouth. "Cuffs."

The same special police officer handed over his cuffs. "I'll get some of the others to see to the bodyguards, sir."

"Good. Who's got the perimeter?"

"Aaron and Kinesha, sir."

"Good."

"We've also called for a van to transport the prisoners."

Kincade gave him a tight, approving smile. "Excellent. Get me some men down here for these three, and remember. Do *not* remove the tape from Jennings's mouth."

"Understood, sir." The officer saluted and strode off quickly.

"The Hunters can learn something from your men," Barney commented quietly.

"Ours can learn something from you as well." Kincade watched as four officers came down and efficiently gathered not only the bodyguards and Jennings, but the errant pinky finger. That officer looked a little green around the gills. "You'll get used to it, Pepper."

She stuck her tongue out at Kincade.

Kincade scowled at her. "Pepper. Not now."

She sighed. "Yes, sir." She trudged after the other officers, her shoulders slumped.

"Newbie?"

"Worse. A relative." Kincade turned back to the safe room. "Kris must have thought we'd never find this little room of hers."

"She must have thought the same thing about her hidden office." Unlike the office, the safe room had nothing in it but a chair, some water and some snacks. "This is for no more than a day, at best."

"She would have had to sneak out sooner or later, and we would have had her." Kincade put his hands on his hips and looked around. "We've already seized her computer, laptop and tablet PC. We'll check her person for her phone. We'll have Ángel crack them and see what's inside."

"An-hell?"

Kincade rolled his eyes. "Ángel Baez, Sebastian's self-proclaimed second best friend. He's the best hacke…um, *programmer* I know of. Sebastian calls him his guardian Angel."

"Once we have more names, we make more arrests?" Barney rubbed his hands together. "I could grow to like this."

Kincade chuckled. "Nope. You're going to go back home and deal with setting up that Hunter school you wanted to do." He led the way up the stairs and back into the huge kitchen.

"Sebastian said I'd have to go through the Senate to get it approved."

"Fuck that. I approve, and I'm putting it under a joint Hunter-Leo's forces training program that will allow us to work together in cases such as this one. Your unique talents and our forces' equipment and teamwork will be mutually beneficial all around."

And Kincade Lowe had that kind of authority as the leader of the Leo's Special Forces. "And I'll be in charge of this?"

Kincade nodded slowly. "I'll send someone to deal with the Special Forces training while you handle the Hunter training. This is an assignment directly from me, not from the Senate. Prove this works, and the Senate will have no reason to override me when I make the Hunter school official."

Barney blinked. "Clever bastard."

"Hey, now. Parents are happily mated, thank you."

Barney and Kincade left the house, discussing their plans while the prisoners were placed in the SUVs. Other members of the Special Forces were combing the mansion, carrying out boxes of possible evidence.

Barney could definitely see the Hunters working with these guys, but like the Hunters, there weren't enough of the Special Forces to fully police the shifter world. The Hunters filled in the gaps somewhat, but if the SF guys had been there when Casey Lee and Derrick were after Chloe, Dr. Woods might never have been forced to fight Derrick. They'd have been arrested long before then.

Something else to discuss with Kincade when the time was right.

Chapter Thirty-One

"Barney!" Heather ran to him and leapt into his arms. "Oh my God, are you okay?" She growled when she found his singed patch of hair. "I'm gonna kill a fucker."

He laughed as if she was joking. "It's okay. I healed it." His hands were on her ass as he hefted her higher.

She pushed his cowboy hat back just enough to kiss him. "You were under heavy gunfire."

He nodded. "Yup."

"You got shot. Again."

"Yup." He started walking toward the stairway, nodding once to the Leo. "I think my baby needs me."

Sebastian laughed and waved them off. "I'll see you two in the morning." He and Kincade walked off, talking quietly to each other.

"All right, let it out."

Let it out? Grr. She was doing paperwork while someone nearly shot his head off. She glared at him for a moment, shoved the shoulder of his coat out of the way and bit into the mark she'd left behind.

Mine.

And if he doesn't understand that, then he needs to get with the program real fast.

"Fuck," he moaned. "I'm gonna drop you if you don't let go."

She snarled around the shirt and flesh, unwilling to let him go.

He pushed into their bedroom. "You're gonna get it now."

Like she cared. She needed him to prove that he was all right, and if that meant fucking her through the mattress, well, that was fine with her.

He barely shut the door behind them before he had her up on the bureau, her jeans off and her pussy in his mouth. She bit her lip and banged her head on the mirror behind her.

Gods, the man had a magic mouth on him. She pulled her legs wider, holding herself open for him, giving him all her trust.

He cupped her ass, keeping her from falling as she writhed on the bureau. She looked down at him, watching him as he pleasured her. It only intensified the desire he was building inside her. She rocked against him, holding on to his head, feeling where he'd been hurt when her fingers brushed over his ears. Closing her eyes she reminded herself that he was alive, that his mouth was on her, wanting her, only her. She was the only one who could heal him after a Hunt.

He growled against her, the vibrations sending her soaring, releasing the tension she'd been under. Her toes curled, her hands clenching his hair as the orgasm washed over her, leaving her breathless.

"More," he muttered against her thigh, leaving a wet kiss behind. "Come for me more."

"Oh, boy," she breathed as he hefted her up once more. She had the feeling she was in for the ride of her life. Maybe biting him for so long had been a mistake…

Her thoughts stuttered to a stop when he put her in a chair, her legs over the arms. He knelt before her, his eyes brown, his gaze firmly fixed on her breasts. He took hold of them both, squeezing them, kneading them. He rolled her nipples between his fingers, tugging on them. He watched her reactions to each of his movements, adjusting himself when he thought she didn't like something.

"Please," she begged. She didn't know whether she wanted more attention on her breasts or if she wanted his mouth back on her pussy. Both sounded really fantastic.

He took a nipple into his mouth, loving on it, nipping at it. His fangs grazed the areola, the little nip of pain driving her wild. It was a craving, a need to have his fangs embed themselves in her flesh, giving her another point he could caress and touch and bring her to ecstasy with.

He switched sides, giving her right breast the same attention. He loved on her, worshipping her body as he kissed his way down her stomach. His claws grazed her sides, but not a scratch was left to mar her skin.

Her Bear was being careful with her.

When he reached her clit she couldn't hold back. "Yes, please."

He responded by kissing both thighs before licking her pussy. She quivered at his touch, more than ready to give him what he was asking for. She wanted to come, wanted to feel that ecstasy take her over again and again. She needed him like air, and he had no idea.

He took her clit in his mouth and sucked, robbing her of breath. She bit her lip and began rubbing her breasts, amazed at the reaction he had when she did so.

He began sucking on her harder, licking her like he wanted to devour her. He rubbed her with his fingers before fucking her with them. All the while his tongue, his magical tongue, continued to toy with her, bringing her to the brink over and over before pulling back, slowing down. He was forcing her to go at his pace, keeping the orgasm at bay with carefully orchestrated strokes.

"Need you," she whispered. She stroked a finger over his mark, hoping it would drive him even crazier.

It did. He let go, and this time he didn't pull back when she began to shake with her impending orgasm. She cried out as he stroked her to completion, her vision going dark as pleasure overrode every one of her senses.

When she came back down he was unbuttoning his jeans. "Gotta have you."

"How do you want me?"

The rumble in his chest made her shiver. "Turn over."

She wasn't sure how that was supposed to work, but she tried. She turned over, keeping her knees on the chair, her arms over the back.

He slipped inside her, moving her thighs a bit farther apart until they were right up against the arms of the chair. He grabbed her by the hips and began fucking her, pushing at her shoulders until her breasts were rubbing up against the fabric of the chair with each thrust.

The added sensation was incredible. He filled her, overwhelmed her to her core. Her breasts felt tight, tingly, her whole body riding him as he filled her. She could feel his claws dimpling her skin and his jeans grazing her ass. She pushed back against him, fucking him back. Her hands tightened on the back of the chair, and she could hear it creaking as Barney thrust harder.

He reached around, stroking her clit as he fucked her, driving her wild with sensation. It was too much, too new, too fucking fantastic not to let go. She threw her head back, enjoying the way he grabbed hold of her hair, letting her hip go in favor of tugging on it briefly.

Eventually she'd let him do that, pull on it when he wanted, but he stopped before she could say anything. His hand was back on her hip, digging in once more.

She turned her head to look at him. He was staring at where they were joined, watching himself fuck her. His other hand continued to pleasure her, stroking her clit in time to his thrusts. "Come on my cock, sweetheart. Squeeze me tight."

She moved against him, her vision glazing over as a low, slow throb began to build inside her. "Barney," she breathed, closing her eyes as the orgasm washed over her. She barely heard some fabric tear as her whole body clenched, robbing her not only of breath but of thought.

God, how could it keep getting better?

"Yes," he hissed, sliding out of her. Before she could protest he picked her up and put her on the bed. "Hands and knees."

She did as asked, wondering how this position would feel.

Barney didn't leave her waiting for long. He slid inside her, grabbing her waist and fucking her hard. She fell down on her elbows, her face in the pillow, the tips of her breasts barely grazing the sheets. She couldn't hold back her cries this time. Her Fox wouldn't let her. It wanted their mate to know that he was pleasing her, giving her what she needed. He was so deep, so hard, and he felt so goddamn amazing. She held on to the bottom of the headboard, her body rocking along with her mate's as he took her.

Had he been holding back with her? Because this. Was. *Amazing.* No pain, just pure, unadulterated pleasure ran through her, curling her toes and driving her wild. Her claws came out, ripping at the sheets like a wild thing, demanding her mate take her, consume her until there was nothing left but them.

He bent until his chin was rubbing against her mark, his stubble rubbing it with every deep, hard thrust. She could hear their bodies slapping together, sweat and sex mingling together on their damp flesh.

"So good," he muttered, his breath stroking her ear. "Gonna come."

She whimpered, dragging her claws through the fabric beneath her. "Bite me."

Teeth met flesh, and Heather went soaring over the edge, screaming into a pillow as she came so hard she saw stars. She was on fire, every nerve ending tingling with the pleasure she took from him. Every fiber of her being clenched as it went on and on, consuming her, body and soul.

When the stars cleared away and she could move again, she let go of the pillow. Licking her lips, she turned, only to find that Barney was still in the throes of passion. His head was tilted back, his hips hammering against her ass as he came.

She smiled and put her head on her arms, watching him come down from his own high.

He blinked down at her. Both of them were out of breath, sticky and sweaty, and she couldn't have been happier.

"You are so beautiful."

Maybe she could. The reverent look in his eyes, the way he stroked her hair, told her more than any words could say. "You too."

That made him smile. "Uh-huh. Pretty like an elf, right?" He pulled out of her, maneuvering them both so that they lay on their sides. His arm was under her head, his hand grazing up and down her side.

She rolled her eyes. "Okay, Faramir pretty."

Barney's brows rose. "Not Boromir?"

She poked him in the chest. "Boromir *dies*, asshole."

"Right. No dying." He winced and rubbed where she'd poked. "Maybe do that without the claws next time, huh?"

"Did I get my point across?" It was hard to be mad at him when her whole body was sated. All she really wanted to do was curl up and sleep.

He kissed the tip of her nose. "As you wish."

She choked on her own spit. "What?" She might be young, but she knew what that meant. She'd seen *The Princess Bride* more than once with her brother and sister. Hell, she'd cried at the end more than once.

He chuckled and pulled her closer. "Go to sleep, little vixen. We've got a long day ahead of us tomorrow."

She snuggled up against him and whispered against his chest. She knew the best way to soothe the heart he'd just bared before her. "As you wish."

Needless to say there wasn't much sleep going on that night. And by the end of it, both knew they were thoroughly and completely loved.

Chapter Thirty-Two

"I want to thank you all for coming," Max Cannon said formally. The Puma Alpha was flanked by his Curana, or co-Alpha, Emma, and his Beta, Simon Holt. More than just the Puma Pride had arrived at the meeting the Alpha had set up. Barney had watched as Heather's entire clan, including their mates, had filed in. Some shifters from the local college had also arrived, restlessly watching the rest of the shifters in the room.

Barney and Heather had been back in Halle for little more than a week when Max sent out the order for a mandatory Pride meeting, to be held on Pride lands rather than in the Alpha's home. Now Barney understood why. This many shifters would never have fit in the Alpha's lovely home. Perhaps if the Freidelinde mansion were still available he'd have been able to hold the meeting in the ballroom there, but no.

Jamie Howard was, of course, nowhere in sight, but Barney had the feeling he was there somewhere in the shadows. After all, Hope Walsh *was* there, standing between Sarah Anderson and Becky Holt. She was trembling, barely standing up, but behind her he caught sight of powder-blue hair. Her twin, Glory, was right there, whispering in her ear, soothing her while Ryan stood guard over them all.

Nothing would get through Ryan to those women.

Casey Lee and Derrick had agreed to join Kincade's Special Forces. He'd been impressed with their work, and agreed to allow them to become part of Barney's school. They were currently with Kincade, going through some training before coming back to Halle. Barney was happy for them. They both deserved the recognition Kincade was giving them.

His attention returned to the Alpha when Max began speaking once more. "While I know it's unusual to hold a Pride meeting with members of the community who aren't Pride, the issue I'm about to discuss concerns us all." Max was looking around the meadow, watching each of the shifters for their reactions. Barney had seen Alphas in action before, but there was something about Max that was different. He'd accepted people into the Pride who weren't Pumas, he enjoyed a close relationship with a Wolf Alpha, and he'd proven himself more than once to be concerned not only about his own people but those who lived in his town. "I've received a warning from the Leo."

Gasps of shock followed his pronouncement, followed by whispers.

"I know, it's rare for the Leo to contact anyone, but he's sent out a mass email to all of the Alphas of Prides and Packs. He's asked us to contact as many shifters as we can to spread the word." Max sounded calm, but there was a faint hint of his power in the air, enough to let Barney know that the Alpha was anything but calm. He was going into protection mode. Barney knew enough about Max after having been in Halle for a few months to gauge the man's actions. If he was right, Halle was about to rally around its most vulnerable members: the children.

Barney watched the shifters absorb Max's pronouncement, their gazes returning to Max as he continued to speak. "It seems there is a group of people who believe the white shifters, like our Chloe and Julian—" Max pointed them out in the crowd, "—do not deserve to live." More murmurs, some confused, some angry. Eric Bunsun looked ready to burst in anger as he sidled next to Tabby. His sister-in-law was holding Wren close to her. "In fact, they've been trying to prevent the white shifters from even existing by systematically killing those who have even the *potential* to become white shifters."

Heather grabbed hold of his arm, her fingers trembling. "It's starting," she whispered.

"What is?" What the hell was she talking about?

She looked up at him, her expression tearing at his heart. "The war. They've been secretly killing for years, but now it's out in the open. Their only choices are to go underground, or…"

"War." Barney's back stiffened as he glanced around at the crowd. "Fuck. You think the Senate will try and do something about the Leo's actions?"

"Not all of them, but yes." She stroked his arm. "Carl will side with us, but who knows about the others?"

"We've got to get the list of names from Senator Jennings," Barney growled. "So far, the Leo hasn't managed to get anything out of her. After the duct tape was removed she refused to talk, even when the Leo ordered her to."

"How?"

He could understand Heather's confusion. The Leo *had* to be obeyed, no matter what. "She somehow drugged herself. Kincade still doesn't know who's funneling her the drugs. When I spoke to him yesterday he was beyond pissed."

"I bet." She scratched at his arm. "Shh. Max is speaking again."

"I know that a number of you have no clue what the hell makes the white shifters so special, or why someone would want them dead." He held up his hand to stop the flow of questions that were suddenly being flung at him. "I want to reassure you that the Leo is now aware of this plot, and is asking us, as the brothers and sisters and families of these precious members of our Pride, to be careful. Be vigilant. Until this is settled, no one is safe."

"Who's doing this?" A voice somewhere from the college crowd bellowed.

"Yeah, who do we have to kill?" one of the Bear clan, Keith maybe, shouted at Max. "Because they aren't touching another member of my family ever again."

Barney smiled as Max looked toward him. "Barney, would you mind coming over here?" He gestured toward Barney. "James 'Barney' Barnwell is a Hunter, and has been working on this problem since we first discovered it."

Barney joined the Alpha, keeping Heather close to his side. He hadn't been able to let her go since seeing her name on that damn list. While he knew she'd never be the white Fox, seeing it had jarred him badly. "I can answer that." He nodded to Max, who nodded back. "There's an investigation ongoing, but until we know who is behind it, there's not much I can tell. I do know that one of the perpetrators is the Ocelot Senator, Kris Jennings."

Complete silence. "The Senate is doing this?"

The fear behind that question was understandable. "We don't know." He so did, but he wasn't going to point the finger at the entire Senate when he was willing to bet it was only a few of them involved. "As far as I know, she acted alone. She is currently being held by the Leo's Special Forces, who are questioning her further."

More whispers.

"Kincade Lowe is at the head of this investigation," Barney continued, speaking a little louder to be heard over the continuing chatter. "I'm going to be working with him on this closely. This warning is more than important, as we have a bigger concentration of white shifters in Halle than has been seen in centuries."

One of the college students raised her hand. "Why do white shifters even exist? What's their purpose?"

He smiled. "Once upon a time, the white shifters *were* the Senate. They advised the Leo through their contacts with the spirit world, and sometimes the Leo acted on that advice, depending on whether or not it was important to all shifters. The Leo guides and guards us all, while the Senators are supposed to do the same for their individual species."

Chloe Williams looked shell-shocked. They hadn't bothered to tell her what her new status would eventually be. Her mate was whispering in her ear and holding her close.

Julian just smiled, like he'd known something like this was coming. He probably did, the smug bastard.

Barney acknowledged another raised hand. This was beginning to remind him of a press conference rather than a Pride gathering. "Yes?"

"How do we know who needs protection?" It was a girl, standing alone, just off the group of college kids.

"Those of mixed lineage, like half Bear, half Wolf." He pointed toward Tabby, who was holding her baby. "Wren Bunsun, for example."

The girl looked at Tabby. "The one with the green hair?"

"No. The baby." Barney held up his hands as some of them cried out in horror. "Yes, Wren Bunsun *is* a target. Alex and Tabitha are well aware of it and are guarding her closely." He felt Heather snuggling closer to him. "The attack that nearly killed Chloe Williams was, we believe, due to her having a Bear father and a Fox mother. Why her, and not her brother Keith or her sister Tiffany, is still something we need to figure out."

"But we will," Heather said, surprising him. "Once we've fully grasped the key, we'll know what to do and who to protect."

The key. His Heather really had been the key that opened the door. It was up to Barney to figure out where it led. She'd been right all along. He'd have to tell her, even if she would hold it over his head for the rest of their lives.

"Anyone with mixed blood, even if it was your grandparents, needs to come forward and let Max know," Barney continued.

"I'll make sure you're protected." Max gestured toward his Marshal, Adrian Giordano, and the Marshal's Second, Gabriel Anderson. "We'll arrange protection for all for all of you, even if you do not join our Pride."

"Why are you doing this?" One of the college students stepped forward. "You don't owe us protection."

Max smiled. "The moment you entered the college you entered my territory, with my permission. It's up to me to ensure your safety until such a time as you rejoin your Pride, Pack or family group, or strike out on your own."

Gabriel Anderson spoke next. "We're giving you a special number to call if you encounter any trouble. It will bring the wrath of God down on whoever is attacking you, so use it wisely."

"It will only be given to those of mixed lineage, like Chloe, Heather and Wren, whose parents will hold the number for her," Adrian added. His mate, Sheri, was in the crowd, her seeing-eye dog at her side. She wore a hat and sunglasses, her arms covered by a light shawl. She was an albino and would burn easily in the sunlight.

"When we have more information for you we'll be letting you know via a newsletter we plan on setting up. All of you are required to subscribe to it." Emma was speaking, her throaty voice reaching every part of the meadow. Her own power began to swirl around her, more than a match for her Alpha's. "You *will* be checked up on regularly. You *will* respond when we text you. I don't care if you're in the middle of the best fu—"

Max's hand slapped over his mate's mouth. "Children, dear."

She removed his hand, glaring up at him even as she changed what she'd been about to say. "Happy fun times of your life, *you will respond*. Do you understand me?"

"Because if you don't respond," Max added gleefully, "the entire Pride will turn out to look for you."

The college students looked horrified. The Bunsun-Williams clan looked relieved, while the Pride seemed to take it in stride. If one of their own was in danger, and they responded, no questions asked.

"Be aware that Rick Lowell of the Red Wolf Pack, Grace Benedetto of the Philadelphia Lion Pride and Nick Consiglione of the New York Coyotes are also giving a similar speeches to their Packs and Pride. All across the nation, the word is spreading." Max stared at his people, and Barney could see the determination in the Alpha's gaze. "I'm sorry this is necessary, but in order to make certain some are safe, we all need to be vigilant."

Gabriel had some of his cops, also shifters, start handing out flyers. "On this sheet is the URL for the newsletter. Those of you with mixed blood will receive a separate paper with the emergency number listed on it. Please keep these in a safe place. Don't let any humans get hold of either of them." He glared particularly at the college students. "Not girlfriends, boyfriends, buddies you've known since kindergarten. No one."

"If you're mated and he or she is not present, feel free to share the information," Emma added. "But only with them."

"Barney?" Heather tugged on his arm. "Do you think all of the mixed-blood shifters will come forward?"

He shook his head. "Hell no. Some of them won't believe it, while others will try to hide, thinking they're better off on their own. Some will think this is a trick to expose themselves to the ones killing them."

She closed her eyes wearily. "They'll be killed."

"More than likely, yes, unless we can get them to believe."

"Everyone, if you have any further questions, please direct them either to Gabe, Adrian or Barney," Max yelled. The murmurs of the crowd were becoming louder, almost drowning out the Alpha's words. "Their emails are on the flyer we just handed out to you."

"What?" Barney grabbed a flyer from a passing cop and stared at it. "Fuck my life."

Heather giggled. "Welcome to the Pride."

Chapter Thirty-Three

Heather was on her way to work. Things hadn't become normal again, not by a long shot, but Barney was far too busy with his own work to stop her from going to her own. She was looking forward to a nice, relaxing day of tattoos and bullshitting with the girls. It felt like a lifetime had passed since she'd done that.

She pulled into the parking lot of Cynful, careful to park under a streetlight. Mrs. H, the owner of the building, had placed a large H on the streetlight, telling Heather it was her spot. Mrs. H didn't like it when Heather, the youngest of the Cynful girls, had to leave at night, as she was the only one whose mate didn't come to pick her up. This was Mrs. H's way of protecting Heather, and Heather was grateful for it.

She got out of the car and checked to make sure she had everything with her. Her sketchbook she'd shoved in her oversized purse, along with some drawing pencils. She hadn't been in the mood to take her entire kit with her, so she'd only brought the basics.

Smiling, she turned away from her car, clicking the button on the key to make sure it locked. She heard the telltale *beep-beep* and looked up, ready for her day to start.

Only to have it stop dead in its tracks.

Jamie Howard stood not five feet from her. His hands were loose at his sides, his feet shoulder-width apart. He was dressed in worn jeans and a gray tank top, and on his feet were a pair of work boots. His gaze was fixed on her, his eyes pure silver, as was his hair.

The white Puma had come to speak to her, and he was scary as hell.

"Good afternoon, Heather." Jamie spoke softly, but there was a menace in his tone, a chill that struck her to the bone. His expression cynical. "I have a message for your mate."

"Oh?" She tried to remain calm, but her heart began to race as she stared at Dr. Howard.

He smiled. "Don't be afraid." His tone was soft, almost soothing, but the menace pouring off of him negated any sense of safety she might have had. "I won't hurt *you*."

Her back immediately stiffened. "But you'll hurt my mate?"

He tilted his head, the gesture cat-like. His Puma must be riding him hard. "Only if he gets in my way."

"You were at the meeting two days ago?" Barney had told her he suspected Dr. Howard was hidden somewhere, either in the crowd or among the trees ringing the meadow. He hadn't bothered to try and find the man because he didn't view him as a threat.

"Yes, I was. I heard what my Alpha had to say." His hands twitched, and she saw his claws emerging. "The Leo acted too quickly."

A chill ran down her spine. "What do you mean?"

He looked away with a grimace as his whole body shuddered. "I don't give a fuck how many of you die." His tone was cold. "None of you matter to me."

"Hope," Heather whispered.

He glared at her. "Hope." That shudder racked him again. "Nothing can happen to Hope."

"She's not of mixed lineage, so she should be safe."

He laughed, and there was no humor in it. "But I am."

"And she could be used against you." Heather nodded. "I understand."

"Good. Then you'll understand what I'm about to say." He stared at her, his silver eyes glittering with sudden rage. "I've been forced to step in sooner than I'd planned, thanks to your mate and the Leo. Things will escalate much faster than either anticipated, all because they let the cat out of the bag."

"We thought—"

"I know what you thought," he interrupted roughly. "If we put what was shadowed into the light, then they'll be helpless." He tsk'd. "Guess what? All you did was piss people off. Worse, some of those who are giving out the warning the Leo so carefully crafted? They're going to use it as an excuse."

"To do what?"

"Kill that which they don't understand." His expression became dull, almost lifeless. "People like me. They'll do the work of those Senators for them rather than help those in need."

"Max is different. Halle is different." Heather took a step toward Dr. Howard. "We won't let anything happen to either you or Hope."

That dull, lifeless look disappeared, replaced with a smile that was almost gentle. "You're so young. So naïve." It took only two steps for him to reach her. He touched her cheek, his claws scraping across her skin. "They will bleed you dry just to get to your mate."

She stood perfectly still even when his claws came dangerously close to her eyes. "I'll help protect Hope. And you. No matter what."

He shook his head and took a step back, his hand finally leaving her face. "You'll try, but you'll fail. I've seen it." He looked haunted. "No. It's going to be up to me to act now, before things get too far out of hand and the whole world loses what you're fighting for."

"What do you mean?" He knew something he wasn't telling.

"Do you understand what it is the spirits are fighting for?" That cynical look was back on his face. "Do you even have a clue?"

"The white shifters talk to the spirits. Through those shifters, they can communicate with the Leo, giving advice and orders to the rest of the shifter world."

His brows rose. "Very good. But that's not all."

"No?"

"Like all politicians, they've hidden something from you. Something very important." Dr. Howard leaned toward her, touching her face once more. "You see, if all the white shifters die, the line of the Leo dies. And if that happens, the death of the shifter world is inevitable."

Heather's eyes went wide. "What?"

He nodded, standing so close she could feel his breath on her cheek. "Our children will be born human."

"Holy fuck. We lose our animals."

"Now you understand how stupid the Senate is being?"

"They don't know, do they?" Heather couldn't even see Dr. Howard anymore. She was too caught up in following the thought he'd implanted in her. "To them, it's just a way to gain control of us."

"And because they can't hear the spirits, they have no idea what will happen if that connection is lost." Jamie stepped back again, releasing her. "And the fight will be here, in Halle, where the white shifters are gathering for a final stand."

She stared at him, horrified. "More of them will come seeking shelter."

"And Max. Max will wind up taking care of them all." He frowned, looking at the ground. "I have no choice but to step in and keep the white shifters safe."

"Because you are one?" Heather tried to sound sympathetic, but really, he was still scaring the fuck out of her.

"No." He lifted his head, and she could see tears in his eyes. "Because Marie would want me to." He turned on his heel and began to leave the parking lot. "Heather?"

"Yeah?" God, he was hurting so badly, and there was nothing she could do for him.

"If you die, stay dead. And if anyone brings you back, slit your goddamn throat." He turned and looked at her one last time. "Because living without your other half is living in hell."

And he was gone, disappearing between the buildings as if he'd never been there.

"Whoa." She stepped back until she could lean against her car, breathing heavily. Her hands were shaking as she called Barney. "Guess who just visited me?"

"The Ghost of Christmas Past?" Barney shushed someone who yelled out his name.

"Jamie Howard."

Silence. "I'm on my way."

Before she could stop him he'd hung up.

Suddenly being alone in the parking lot didn't feel like a good idea. Rubbing her arms to chase away the chill, she sprinted around the building and to the front door of Cynful.

She yanked it open, setting off the bell at the top, and dashed inside. Cyn was there, looking startled. Behind the curtains she could hear the buzz of a tattoo gun. Little Wren was on the counter next to Cyn, whose claws were out.

A spate of Spanish was hurled at her before she could take a breath.

"Hi." Heather waved her shaking hand at Cyn. "Jamie Howard stopped by to say hello."

Cyn picked up the baby carrier and put it behind the counter. "Is he still here?"

"No, and I don't think he'd hurt Wren." She held up her hands. "Let me tell it all once Barney gets here, okay?"

Cyn nodded. "I'm calling Julian. Glory's off and Alex is working with your mate on setting up the training grounds." Bunsun Exteriors had offered to set up various training routes for the Hunters and the Special Forces, using plants and hardscape to mimic conditions in other parts of the country. Some of it would be done in a building that someone else was designing via Kincade Lowe's specific requirements. Other parts would be outside that building. And Alpha Lowell of the Red Wolf Pack had given permission for "weekend getaways" at his lodge, where they'd train among the mountains and in snowy conditions.

Cyn picked up the phone, speaking quietly. Heather sat in one of the waiting chairs, still trembling from her encounter.

Cyn came around the counter with the baby. "Here. Watch her. I've got to go speak to Tabby."

Heather smiled down at the sleeping infant. "Will do."

The baby was making some kind of sucking, puckering face. Her little hands were fisted and her little brows furrowed. Her pink knit cap was askew on her head and her adorable black curls were visible. Heather smiled down at her little cousin and touched the baby's cheek. It was so soft, so vulnerable. "Hello, little one."

The baby sighed and relaxed. She watched Wren sleep until Barney and Alex came barreling through the front door.

"You okay?" Barney asked quietly as he crouched down in front of her.

"Yeah, I am." She'd had a little bit of time to relax. Jamie Howard had been warning her of what was coming. He hadn't been threatening her. He'd been *helping* her. "Dr. Howard is…intense."

"That's one word for it," Barney muttered. He moved out of the way as Alex scooped his baby up. "She's fine, Alex."

"I know." But that didn't stop Alex from taking his child through the curtain, where his mate was.

Barney turned his attention back to her just as the bell jingled and Julian stepped in. "Tell me."

"Me too. I want to hear what Jamie said." There was a silver streak in Julian's hair, but his eyes were still dark. He sounded almost happy, but his expression when he said Jamie's name was completely different. He missed the old Jamie, and everyone knew it.

Heather took a deep breath. "He said the Leo made a mistake in announcing everything right from the start, that it will only end in more deaths for the white shifters. He also told me that if the Leo dies, then our children will be born human."

Barney blinked. "Holy fuck."

Heather nodded. "He also said that he thinks those who are doing this have no idea of the consequences of killing the Lowe line. They think it's just power, nothing more, but the Leo is our link to our animals. It's through him that we exist at all."

"You think…" Julian's eyes went wide. "Of course. It makes sense."

"What does?" Heather smiled as Barney took hold of her hands. She hadn't realized they were still shaking.

Julian sat down in the other chair, his gaze on Heather. There was a flicker of silver. "That's why the Leo can't talk to the spirits. He's a conduit."

Barney and Heather exchanged a confused glance, but it was Cyn who spoke. "In English, *mi corazón*."

"He's channeling the power of the spirits into us, the descendants of the first shifters," Julian replied faintly. He still seemed stunned by his own revelation. "Without that cornerstone, the Leo, the whole thing crumbles to dust. We lose our connection to our animals, and thus our children are born human."

"There's nothing wrong with being human," Cyn replied.

"No, there isn't." Julian stared at his mate. "Now, imagine losing your Bear forever."

Her eyes went wide, and she shivered.

Heather could understand. Her Fox was yipping in distress, and the urge to soothe it, to reassure it that they'd never be apart, was so strong she almost shifted right then and there. "Hell."

"How did Jamie know when no one else did?" Barney was staring out the window, but she could see the wheels turning. "Because he's the white Puma?"

"Who knows?" Julian shrugged. "The rules the spirits live by are different from ours. Perhaps it was simply time we knew, and the spirits allowed it. Or perhaps Puma broke the rules to make sure we lived, and will be punished for it. Without talking to Bear, I can't answer that."

"And it looks like you've been a busy boy already," Cyn grunted. She stepped from behind the counter and touched the streak of silver in her mate's hair. "No spirit jaunts for you until you rest, *cariño*."

"Yes, ma'am," Julian replied, leaning into his mate's touch.

"Now I'm really worried." Cyn shook her head. "Go in the back and get something to drink." She turned to Barney and Heather as Julian nodded, stood and headed for the employees' area. "Barney, you need to let Max know what Jamie said. Heather, you think you can work today?"

She took a deep breath. "Yeah, I think so."

"Good. Go clean your station. You'll be tatting someone today."

Barney kissed her cheek. "Good luck, sweetheart." He turned to Cyn. "Call me if anything, and I mean *anything*, seems out of place."

"Will do." She pointed out the window. "We've got a guard out there, one of Gabe's men, but he must not have seen Jamie."

"I don't care if Rambo is guarding this place. Call me." Barney gave her one last kiss before striding out the door.

Cyn put her hands on her hips. "Okay. Forget all of that. It's time to get your head into the art, got it?"

Heather nodded, but it would take a while for her to forget the words Dr. Howard had said. She'd been right to tell Barney a war was coming.

Now all she had to do was keep her mate safe, and pray it didn't take her family.

About the Author

Dana Marie Bell wrote her first short story when she was thirteen years old. She's now a *USA TODAY* bestselling author with Samhain Publishing and Carina Press. Dana has lived primarily in the Northeast with a brief stint on the U.S. Virgin Island of St. Croix. She lives with her soul mate and husband Dusty, their two maniacal children, two evil ice-cream-stealing cats and a bull terrier that thinks it's a Pekingese. She's been heard to describe herself as "vertically challenged" and "a lapsed brunette". Dana also suffers from ankylosing spondylitis (a progressive inflammatory arthritis that primarily affects the spine), and can be seen walking with a cane or tooling around in her mobility scooter. Her condition was the inspiration for Belle's hip injury in *Steel Beauty*.

You can learn more about Dana at:

www.danamariebell.com

danamariebell.blogspot.com

www.facebook.com/pages/Dana-Marie-Bells-Fan-Page/185916691436341

www.twitter/com/danamariebell

The last Beckett brother is going down.

Warlock Unbound
© 2015 Dana Marie Bell

Heart's Desire, Book 4

If he had a choice, Daniel Beckett would wait to cast the Beckett family mating spell until his life is more settled. But his brothers, worried he's losing himself to his wolf, aren't giving it to him.

Daniel doesn't need a spell to know Kerry Andrews is his mate. With the last of the Godwin warlocks still on the loose, Daniel crosses his fingers that the willful, stubborn, beautiful woman will allow him to protect her.

Kerry is tempted to make Daniel wait, like he's made *her* wait for so long. But the decision is taken out of her hands when things start going horribly wrong. A sleeper hex is activated, putting her life in danger—and the only safe place to run is Daniel's waiting arms.

Once there, Kerry finds a whole new world to explore with her magical mate. But Arthur Godwin is plotting to rip away their newfound happiness. Women who look like Kerry are turning up dead…and it's only a matter of time before the killer's weapon hits its intended prey.

Warning: This title contains explicit sex, graphic language, a growly wizard and the woman who loves him.

He'll fulfill her wildest fantasies… but only if she believes.

Dare to Believe
© 2009 Dana Marie Bell

The Gray Court, Book 1

Leo Dunne has been searching his entire life for the one person born just for him. He finds her working in his own company, but the shy little Ruby Halloway constantly hides from him. He hatches a devilish plot with her best friend to bring her out of her shell, and the result proves her desire is more than a match for his own.

Ruby has had the hots for her boss for some time now, but she knows business and pleasure shouldn't mix. While that can't stop a girl from dreaming, she sticks by her guns and does her best never to be alone with the handsome CEO. Until the company masquerade party, where she discovers a passion with him that leaves a mark on her soul.

A family emergency calls Leo away, and rather than spend one night out of Ruby's arms, he convinces her to go with him. With his brother's life on the line, it's vital she learn how to deal with who, and what, her new lover really is… before it's too late.

Warning: This book contains explicit sex, graphic language, some violence, a bit of bondage, and a Sidhe Lord determined to claim and protect what is his.

FANTASY ~ PARANORMAL ~ CONTEMPORARY ~ SCIENCE FICTION

SUSPENSE ~ LGBT ~ CYBERPUNK ~ STEAMPUNK ~ REGENCY ~ WESTERN ~ FANTASY ~ PARANORMAL ~ URBAN FANTASY

FANTASY ~ PARANORMAL ~ CONTEMPORARY ~ SCIENCE FICTION ~ HISTORICAL ~ WESTERN ~ ALTERNATE WORLDS

Your favorite romance genres in print and ebook from samhainromance.com

It's all about the story...

SUSPENSE ~ LGBT ~ CYBERPUNK ~ STEAMPUNK ~ POST APOCALYPTIC

It's all about the story...

Romance

HORROR

www.samhainpublishing.com

CPSIA information can be obtained at www.ICGtesting.com
Printed in the USA
LVOW11s1817220216

476212LV00004B/350/P